Adv

The Brea

'A... .... vel – the music of Lisa Allen-Agostini's writing voice is gloriously specific to Trinidad, yet this heart-wrenching story of a woman both liberated and in need of liberation has universal resonance. The powerful themes that emerge are both unpredictable and unforgettable, dealing with the masquerade of everyday love as well as hidden secrets that are the legacy of family.' – Margaret Busby

'As with its protagonist, Alethea, this book strips you down to raw nerve to build you back up again. Allen-Agostini has an unswerving eye with so much: the legacies of familial and sexual violence; the chronic self-suppression of the survivors; and finally, the life-saving and precious human urge to offer true love and friendship.' – Nalo Hopkinson

'This is the kind of novel where you dip into the first page and don't come up for breath until the last; the surface of the writing is so smooth that you fall right in. This is a thoroughly enjoyable read!' – Kei Miller

THE BREAD THE DEVIL KNEAD

LISA ALLEN-AGOSTINI

First published in 2021 by
Myriad Editions
www.myriadeditions.com

Myriad Editions
An imprint of New Internationalist Publications
The Old Music Hall, 106–108 Cowley Rd,
Oxford OX41JE

Reprinted 2022
3 5 7 9 10 8 6 4

A CIP catalogue record for this book
is available from the British Library

ISBN (paperback): 978-1-912408-99-3
ISBN (ebook): 978-1-912408-98-6

This is a work of fiction.
Names, characters, places, businesses, locales, events and incidents
are the products of the author's imagination or have been used in
a fictitious manner. Any resemblance to actual persons, living or
dead, or actual events is purely coincidental.

Designed and typeset in Sabon
by www.twenty-sixletters.com

Printed and bound in Great Britain
by Clays Ltd, Elcograf S.p.A

For Wayne Brown

ONE

When I wake up that morning, oh, God, my back and my belly was hurting. But I didn't want to make no noise and wake up Leo, so I bite my lip hard to make sure I didn't bawl out for pain. Slow slow slow I turn on the bed and swing my foot over the side, and get up like if is eggs I sitting on and I feel with my foot for my rubber slippers before I stand up.

It was dark in the bedroom, dayclean still a good hour away. I hear the neighbour cock crowing anyway, as though he watch break. I didn't switch on the light because I living here five years and I could find anything here with my eyes close. I reach under the bed by the ashtray for my pack of cigarettes and lighter, slip them in my duster pocket and tiptoe out the room. When I reach the door, I remember the book I was reading last night before Leo come home. Yes. Look it there where he did fling it by the wardrobe. I bite my lip again when I bend down to pick it up. I close the bedroom door behind me soft soft.

In the kitchen, rubbish was falling out of the old grocery bag in the corner by the back door, and it had a smell like stale fish and cigarette in the air. The stove had a crust on it – split peas boil over on top of the black grease coating the white enamel. I didn't even bother to suck my teeth. I pick up my copper-bottom kettle, shiny, bright chrome, full it with water and use my lighter to light the stove.

As I waiting for the water to boil I sit down and start back reading my book. The table nasty, like the stove. I feel long time it used to be red like the cigarette pack – carmine? A nice word, carmine – but now it just kind of fadey-orangey colour. Tangerine. Right in the centre of the table it had a big circle of bright red – carmine! – as though it had a flowerpot on the table for years and years. But when I move here it didn't have no flowerpot there. Leo mustbe break it.

I light a cigarette and take a long drag. That first cigarette does go straight to my head, every time. I was a little dizzy until I take the next drag. I ash the cigarette in a dirty coffee mug on the table, and the ashes float in the black coffee still in the cup.

The book I was reading wasn't Tolstoy, just some murder mystery I borrow from the library. The detective was a woman who had a bookshop in London. This is how I does see the world: by reading books. I does go to London, Hong Kong, Siberia, even, when I read a book. I does meet all kind of people. Learn all kinds of words. Live all kinds of lives.

Thank God for books.

The kettle start to boil and I jump up quick quick before it could whistle too much and wake up Leo. I stand up by the sink to wash the same cup I was ashing the cigarette in. The rag I was using was a old piece of jersey. It had a print on it that say *Prop-somethingsomething-versi-somethingsomething-consin. Property of the University of Wisconsin*, it used to say,

2

before the SqEzy and Vim fade out the print. It had a million other jerseys like it cut up in pieces. We does use them to wash wares, wash windows, clean the furnitures when we cleaning. Which is hardly ever.

I pick up the sugar pan to sweeten the tea, but the pan was empty. I didn't bother to look for milk; I drink the tea black and strong and bitter. Just like Leo. I laugh inside my head. The tea edge my teeth and burn my tongue.

The woman detective in the book was going to a estate sale in the country to see if she find any first editions and she meet a handsome man in the big old house which part she went. I was just getting back into the story when the stupid rooster next door crow again and remind me I had was to go to work.

Every time I watch that bathroom it does crawl my blood, but Leo lie if he feel I cleaning it. He could do what. I don't care. I not scrubbing that moss and mildew off the wall for he lazy ass. If he beat me, he beat me.

I hang the duster on the towel rail, scrub my mouth looking in the mirror but not really seeing the thin, white face, long, straight brown hair, hazel eyes, the mouth men does call rude. I have a small waist and a flat belly, but right now that belly was black and blue and red and green, depending on what bruises you was looking at: the older ones was lighter; the ones from last night was still red.

Sun now starting to think about coming up. A greyish light was glowing through the cobwebs in the ventilation blocks high up on the wall of the bathroom. I bathe myself with my rag and some cheap vanilla body wash – real gentle when I rubbing my belly and back – and rinse off under the one tap gushing cold water from the bathroom wall. I had my slippers on still.

I know is really one thing I have that I could count on, and that is my looks. I going on forty but you would never know it, because every morning and night God spare life I does cleanse and tone and moisturise from head to foot. I have special cream for my hair, my face, my hand, my body, my foot. Is not that I vain. I does think of it as an investment. If you had a nice car, ent you would take care of it? Depreciation is a hell of a thing.

I creep back inside the bedroom and, in the dawn peeping through the curtains by the window, I put on my underwears. I does iron on a weekend and so is just to ease out a shirt, a skirt and some shoes from the wardrobe, take my handbag from the kitchen table, stuff the book in it and I gone before Leo could even turn twice.

In this neighbourhood you doesn't have to lock your door. Everybody know you and everybody know your business; so everybody know we didn't have nothing to thief. I push in the back door and walk out to the front yard. My two little neighbours was there already, dragging theyself down the road.

'Happy New Year,' I tell them.

The girl didn't watch me in my eye. 'Happy New Year, Miss Allie.' She say it like she eating aloes.

'Ty, you ready for the first day of school?'

He and all watching me funny. 'Yes, Miss Allie.' He walk quiet for a little while, and then he hitch up the big big book bag on he back before he talk again. 'Miss Allie, last night, my mother say Uncle Leo just like he father—'

He sister jump in one time, 'Hush your mouth!'

'But, Natalie!'

Natalie hit him one cut eye and grab he hand rough rough and pull him like he is a sack of rice. 'Mind your business,' I hear she tell she brother.

Me, I do like nothing didn't happen. I plaster a smile on my face and step up my pace to pass them on the road. 'Have a great day!' I say. Is not my place to teach piss-in-tail children their manners.

4

When I reach the main road the sun was up and the road was busy already. I put out my hand to stop a maxi and one pull up one time, giving a next maxi a bad-drive, fus he hurry to catch this one passenger.

When I sit down in the back seat of the little bus, I keep my knees together tight tight and didn't turn right or left. I staring in front at the 2004 calendar the driver still have stick up over he head. I could see, out the corner of my eye, a little girl in pigtails and ribbons watching me with she eye big big. She was probably wondering what a white lady was doing taking maxi. I didn't study she. I pull out my book from my handbag and start to read.

Well, pretend to read.

In truth, I was going down the rabbit hole in my head.

Ever since I was small, when I get licks I does picture myself disappearing inside a black hole. The black hole does swallow up everything, starting with my navel and sucking everything down with it. This morning the black hole pick up the places where Leo cuff and kick me the night before, the places where he hold me down and force me to do what he does call making love, the places with the nasty kitchen and the overflowing rubbish bag and the mossy bathroom and the neighbours talking behind my back and the mud on the road and the cussing maxi driver and the gaping little girl...everything get suck down inside that black hole and I was staring at the page of the book like it was blank or infinity.

The maxi mustbe stop. Next thing I know, is because somebody shaking my shoulder and saying, 'Miss Allie! Happy New Year!'

The black hole close up like water going down a drain.

It was Tamika, a girl I does work with. She black eyes was sparkling and she teeth look extra white when she smile, splitting she dark brown face from ear to ear.

'Aye, happy New Year! But what you doing on this side?'

I wouldn't say we was close friends, but we was friendly enough for me to know she was living Chaguanas, not Carenage.

She slide in next to me and kiss me on the cheek. As she reach to put she purse on she lap, I spot a little twinkling on she left hand.

'Hmmm, like somebody had a very happy New Year!' I tell she, grinning.

'Girl,' she say. She hold out she hand and turning it left and right so the little diamond could catch the light. 'Curtis and me get engage. Christmas.'

'All you set a date yet?'

'Girl, you rushing me, or what? No, no date. But I move in by he this weekend.'

'That is why you down here? Where all you living?'

'In he mother house, up in La Horquette.' Tamika skin up she face a little bit. 'That woman like she don't like the best bone in my body.'

'And you know you have plenty bones,' I tell she. I does tease Tamika all the time because she bony and long. She used to be a dancer and she still have the body for it. I try to get she to do some modelling for the shop, for a ad for the papers, but she was never interested – is only 'Curtis this' and 'Curtis that'. I used to feel like that about Leo, too, once upon a time. He say he want to carry me out on a evening and like a fool I drop everything: Leo want me. Leo love me. Leo need me.

I watch the sea slide by the maxi as we speed down the highway towards the city, listening with half a ear to Tamika chattering away about the engagement and she soon-to-be mother-in-law and how Curtis was so generous and rayrayray. Even on this western peninsula, you could still see spectacular colours on the water when the sun coming up: a little pink, a little silver, a little blue, a little gold. Waves was washing up on the shore in between the mangrove growing in the water on the side of the highway. A man was bathing a horse in the sea, leading it in by the reins. I feel sorry for the horse. That water mustbe damn cold at that hour.

'And you?' Tamika jook my waist with she elbow. 'What you get for Christmas?'

'Nothing,' I say, eating the pain when she bounce me. That was one of Leo favourite spots, too. I wish I could have go back in the black hole again.

'Nothing? Or you don't want to tell me?' Tamika say, like she was trying to get back at me for the bony joke.

I make up my mind just like that. I don't know what fly in my head. I never tell nobody about this before, but just so, just so I decide I go tell Tamika. 'You know what? I go show you what I get for Christmas. Leo give me. When we reach in work, I go show you.'

A Bobo Shanti rasta man sitting on the other side of Tamika, he hair tie up in a turban, raise he eyebrow and give we a reproachful look from the side of he eye. He mustbe feel is some sex thing I talking about.

Oh, brother man, if you only know, I tell myself.

We come out the maxi with everybody else and join the river of people flowing from South Quay to Broadway. Seven in the morning, first workday of the year, and town was already jumping: little school children ent reaching my hip, weigh down with bags bigger than them, jostling with full grown man and woman. Everybody hurrying to reach to school, work, government office or wherever they was going. Tamika in she orange work polo jersey and jeans, and me in my shirt and skirt blend right in as we cross the road by Cipriani statue and walk half a block to On the Town. Is two years now I is store manager; Tamika is a sales clerk. We does sell clothes and accessories, mostly cheap Chinese thing we boss

7

wife does order. The boss wife little on the tacky side, but she bright for so. The clothes does be bright bright bright and a little on the tacky side, just like she.

I unlock the big metal grill and roll it up to reach the shop door. I walk inside first. Tamika come in after me and I hand she the big, jangling bunch of keys to lock back the street door, and both of we gone in the back by the kitchen. I put on the kettle and put out some cups, and she take out a open tin of condensed milk, the pack of Crix and the small small block of cheese from the little fridge. She cut up squares of cheddar and put about ten biscuit on a plate while I make the tea. This time I put sugar and milk in mine until it was sweet and light. I give she she cup with a spoon and put the milk on the table.

'So, what is this big secret thing Leo give you for Christmas?' Tamika sit down by the table and take a bite from she Crix and watch me mischievously, she eyes practically sparkling.

I still standing up by the kettle. I suck my teeth and set up myself to show she. My belly boiling, fus I nervous. But outside, I was cool. 'Curiosity kill the cat, eh, Miss Tamika.' I pull my shirt out my waistband.

'What is this!' Tamika was squeaking, excited like a little child in a birthday party as she sipping she tea.

I feel she figure it was a navel ring or a tattoo I going and show she. She didn't notice my face was serious like a police in court.

When I unbutton the shirt, she put down she tea and she hand start to shake.

'Miss Allie! What the hell?'

'You see? Leo give me.' I shake my shoulders in a shrug and button back up the shirt.

Tamika ent say a word. She just sit down there with she lip quivering and she eye fulling up with water. I sit down and try to eat my Crix and cheese.

Finally, tears rolling down she face, she say soft soft, 'You call the police?'

'Police? You joking? What police go do? Say is man and woman business and leave me to get more cutass?'

'No, girl,' Tamika say, in a rush. 'Things different now. They does actually help—'

I hold up my hand and stop she right there. 'If Leo only know I call police for he, is even more licks I go get.'

The Crix pack on the table start unfolding for itself as the plastic try to find back the shape it want to be in, even though I roll it and twist it up to make it stay close.

Tamika reach and pick it up. She get up and put it back in the fridge with the cheese and the milk. She sit back down. She didn't say nothing. She didn't watch me in my eye. All kind of expressions was passing on she face: horror, disgust, sorrow, but then rage settle around she mouth and draw out she eyes to finally look at me. 'Why you does stay, Miss Allie?'

'You know, that is the first question people does ask?' My throat was dry. I take up the cup with my two hand to keep from trembling and throwing down the tea. I sip some before I talk. I feel like she was accusing me. I hear it from doctor and nurse already, as though by staying I was saying I want to get licks. 'Nobody doesn't ask, "Why he don't stop beating you?" As if somehow is a normal thing for a man to beat a woman. Yet it not normal for a woman to stay with a man who beating she? If is the woman fault for staying, not the man fault for lashing she, beating woman come normal, then.'

Tamika still sit down quiet. Water full up in she eye again. She shake she head hard, maybe to say, No, it not normal. But she didn't open she mouth to tell me nothing.

'He doesn't always be so,' I say. It was partly true. 'When we meet, he was nice. He was sweet. If you see that man. Hard body for days. And, oh gorm, girl, that smile. A hundred watts he could turn on and off when he want and I ain't lie,

9

he hook me with he voice. You know he's a singer. Voice like butter.' I smile to remember them days.

She shake she head. 'I know he's a big famous singer. And he handsome. To look at him you would never know he is a monster, eh?'

That make me jump. 'No, Tamika. He's not a monster. He like to lash and he like to…' I study if I could really tell this girl all the thing Leo does do me. But if she react like that when she only see the bruises on my body, she go dead if she know the rest. My turn to shake my head. 'No, he's not no monster. He take care of me. He put me in house, a real house. I never meet a man who love me so much.' I watch she. My eyes was dry. 'He still love me,' I say confidently, though I wonder if I self believe it.

'And you? You still love he?' she challenge me, looking straight in my eye.

A hard question for so early in the morning. And what is love? I human, I have feelings. I with the man. Of course I love him. Yet, the way he love me does make me hate myself.

He very imperfect, is true. But how to tell Tamika that, as far as I concern, it ent have no such thing as a good man anyway? One man I had was locho for spite, sitting down there waiting for me to mind him and not getting up to get for heself. One man was under he mother skirt; he couldn't say boo unless he mother tell him say boo. She used to buy down to he drawers for him. I had plenty horner man, sniffing behind every woman bottom they see. Some boldface exes bring their women in we place and bull them in we bed. Hence the 'exes'. Is not that I vex they have woman, but, oh gorm! It have rules for this thing, man. Another one love he boys more than he love me, liming, drinking and playing football with them like that was he work. He didn't have no time or energy for me when the night come.

All of them used to lash.

Leo have he ways, me ent say no. Yes, he does horn, but so what? I accustom and what don't kill does fatten. As long as he have enough leave over for me to get my share. That share was worth a lot, to me. Even with the licks and the rest of it, when he wasn't hurting me, he was my best lover. For me, that was good enough.

If I still love him? Simplest answer: 'Yes,' I say. In my head, I tack on, Sometimes.

We eat we biscuit and drink we tea and she wipe she face and fix back she eyeliner. We didn't say nothing again. By the time the two next girls who does work with we, Ann and Janelle, come knocking on the door, it was nearly time to open up the shop. I put my hair up in a ponytail and put on some lipstick and slap on a smile. It was eight o'clock.

The week after New Year's does start kind of slow in we shop. Nobody not coming in for Christmas lime clothes or Old Year's night dress, and it just a little too early for the Carnival fete clothes to sell. The four of we does busy weself with stock taking and tidying up the racks in between the odd customer or two. As it was slow, when Ann take she break I figure was a good time to duck out. I tell Tamika I coming back, and I make my way to Prince Street corner where the main branch of On the Town was. I walk right in.

This shop was almost the same as we own – same cheap clothes, same sales staff in orange polo jersey and jeans – but bigger. They had a stock room upstairs and that is where I make a tack for as I enter the shop, but not before I stop by a cow-eye, fat dougla girl.

As usual when I talking to staff and strangers, I put on my best town accent. Just because I is a country bookie don't mean I does always talk like one. 'Marie, could you go to the other branch to help Tamika, please? I'd like to have a meeting with Mr Sharma.'

Marie roll up she eyes, round and brown and placid like a cow own and she turn she big backside and walk out the store without answering me. What I do the girl I don't know, but she never like me. Is a reaction I accustom with. Some women will flat out tell you they don't trust red woman, and because my skin light colour they feel like I feel I better than them. That is bullshit, but you couldn't tell that to Marie, a dark-skin girl with curly black hair. On top of all the colour thing, she mustbe feel I take she work: if I didn't come she would have been the manager of the next town branch because she working for the company so long. She watch me slight, as if I get my work because I is a pretty local white girl and the boss like me, not because I is a big woman with years of experience in sales and management. I never went much school, but I learn from working my way up – and not on my back, neither. She want to manage shop? Why she didn't go San Fernando when they open the South branch? I steups in my mind.

Climbing up the narrow stairs at the back of the shop, I squeeze past bales of clothes that didn't unpack yet and one or two naked mannequin with unreasonably big breasts and bottom. That was the latest thing: mannequin that look more like Marie than like me or Tamika. The idea was that Caribbean woman have plenty curves so the mannequins should have plenty curves, too. Didn't matter much to me. Whatever the mannequin look like I would dress it and sell the clothes either way.

I knock on the door and walk in one time, saying, 'Is me. Happy New Year.'

My boss face spread out in a smile as he see me. Bobby Sharma had big teeth in a wide, Brahmin face. He look a little like a shark with them teeth, I always thought: hungry and sneaky.

Bobby get up one time and come around the desk. It had all kind of clutter on it – papers, ledgers, files, and garment samples. Even the office had a few bundles of clothes and a mannequin. He had to slide between them and the desk to reach me and hug me up.

'Take it easy,' I say, screwing up my face when he wrap he arms around my body. 'That hurting.'

'Hurting?' He face set up just so. 'He beating you again?'

'That is not your business,' I tell he.

Bobby hush he mouth and start to unbutton my shirt. I slap he hand away. He move he hand to my thigh, slipping it up between my legs and touching my panty before I could react.

I jump and do a kind of duck and slide – slither – away from he hand. 'You didn't even lock the door,' I say, pulling my skirt back down and sitting in one of the two chairs on that side of the desk.

He lock the door and, raising my hair off my back, kiss my neck soft and wet. I shiver, because he damn well know the spot.

'Bobby, we don't have time for this. I have to talk to you about the shop.'

'The shop could wait. Ten minutes,' he say, putting he hand down inside a cup of my bra and pinching the nipple.

'Five,' I say.

'Ten,' he insist.

I stand up and pull my skirt hem up to my waist, bending forward over the desk. 'Five,' I say again.

TWO

Eight minutes later I straighten my skirt and do my best to smooth down the hair he ramfle up. As I sit down again he shuffle back around to he side of the desk and settle in a tufted black leather executive chair. It look like it could be in a *MACO Caribbean* magazine.

'That new,' I say.

He stroke the leather armrest. 'Christmas present.'

'Sita?'

He purse he lips but didn't answer. Of course it was from Sita. Who else?

'It very nice. I sure she want you to work very hard this year to earn it,' I tell him, with a little savage smile on my lips.

He ignore me. 'What you want to discuss about the shop?'

Down to brass tacks one time, I start to explain that the shop need a new window display.

'Fire Fete coming. Ent we did order a shipment of red and orange clothes? I suppose that is what in them bales outside.'

He nod.

'I want to bring in Jerry to do the window, something really spectacular. We have to get rid of them clothes somehow.' Is grin I was grinning by now. Since I working there I telling him Sita don't have no taste, but he say he hands tie. Is Sita who have the money, not Bobby. What Sita want, Sita get, and if that mean ordering hundreds of pieces that can't sell, he don't business with that.

'I feel,' I continue, 'we could push the red clothes for Fire Fete. We might as well. Or is clearance sale for Easter.'

Bobby hair short and black, cut like he's a soldier. When he agitated, he does run he hand over it as though he stroking a cat. He do that for a few seconds and then pick up the handset for the beige telephone on top he desk and dial two numbers. 'Ahm, Marie there?'

'I send Marie down the road to hold on for me,' I jump in, just as a woman on the line say, 'No, Mr Sharma.' I hear the squeaky little voice and figure it was Shaniqua, one of the shop girls downstairs.

He suck he teeth. 'Marie know the inventory like the back of she hand, man.' He suck he teeth again, then hang up the phone and dial another, longer number. 'Marie, I need you up here for this meeting with Miss Lopez. Come up now.'

That wouldn't make Marie like me any better, I tell myself. First I send she down the road, then he call she to come back up the road. It wasn't a long walk – just two blocks – but I know she done didn't like my head already and that would be one more thing to hold against me.

He hang up the phone and lean back in he new leather chair, rocking back and forth and looking at me with he pretty amber eyes, smiling with he shark teeth showing. As if he remember something, he snap he finger and pick up a parcel from under the desk.

'Here,' he say. 'This is for you.'

Inside the bag it had a brand new cell phone still in the box. I hand him back one time. 'You want Leo kill me?'

'What he killing you for? Is for work, Alethea. Just for work.'

'You feel he stupid.'

'No, I feel that he has to understand his wife is a working woman and she has responsibilities. When you home, Allie,' he say, dropping he voice, 'I doesn't know if you alive or dead. I nearly kill myself over the Christmas, worrying about what that man was doing you out there behind God back.'

'Carenage not behind God back, Bobby. There are roads, streetlights, running water and everything.'

'You know what I mean.' Again, he tone change. This time it was what books does call wheedling. 'Girl, let me put you in a apartment, nah. Let me get you away from that man. You would have everything. I would pay your rent, you would have phone, cable, a car, even a swimming pool, if that is what you want. Just—'

I cut him off, 'I would have the people-man, that is what I would have. I am not your whore, Bobby.' You could have slice meat with the razor edge of my voice. The town accent come back strong strong. 'I work for you, making a shop manager's salary – good, but not great. If people were to see me in a nice house, driving a nice car and living large, what do you think they would say? What other conclusion would they come to but that I was sleeping with the boss?'

'But you are sleeping with the boss!'

I shake my head. 'I sleeping with you because I want to, not because I have to. If you put me in house that is another level of obligation, a level I am not willing to live with. Because when Sita calls for her husband, you will run to answer.'

He eyes was sad sad because he know it was the truth.

'Leo might be a beast. I might be living in hell. But is my beast and my hell and I don't have to answer to Sita Sharma for any of it. Talk done.' Pushing the phone back towards him over the crowded desk, I fold my arms and set up my face.

Still, he push the phone back to me. 'Take it. I giving all the managers anyway. Is not you alone.' He switch back to business and pick up the telephone on he desk again. 'Is Jerry you want to do the window, you say?'

By the time Marie knock on the door, me and Bobby done talk to Jerry about starting the window the next day.

'Come!' Bobby call out, forgetting he did lock the door. Of course, that was one more mark against me when I had was to get up and unlock the door for she to come inside with she sour face. She mustbe was wondering what kind of 'business' we was talking so that we had to lock the door.

'Ann come back yet?'

'Yes, Miss Allie,' she say. 'She now reach back.' In front of Bobby she was sweet like a paradise plum, fanning sheself with one hand and using the next hand to pat away the little sweat she was sweating, to emphasise how quick she run up the road when he call she. 'I see you get your cell phone,' Marie say to me, before turning to Bobby. 'You show her the bags?'

'Oh!' Bobby start to grin, picking through the stacks of things on the desk to find a silver-colour plastic handle-bag with *On the Town* print on it. 'You like it?'

'Actually, yes,' I say, surprising even me. Nothing Sita put she hand on does be nice or tasteful and this bag come as a shock because it was both.

'Is I who design it,' Marie say, gloating. She cow eye watch me innocent, but I know and she know exactly what I was thinking just before.

17

'Very nice,' I say. 'Good job, Marie.' I give she a big grin. Let she put that in she pipe and smoke it.

All that pass voosh over Bobby head. He turn to Marie and ask she to bring samples from the bales for me to see what we had to work with.

By the time we done pick the samples, Bobby watch the clock on the wall and say he had a appointment just now and he had to go. He leave me and Marie in the office. One time, I tell she call a stock boy and start to pack up things for we branch.

As we waiting she didn't waste a second before she start to gossip. 'I see Tamika get engage,' she say, the cow eye watching me from underneath she eyelash.

'Uh huh,' I say, playing like I busy with the handle bags.

The stock boy come pounding up the stairs like a horse.

'Mark,' I say, 'please pack out a dozen each of these samples, in all sizes, and deliver them to the other branch.'

'Yes, Miss Allie.' He grab the samples from my hand and went to work. We follow him outside, watching him pull out slippery satin, Spandex and polyester garments in shades of red and orange, from coral to terracotta. Some them actually wasn't so bad, I tell myself. Sita mustbe getting some taste after all.

As he start to pack them up in brown boxes, Marie come back with the gossiping. 'Is the same fella she engage to? How he name...Curtis?'

'Uh huh,' I say again.

'Hmmm,' she murmur. The single sound had a world of meaning in it.

I hit she one cut eye.

'Is just that I hear he with Tiny, nah,' she say, hasty, as though she fraid I hit she for truth.

I doesn't like to gossip, but this was news that Tamika could probably use, so I take the bait. 'Tiny who?' I try to make it sound casual, but Marie damn well know I was interested.

'You don't remember Tiny? She used to work here, but she went over by Hadeed and them in September. A fine fine dark-skin girl with a gold teeth. She does have she hair in braids.'

I frown. The name didn't ring a bell but the description was familiar. 'You mean...' I was groping for the name I know she by. 'Alicia?'

'Yes, Alicia. But everybody does call she Tiny. I hear she and Curtis was by Smokey and Bunty the other night and she was sitting down in he lap. I hear they was kissing up and thing,' Marie say. She try to sound innocent, but it had pure venom dripping from them big, square teeth when she smile.

'He has one of those faces, you know?' I smiled right back at her. 'I'm sure it wasn't him.'

She give me a sceptical look. 'If you say so. That is your friend, not mines.'

The stock boy walk out the store pushing a dolly of goods. I walk out behind him just in time to see Bobby climb in Sita gold BMW and kiss he wife hello. In spite of myself I feel a how. I mean, I wasn't a stone. The man was still my lover. Sita, bleach-blonde hair press out straight straight, and wearing big Versace shades on she head, fix she lipstick before she drive off. Neither of them see me.

I follow Mark down to the shop. When he start to unload he start to chat up Tamika one time.

'Princess,' he say, oozing charm. He wasn't a bad looking boy, but he was a boy, only eighteen or nineteen, if I remember properly. Tamika didn't take him on so he shift to Janelle, a short, brown-skin girl with a big bottom. She was more he age, and she giggle at the chats he give she, lapping up every unctuous compliment. Good word, I tell myself. Unctuous. I wonder if I was ever so young and foolish like Janelle.

Going back to my perch by the cash register, I ask Tamika how things went while I was gone.

'Not bad, you know. Surprising for this time of year. You know how people does like to spend out all their money over the Christmas and not have a red cent leave back for January,' she say. 'But like somebody get a bonus. A lady come in and pick out a set of clothes for she niece. I think is she niece, anyway. Plus they promise to come back just now – they gone and look for sneakers and the child want a jersey to match.'

We spend the rest of the morning unpacking stock and discussing plans for the window. Although the next store bigger, we does get more traffic because we almost at the bottom of Frederick Street, prime real estate for the retail outlets in the city because the marish and the parish had to pass there twice a day to go home. But don't look for no designer brands on lower Frederick Street. Is strictly knockoff and cheap thing. Downtown wasn't no spot for no exclusive boutique, and even the tacky clothes used to sell. Every stale bun have its rancid cheese, as they say.

I hear Ann, Janelle and Tamika chattering in the corner, shooting glances at me every couple of sentences. It didn't have no customers in the store for the time being, so I come down from my perch and went to hear what they was talking about.

'Is Fire Fete,' Tamika explain. 'I telling them you would never go that kind of party, but they saying everybody going so why you can't come.'

'In the first place,' I say, 'who is "everybody"?'

'All the On the Town staff,' Ann put in. 'We buying tickets early to get the discount. Mark was telling we. Mr Sharma sponsoring a flag and everything.'

'Really?'

'Yes, and we go have cooler, and drinks and one big section. With the stock boys and all the girls is eleven people.

A dozen if you coming. Plus them from the branch in South,' Janelle say.

'Don't forget who bringing they man,' Tamika say, holding up she little diamond to make she point.

Everybody laugh.

'Yes, Miss Tamika,' Ann say. 'Curtis and all could come.'

'The point is,' Janelle say, 'we could have a nice lime. But Tamika say you doesn't go them kind of fete.'

'I don't go to any kind of fete,' I admit. 'I's not really a Carnival person.'

'Oh, gosh,' Tamika say, 'pull that stick out your bamsee and come, nah!'

While Janelle and Ann look like they frighten to react first, I buss out in a scandalous laugh. 'So that is what you think, eh! Well, all right, Miss Tamika. I will come.'

'For truth?'

'Yes, for truth. My first Fire Fete,' I say, and while them giggling behind the clothes rack I straightening the merchandise to do like I not feeling shame. I look around the store, watching out for customers. A Indian woman and a little girl – I saying little girl but she mustbe was about thirteen, fourteen years – walk in and start to scan the store for help. Before they could say a word I leave the staff, walk up behind the customers and say, 'Can I help you, ladies?'

The big woman had a strong American accent over a island twang. 'Yes, thank you,' she say. 'We were here a little while ago and I told the sales girl we'd be back...here we are!' She hold up one of we Carnival jersey – one that say *Dead or Alive!* – and ask if we had it in a size to fit the little girl.

'A small? Sure,' I say, and start to flip through the rack to look for the size. The jerseys was hanging on one of them circular racks that does turn, so it didn't take me long to check the neck tags and find the right size. I send the girl in the dressing room with the jersey and turn around to find the big woman watching me hard hard hard, with a frown on she face.

'Wait a minute,' she say, in that Yankee drawl, 'are you from Aranguez?'

She didn't say it like the Spanish, Ah-ran-huez, but like we does say it, Ah-rang-gwez.

It was my turn to watch she hard. 'Jankie?'

'Girlie?'

We hug up long and hard and I think she start to cry a little bit.

'You know how long I ent see—'

'Where the heck did you go—'

Both of we tumbling over one another to say the same thing.

'You first!' she say.

'It so nice to see you!'

I hold she at arm's length and take in everything, from head to foot. The hair dye nearly blonde, the skin lighter than I remember, the black eyes now as hazel brown as if I looking in my own face. Dolce and Gabbana sunglasses hooking back the hair like a bandeau. A plain white cotton voile kurta over what they does call 'boyfriend' jeans – I couldn't make out the brand but I bet it was a Guess, from the stitching and the fabric. Bright orangey-brown Hermès 'hobo' bag – in magazine they does call the colour cognac, if I remember right. One-carat white diamond solitaires, princess cut, in platinum setting, on hand, ears and neck; platinum wedding band with so much round brilliants it almost look like it pave. Khaki canvas wedge-heel sandals – Guess, too, I would say. Perfect French pedicure. The perfume was Light Blue, by Dolce and Gabbana.

She was turning forty, too, I know. But it didn't show on she face. She look like thirty for the most.

22

'You look amazing,' I say. I wasn't lying. My old best friend was buff – I could tell from the arms and the abs when she hug me up – and she skin was smooth and the makeup was perfect, even in the island heat. Not a smudge, not a speck out of place on the look they does call 'nude', but what does really take about a half hour to do, from foundation to setting spray.

'Oh,' she say, waving my comment away like is a fly buzzing around she face. 'But you! I haven't seen you in years!' I know what she would see if she do me the same thing I do she. Natural hair, straight and long just like when I was fifteen; same hazel eyes. Too much foundation, in a colour that was slightly too dark for me. Not looking my age, but not looking great, neither. Cubic zirconias on ears and neck, sterling silver setting. No ring on finger; manicured nails, but no polish. White cotton blouse – maybe Gap? Straight black and white pinstripe skirt, anonymous designer. No stockings, but at least the legs shave. Black slingback pumps, kitten heel, patent leather – Nine West? Or knock off? Hard to tell without checking. Feet soft and scrubbed. Cool Water for women, Davidoff. 'You look amazing, too, Girlie!'

Yeah, right, I tell myself. But she was smiling like she see Christmas, so maybe she wasn't lying. I suppose, compare to plenty women my age on this island, where people doesn't wear sunblock and doesn't take care of theyself really, I was looking damn good.

'Nobody doesn't call me Girlie no more,' I say, almost automatic. 'They does call me Alethea – Allie, for short.'

'Alethea,' she say, remembering it in she mouth. It was always my birth-paper name, but nobody didn't call me that growing up, not even in school. Teachers used to call me Lopez and I was Girlie to everybody else. Is only for exams I use the name at all when I was young.

'So, how are you?' I ask she, genuinely curious. Me ent see she in years but I wasn't surprise she pop up in a shop on Frederick Street that January day. Carnival time all the 'foreign' locals who could afford does come back home to eat roti and doubles and pelau, drink rum and wine down the place for a few weeks before they go back in the cold. I figure Jankie was the same. 'Where were you all this time? When last I saw you, you were in Miami with your mother.'

'Oh my God,' she say, in that high pitch American squeal, like Paris Hilton. 'It's been that long since we've seen each other? I moved from Miami to New York, what, ten years ago? I mean, I'm back in Miami now – we have a nice condo on South Beach – but we were in New York for years. When did you leave...oh, what was the name of the cloth store again?'

'Queensway.'

'Right, of course. When did you leave Queensway? I thought you would be there for life. And what about your mom? And Colin?'

I only smile and shake my head. Mammie? Colin? Not today, nah. I change the topic as though I never hear she. 'Still married to Mr Inalsingh?'

She hold up the big set of diamond on she hand. She smile was bright like glass. 'Twenty-three years.'

Jankie didn't bother to ask about me. My naked hand stay hanging by my side.

She hug me up again. I hug she up back, but all kind of memories was dancing in my head, bad and good. It had a time Jankie and she family come like my lifeline. She was my good good friend in school. She know we was poor, but she didn't know half the thing I used to go through when I wasn't by she. After junior sec, I didn't do no fourteen-plus exam to go in senior comp. What was the point? I wasn't no scholar. She family give me a work in their roti shop.

24

And when I couldn't take it no more and run away from my mother house, is right by Jankie I went, too.

But Jankie married we PE teacher, Mr Inalsingh, and went away and that was the end of that. I see she once or twice in the years in between, but we never keep in touch. Is only Carnival bring she back home, and is only by chance she come in my shop.

A piping little freshwater Yankee voice call from the changing room, 'Aunt Jankie? Would you look at this?'

I carry my old friend in the back to see what the girl want.

The jersey fit she nice – not too tight, although the little tut-tuts was pushing up from the bra in the way that teenage girls' breasts does do. I could tell she was embarrass one time.

'You find it too tight, honey?' I say.

She nod she head, pulling down the jersey hem and worrying at the neckline at the same time.

Jankie say, 'It looks fine. Amanda, this is my dear old friend, Alethea. We went to high school together.'

High school? Since when Aranguez Junior Sec was a high school? But out loud I only say, 'Nice to meet you, Amanda. You must be Ricky's child.'

Amanda look confuse. She never lay eyes on me, never hear word one about me, I bet. 'Nice to meet you, Aunty Althea—'

'Alethea,' I say. 'It's an old-fashioned name. My mom named me after my grandmother. Alethea,' I say again, slow.

'Aunty Alethea.'

'Your Aunty Jankie knew me as Girlie.'

The child face clear up one time. 'Of course! She talks about you all the time. She says you were the prettiest girl in school and she was so jealous of you.'

I laugh out loud for that one. 'Jealous of me?' I shake my head, still laughing. 'Amanda, your aunty had everything:

25

a nice mom, a dad, nice house, nice clothes – really nice clothes! I had nothing she would envy.'

But then I think about the dyed hair, the contact lenses, the bleached skin. Maybe I had something she didn't have, in truth. Maybe she feel I had something to jealous.

People strange, yes.

THREE

When lunchtime reach, Tamika come up to me by the cash register where I was sitting down and ask if I know anything about church wedding.

Well, I had to laugh. 'Me? What I go know about church wedding? Or any wedding? You forget is shack up I shack up?'

She make monkey face at me, skinning up she nose and pushing out she tongue, and tell me she want to go by the Catholic church up the road, if I will come with she. I didn't have nothing better to do with my lunchtime, and the customers still one-one, so I say okay. I give Ann the keys and tell she and Janelle we coming back in about a hour, and me and Tamika step out on Frederick Street and start walking towards the Savannah.

I stop and buy a pack of nuts and a juice from a man on the corner of Queen Street. I try to eat my nuts in peace but Tamika start to talk as soon as we clear the block.

'Hear nah, girl, you have to leave that man, you know.'

'Who, Leo?'

'Yes, Leo! Who else? You feel is the nuts man I there with?'

'Well these nuts kind of dry...'

'Thing to cry you laughing?'

'What you want me do, Tamika? Leave him and go where? And do what?'

'How you mean? You's a big woman. You's a free woman, too. You not married. You don't have no children. You have a good work. You buy house and car and land with he or what?'

I shake my head.

'Well, pack your things and leave.'

'I can't just walk out on him. Is not really he fault.'

Tamika watch me with she eye hard like stone. 'That is a pack of ass. This is abuse. And is he fault. Who fault you think it is?'

I shake my shoulders again. I didn't really want to talk about it any more, but like Tamika wouldn't shut up.

'Is not your fault. Is he hit you. No matter what excuse he make, is not your fault.'

'He feel I have a next man.'

'So what? You could have ten next man. Is not a excuse for he to beat you. Oh gorm, Miss Allie.'

By this time we turn the corner by Hart Street and walking towards the Red House. Woodford Square was full of people, hustling to get their lunch and ignoring the green grass and lush trees over their heads. The sun was high in the sky and I turn my face up to feel the heat. It was nice to get out of the air conditioning for a little while. Tamika pull my hand. 'Aye, I talking to you, girlie.'

'You know,' I say, 'when I was a little girl they used to call me Girlie. They never call me Alethea. They never call me Allie. They just call me Girlie. Like if that is all I ever was.'

'Alethea Lopez,' Tamika say, stern like she is my teacher and I daydreaming in she class, 'you hearing what I saying? You have to leave that man.'

I suck my teeth and continue to dig out the red-skinned peanuts from the brown paper sack in my hand. I eat them whole, skin and all, and take a sip from the box of orange juice. 'Tamika French,' I answer she same way, 'you just say I's a big woman. Let we drop this talk, nah.'

Tamika walk off a little way in front, but by the time we reach the old Fire Station she slow down. 'All right. Whatever you want, boss lady.'

We cut around the Red House and pass Police Headquarters and reach by the Catholic church in a couple of minutes. One or two ladies in office clothes was hustling through the wrought iron gates into the old stone church, and I hear the sound of women raising a hymn inside: 'O Come, All Ye Faithful'.

So much years I spend in church when I was small, but I had to think for a little while to remember that January third is still Christmas, because Epiphany is on January sixth.

Inside the church was cool and dark, and smoky with incense. A young, dark-skin priest was up by the altar, in white vestments, he back to we. Tamika ask one of the women who now come in which part the office was and the woman point to a side door. Tamika leave me by the door.

Old habits does die hard: I dip a finger in the holy water font by the door and genuflect before I sit down on a hard wooden pew quite in the back of the church.

Mass was now starting. I stand up again and I was kind of surprise it was the same words I know from when I was a girl. Was the same confession and all. I recite the words without thinking because I know them by heart, but I didn't really pay no attention to them. You feel I study how I living with Leo and still taking man on the side? Please. Who say God go bother with that? If he had a problem with it he never tell me word one. I sing the Kyrie in the same panty Bobby Sharma pull down that morning.

I was thinking about my mother and how she grow me up staunch staunch Catholic, and how I doesn't go nowhere near a church now, when something about the priest voice catch my ear. I look up and strain to see his face, but it was hard, in the dim light, and with the smoke from the censer the acolyte in a white gown was swinging around... I just couldn't see clear. I laugh at myself. Forty. They does warn you your eyes go fail you. They doesn't mention that your ears go play tricks on you, too.

I didn't go for communion when the time come, although I answer all the old responses that stick in my head since I small. Lord, I am not worthy to receive you, but only say the word and I shall be healed. When the old ladies and them was lining up for communion I tell myself I in church so I might as well kneel down and pray.

At first I didn't know what I was praying for. Idleness? Old habit, more likely. But like I relax into it and my mind start to go over what happen to me over the past week. Christmas was bad. New Years was worse. I relive every kick, cuff, tap and slap Leo give me and I start to really wonder what hell I was living in, and why.

I figure is because I accustom by now why I don't leave Leo. He doesn't make too much money, and the house not exactly nice, although it could have been if somebody take time to clean it and paint it and fix the old break-up window and door. I know that person wouldn't be me. Tell the truth, I was fed up with the house, fed up with the licks. Fed up with Leo and him blaming me for everything. But you ever find yourself down in a canal? It hard to climb out by yourself.

Mass finish – barely half hour long – right after communion and the women scatter like doves halfway through the exit hymn: 'Go Tell It on the Mountain'.

Tamika creep up beside me and say, 'The office was close for mass. Let we go now and see if it open back.'

'You go, nah,' I tell she. 'I go wait here.'

'Oh gorm, Alethea, you promise.'

'When I promise?' I watch she with my eye big big. I never promise nothing. I say I go go with she to the church, but I never promise nothing. But I genuflect again and stand up and walk through the church to the side door which part she say the office was. We went inside the little white annex – concrete, not stone like the church – and sit down on some hard hard chairs where a sour-face old crone tell we to sit down in a outer office and wait. I was checking out she blue hair and wondering what effect she was going for when the priest come in.

Is he recognise me first.

'Girlie?' he say.

JANUARY 1

Alethea's hair was scraped back into two ponytails of curls that hung down her back; the rubber bands holding them were so tight that the skin around her eyes was pulled up and she looked like a Chinee. Black patent leather shoes pinched her feet. The scratchy lace of her Peter Pan collar burned her neck. The velvet dress and her white stockings made her legs and back perspire. Mammie always got into a bad mood when she had to wear a girdle and longline bra, so Alethea didn't mention her own discomfort. It was just for mass, she told herself. She'd be back home and in regular clothes in a little while, eating bread and ham and, maybe, if Mammie wasn't too mad, an apple.

But, of course, mass lasted forever. She was quietly bewildered at the rituals. Fah in his red coat over the white dress, holding up the golden cups and singing things. All the grown-ups in fancy dresses and hats: the women in click-clacking high-heel shoes, thick white powder on their necks, red lipstick, and the men in black suits that smelled like the cupboard. Mammie made her kneel down, stand up, sit down, all the time, dragging her up by the elbow with a jerk when she didn't move fast enough. She wanted to taste thebodyanblood but Mammie put her to sit down and told her to wait – she couldn't follow her up to get it from Fah. When she was a big girl, Mammie said. Just like school, high-heel shoes, lipstick and perfume. When she was a big girl she would do plenty things, just like Mammie.

After mass, Mammie took her to the back of the church where a cloud of fragrance floated around the ladies. They pinched her cheeks and fussed over her hair and kissed her; when she rubbed her cheek Mammie slapped her hand. 'Why you wiping off Miss Lucy kiss, Girlie?' Alethea looked at her palm, streaked red. An old man who smelled like cigarettes put her on his knee and tickled her under her arms. He gave her two twenty-five cents afterwards. Mammie took them and put them in her purse – a sparkling black one with a silver chain for a strap. It was her Good Handbag and Alethea wasn't allowed to touch it, ever. She wondered how she would get her two shillings back from the Good Handbag, if she would be able to go with Mammie and buy hallay or a kaiser ball, or if the press man would pass around that day and she would get a cup of crushed ice, red and sticky with sweet guava syrup.

They walked down the hill from the church, passing through the dead quiet Croisée. The shoes were burning. Alethea's big toe, right in the corner, and the little toe, all along the side, felt like they were on fire. Mammie hushed her up when she started to cry. As she continued, Mammie pinched her arm roughly.

Finally, Mammie stopped and picked her up, warning her, 'Don't put your nasty foot on my nice dress, you hear!' Alethea clung to Mammie's neck with her skinny arms, her thighs clamped around Mammie's waist, and her bony legs sticking straight out behind Mammie's back. Mammie sucked her teeth and pushed Alethea's legs down. 'Why you like to make a pappyshow all the time?'

Alethea didn't know what was a pappyshow. Maybe it had something to do with her father, though she couldn't figure out why holding on to Mammie like that because her feet hurt was going to make her Pappy come and see them. Mammie said that Pappy was dead and wasn't coming back at all, not ever.

The morning sun was already hot and bright. Mammie was soft and strong, and Alethea soon found her head nodding against her mother's shoulder, soothed by the rocking of her walk. When she opened her eyes again, it was to see the high bush of the track leading to their house. She slid down Mammie's chest and leaned sleepily against her as she opened the kitchen door. Mammie stepped inside and came to an abrupt stop. Alethea bounced off her backside and fell on her own bottom, startled.

Between Mammie's legs she could see a man at the kitchen table. He had a sleeping baby boy on his lap. Alethea studied the toddler's small, hard leather shoes and wondered if they hurt his toes when he walked like hers did.

'Happy New Year, Marcia.' His voice was funny. Like the man on the radio singing 'I Heard it Through the Grapevine.' He was small and skinny, with straight black hair, golden skin and eyes like black buttons. His eyebrows were straight lines across his forehead, as thin as his lips.

'Mammie,' Alethea whispered urgently. 'Who is that?'

'Hush your mouth, Girlie, who talking to you?' Mammie hissed.

The strange man stood up, still holding the child, who fussed but went back to sleep when the man rocked him against his chest. 'Shhhh, shhhh, Colin, nice boy,' the man murmured.

Mammie hadn't moved. Alethea peeped around her skirt at the visitors and the motion drew her mother's attention.

'Girlie, get up and go and change your clothes!'

As Alethea scuttled into the next room, she heard Mammie's voice from behind the curtain. Mammie wasn't whispering but she dropped her voice low enough that Alethea had to strain to hear her. She was angry. It sounded like she was biting her words up before she spat them out at the man.

'Where you come out?'

'Marcia. You know I was in New York.'

'And why you didn't stay there!'

'I couldn't come back yet, you know that.'

'Five years I ent see you, not a letter, nothing. And what is that?'

The man was silent. Alethea could imagine the look on Mammie's face: lips drawn in and pushed out, eyes squinted, cheeks hollow with rage.

'What nigger girl you breed to bring this nasty child for me here today?'

'Marcia, don't talk like that.'

'The child black like tar. The mother had to be some black bitch for he to come out so!'

'Marcia!' He no longer sounded like the radio man. He sounded just like Mammie now, and just as vexed. 'This is Colin. I brought him here because his mother…she can't mind him. I was hoping you would take him, but I can see you—'

'Mind him?' Mammie was laughing softly. 'You do your shit in America and expect me to clean up after you? Mind your little nigger baby, eh, big brother?'

The man sucked his teeth. 'You feel you white, or what? You forget Ma blacker than this boy!'

Mammie made no comment.

'Just because we come out looking little whiteish, don't forget you's as much of a nigger as he is.'

Whap!

'You too damn fast!' Mammie screamed.

The baby woke up, crying loudly. The man hushed him again, trying in vain to stop his shrieking, as Mammie jeered, 'Take your nigger baby and get out my house, Allan. Go back to America or go to hell. I don't care. Just don't come back here.'

'Who you feel you is?' The man was shouting now. 'Marcia, I warning you...'

'What you go do me, eh?'

Alethea heard the sound of flesh hitting flesh, and Mammie cried out, 'Oh, God! Oh, God!'

Alethea, stripped to her nylon vest and frilly bottomed panties, peered through the crack between the curtain and the doorframe. Mammie was bending down with her arm over her head, just like Alethea did when Mammie was beating her. The man, Allan, stood a foot in front of her, shouting at her. Snot and tears poured down the baby boy's face.

Alethea's heart melted. Without a thought she pulled the curtain aside and stepped between the adults, reaching for the screaming boy. He jerked back at first, clinging to the man, but Alethea slipped her little hands around his body and tugged gently. The man released him. Alethea clutched the boy.

'Don't mind, baby, don't mind,' Alethea crooned.

Colin stopped yelling and looked into her face. They smiled at each other.

Mammie drew breath to speak, but Allan stopped her with a rough hand on her arm.

In the bedroom, Alethea sang to the boy, 'Clap hand for Girlie till Mammie come, bring cake and sugar plum, give baby some...'

The boy's laughter cut the air.

FOUR

'Girlie?' he say again. And all and a sudden I realise it wasn't my ears playing tricks on me in the church at all. Like Jankie put goat mouth on me when she ask about my family because look, Colin, the same Colin who name she call. I close my eyes and I could almost smell baby powder, Farex and milk.

My eyes was still close when I say for the second time that day, 'Nobody doesn't call me that no more. My name is Alethea.'

'It is you!' Colin come up around the hard chair I was sitting on and drag me to stand up and hug me up tight tight tight. He mustbe didn't notice I wasn't hugging him back, fus he busy rocking from side to side. I feel tears dripping on my forehead. He get taller since I see him last.

I wasn't smelling Farex no more, just church incense and deodorant and man-smell. Colin – Father Colin – already take off he white Christmas vestments and had on a ordinary jersey and khaki pants. The jersey was light blue and it make him look like the schoolboy he was the last time I see him. He had on sandals and socks. He was really a priest for truth. A young one, but still. Colin. A whole priest.

I give Tamika a glance. She mouth and she eye open big big.

'Close your mouth,' I say. 'You looking—'

'—like a wabine!' Colin finish, and start to laugh. 'Mammie used to say that all the time!' I notice he had a kind of twang, a little Yankee something on top of the college accent I remember. St Mary's by way of Aranguez get mix up with America.

'Tamika, this is my brother, Colin. Father Reece.'

'Jackson,' he say, correcting me. 'Father Colin Jackson.'

I screw up my face in a frown because I didn't know him by that name at all. As far as I know, he name Reece, just like he father.

He see my confusion and say, 'I dropped his name, Alethea. I took my mother's name, Jackson, when I went to the States to seminary.'

'Or hor,' I say, soft. I wonder why he do that. He father was a nasty man, but I didn't know Colin know that. 'Ahmm, Father Colin, this is my friend Tamika French. She want to find out about getting married.'

I could see Colin barely wanted to drag he eye off me, but he force heself to turn to Tamika. 'Congratulations! The church requires you to give six months' notice before a wedding...' He carry we inside he private office, close the door and put we to sit down.

Them start talking and I drift off, not really studying what they saying. It wasn't my wedding.

I glance around he office. The walls was plain white. Not a picture in sight, unless you count the *Jesus, I trust in You* poster they laminate on a piece of board. A big, wood crucifix, Jesus dripping red red blood (Carmine, I tell myself, then change my mind: Crimson) from actual nails in he hand and foot. A whiteboard with Colin schedule on it – although it was only the third of January, it was done full up with wedding, baptism and blessing this and that. No wonder they does need six months' notice.

It had a bookcase in one corner and as they was talking I get up and wander over to it. Mostly church books: a Bible, a Missal, books on scripture and what look like dozens of Living Faith booklets arrange by date, going back five years. In case somebody miss one, I suppose. Not a novel in sight. Not the Colin I remember at all. That boy always had a book in he hand; that is where I pick up my thing about reading.

I see a book about baby names – for people who going and baptise their children, I suppose – and pick it up.

'Would you like to borrow something?' Colin ask me, interrupting what he was telling Tamika. 'We lend to parishioners.'

'I'm not a parishioner, Father,' I say. But I soften it with a smile. My little Colin get so big.

'You don't have to call me Father, then,' he shoot back. 'What is your parish, Girl— Alethea?'

'I don't have one, Colin,' I answer back. 'I stop going to church when I leave home. Mammie was the *poteau d'eglise*, not me.'

He nod he head and leave it at that. I flip through the book. In a few minutes I hear Tamika chair drag. She stand up, shake he hand and promise to come back with Curtis.

'Come back any time,' Colin tell she. 'Any time at all.' I glance over my shoulder and notice he wasn't watching she when he say it.

'That is your brother?' Tamika sound as if I tell she the moon pink and cover down in fairy dust. 'How he so...'

39

'Black?' I know just what she was thinking. Me with my whitish looking self couldn't possibly be that black black man sister. Colin skin was just as I remember, dark like good mahogany, shining from the inside like how I remember we grandmother skin. 'Yes. Well, no.'

'Ah, ha. I know it!'

I suck my teeth. By this time we was walking out the churchyard, hustling to get back to work. 'He is my adopted brother. He is really my cousin on my mother side. He father and my mother is brother and sister, but he father bring him by we when Colin was a baby and never take him back. So we grow as brother and sister.'

'Or hor,' Tamika drawl out. It wasn't so uncommon in this country for people to raise other people children. 'So he is not really your brother.'

I suck my teeth again. 'We grow together. We eat the same licks from Mammie. We sleep in the same pissy bed. We even wear the same clothes – when a shirt get too small for me he had to take it, unless it had a frill or something, and then when he start to get bigger than me I wear he clothes when they get too small for he. That is my brother. All the brother I ever had, anyway.'

She digest that for a little while, striding down the road with she long long legs and forcing me to trot to catch up with she. She build like a racehorse and I like a miniature pony.

'But you all not in touch?'

'No.'

'How come?'

'Long story.' I answer she short, partly because it was really a long story – twenty-three years is a long time for truth – and partly because I couldn't talk because I was out of breath. I trotting to keep up while she sashaying down the road.

'Oh.' She hush for a little while and we walk along, me nearly running – cantering – by now. Town had its own sound, a music that take over we silence as we cross St Vincent Street again: the sound of cars driving, people cussing, songs playing, vendors calling. I let it seep into my soul for a little while.

FIVE

I does read magazine almost as much as I does read book. I love a fashion magazine. *Allure*, *Elle*, *Vogue*, *Marie Claire*. *In Style* is my favourite because it does show you how to do makeup and hair and thing, and how to look like you wearing expensive clothes when you really wearing a knock off. Is a habit I have since I was working in the cloth store.

Them magazine teach me something else too: it ent have nothing sadder in this world than a pretty woman turning forty. All them magazine full of advertisement for lifting, tightening, wrinkle-reducing, anti-aging cream, serum, injection, and surgery. A woman turning forty would do any damn thing to stop it, I used to think. Now that I turning forty myself, I not so sure. Forty don't sound so bad when you is thirty-nine and eleven months and some days – is just a number and the face you does see staring back at you in the mirror not as important as the memories in the mind behind it.

Trouble with me is that most of the memories was bad.

All I ever know in my life was licks. If I had friends I would have tell them that I grow up on more licks than food. I don't have much friends, though. I does keep to myself, more or less. I can't say I is friends with too much men – men mostly good for one thing and that one thing is not conversation – and, to me, women not dependable. They does always go and leave you.

Coming and telling Tamika what I tell she that morning, showing she what I show she, that wasn't my style. I don't know what get in my head to do that. I does eat my biscuit and hush my mouth, just as Mammie grow me. You ever hear them Americans say on TV, 'What happens in Vegas stays in Vegas?' Just say my whole life is Vegas, and I never leave it.

When the shop phone ring just before the end of the day, about quarter to six, I say it was Bobby. I wasn't in no mood for he and he old talk, so I tell Tamika take it while I went to collect my bag from the kitchen which part we lockers was. I was surprise when she say is for me, and it wasn't Bobby.

'Who?' I whisper.

'The priest,' she whisper back.

'Hello?'

'Girlie,' he say.

'Alethea,' I reply.

'Alethea. How are you?'

'Fine, thanks. You?'

'You left so quickly today. I had hoped to talk to you—'

'Colin, what you want?'

That stop he cold.

'I have to go,' I tell the silence on the other side of the phone, and hang up.

Tamika watch me hard. 'Why you talk to him like that? He only want to make contact, Allie.'

I suck my teeth. Make contact for what? Mammie dead and gone. The only thing we had was to talk about again was he father – and that and God face Colin would never see. Even if he was a priest.

Ann and Janelle was done gone already. I walk out the shop behind Tamika and lock the glass door, pulling down the security gate with a brag-a-dang.

I light a cigarette one time.

The river of people was flowing down Frederick Street now. The faces look the same, though. Everybody tight and tense, anticipating the traffic to go home, bustling along the pavement. I had my own reasons to walk fast. Leo didn't like me reaching home late.

As I was trudging down the pavement towards the Promenade – trudging, good one – Tamika didn't say much. She was smiling, stepping with a bounce. She had something nice to go home to.

Maybe I should tell she what Marie say about Tiny and Curtis, I was thinking. Maybe. But what she didn't know wouldn't hurt she, nah. Out of all them people who was hustling to go home, she was one of the few who was smiling, one of the few who wasn't looking dog tired and ready to fall down, fus they fed of the same old same old life they does go home to day in and day out. Is love had she walking so. Who is me to buss she bubble? Besides, Marie is a old gossip and for all I know she could just be trying to make trouble. I wouldn't put it past she. She had a malicious streak.

One of the trees on the Promenade seem to explode into black feathers as we pass underneath it. Like a thousand birds was living in it, waiting for sunset for them to come out and sing. The air was suddenly full of chattering, chirping and tweeting as them birds fly out. It take a good minute or two for them to finish and then it was just town again, the cars, the music, the people. A one-minute miracle of flight and sound.

I wonder if Colin would like that.

Then I catch myself. Colin? Chuts.

Instead, I think about Tamika again. She was still smiling.

We join the crowd jostling for maxi by the terminal, a little knot of flesh and sweat pushing, then shrinking when one maxi pull off, and growing thick again when a new one pull up.

'Carenage! Carenage!' a tout sing out, as if he had to announce what was plain to see on a sign in the maxi front window. Me and Tamika angle weself to get in the maxi, behind a schoolboy and he mother holding hands and a old granny with a stick. It didn't have no privilege in this line. Granny push hard like anybody else and she stick handle catch me in one of my bruises. I grit my teeth and push back. Tamika, because she thin, slip inside first, a body or two before me. She sit down in the back of the bus and wave to me when I pop through the crowd like a cork from a bottle, putting my foot on the step of the maxi and letting the pressure shove me up from behind.

'Why these people can't line up?' Tamika say.

I go to say, Now that you inside you go ask that? But I keep my mouth shut and pull out my book. Tamika take the hint and she didn't say nothing as the twenty-five-seater bus swerve out of the Carenage bay of the terminal and into the traffic heading west from the city.

I had the book on my lap but I wasn't reading. I watch the sun pour itself into the gulf, turning the blue sky and blue sea orange, purple, pink, red. Azure, tangerine, magenta, lavender, scarlet. Same colours, different words. God was painting a picture for we, if only we would watch it.

All and a sudden I change my mind about talking and turn to Tamika.

45

'You sure, girl?'

'About what?' She had the blackest eyes. When she turn them to watch me I nearly couldn't say nothing again. She look so trusting. I doubt I ever look that trusting in my life.

'About Curtis. About getting married.'

'Positive,' she say.

That was that. Let the cow haul she ass. Tamika was getting married, by hook or by crook.

Tamika come out before me and wave bye-bye from the pavement as the maxi drive off. I wave back. My other hand was on the book, on top of the handbag and the On the Town handle bag in my lap. The phone was inside the bag. I shake a little bit to think about what Leo would say or do when he see the phone. I know it wouldn't be nothing good.

Walking in the house through the kitchen door, like I accustom, I stop short. The kitchen was sparkling clean. The stove I leave this morning nasty with old split peas and years of black, oily gunk was spotless, glittering white, with pots and pans on the stovetop. The garbage bag by the door was gone, and all the rubbish falling out of it gone too. Not a dirty cup or spoon in the sink. Even the fridge get a good wipe down and was shining.

A plate was cover down on the table and I could smell a stew. I stand up in the doorway in a kind of shock and when I hear Leo voice right behind me I jump about a foot in the air.

'Babes,' he purr, right in my ear, 'take it easy. Is only me.'

He nudge me inside by pressing he whole bare chest against my back, and sweep my handbag and the plastic bag with the phone from my fist, hanging them on the back of a kitchen chair.

'Come, come,' he say. He was jovial, as if he entertaining a guest. I could smell a little rum on he breath. 'Come in the drawing room.'

The shabby drawing room and all get a clean out. No old newspapers, no dusty cobwebs on the walls, and the ancient black baby grand piano he parents give him when he was small was gleaming. I wonder where he get furniture polish from.

For a minute I could almost see the nice middle-class house it used to be when he civil servant parents was still alive. Then I blink and it turn back to the tattered place I accustom seeing since I move in there five years ago, long after he parents dead. Leo never buy a damn cushion for heself. Everything there was what he mother and father buy before they dead.

A ashtray was overflowing on top the piano, and a manuscript book was open on the floor next to the shining black piano legs. Leo sit down on the fadey fadey blue velvet stool and rest he two hand on the keys. A little breeze lift the window curtain and a cigarette butt and some ash drift out on to the yellowing ivory and warped ebony. Leo chuff the ash away. He put the book on the fallboard and start to play.

It was a lingering, silvery melody, a school of fishes darting in shallow, sunny waters, a pair of kites dancing in the sky. It was so sweet it make my belly hurt.

He sing. Leo had a voice like thunder when he was beating me, but put a song in he throat and it get mellow one time: thunder turn to rain rolling down a leaf in a deep forest. He sing how much he love me, how precious I was, how he would never let me go.

When he finish, I just watch him. I didn't say a word.

'You like it?' Leo body was hard, with broad shoulders and abdominal muscles like river stone under he silky brown skin. He didn't have much body hair, and he skin was as smooth as the satin boxer shorts he was wearing.

He stand up; I scramble back. My heel catch on the edge of a broken tile and I stumble, flinging out a hand for balance and hitting it hard on the wall. Leo rush to my side.

'Babes!' He take me in he arms and walk me to the kitchen table. 'Sit down, lemme see that.' The back of my hand was red where I hit it. He put a plastic bag of ice from the freezer on top it. 'You have to be more careful, babes.'

I hold the bag on the back of my hand, still saying not a word.

He uncover the plate in front me. A heaping set of food was on the plate: steaming white rice, stew pork and callaloo. The deep green callaloo cover the rice like scum, I think to myself.

'You want pepper?' He stop near the fridge. I shake my head. He put a fork in front of me next to the plate. 'I done eat. You go ahead.' And he sit down and watch me with a broad smile, he hands on the table, palms down.

I manage three forkfuls and a bite of pork before I push the plate aside. By this time my belly was churning. I wanted to vomit.

'It have mauby. You want?' Without waiting for an answer he reach in the fridge for a mug. He put ice in a glass and pour the brown mauby over it. Amber. Froth was floating on top.

The glass was slick in my hand. I take one sip – the mauby was bitter. I skin up my face before I could control the expression. I know he see. I try to sit the glass exactly in the ring of water that show where Leo first put it down for me.

Just so, the plate, the glass and my face went flying to the floor.

Callaloo was dripping from my hair. I had mauby in my eye. My good white blouse was soaking in brown stew and it had rice grains everywhere. Leo step over me on he way to the bedroom.

I lie down there. My ear was starting to swell – I could feel it hot like fire and pounding like a drum. I run my tongue over my teeth to see if they was still in my mouth.

He step over me again on he way out the back door. He did put on a shirt and pants and he shoes was in he hand. He take care not to mash the rice on the floor. He slam the back door and lean against it outside to put on he shoes; I hear the wood creak under he weight. Then I hear gravel crunching under he foot. He was walking away.

Nothing didn't break. I roll over to my knees and, holding on to the sink, make myself stand up.

Ignoring the mess, I strip and went in the shower. I notice with half my attention that he finally scrub the bathroom.

The rice, callaloo and stew sauce swirl down the drain with the body wash and shampoo suds I lather up. I rinse off, walk to the kitchen naked and pick up the same bag of ice, lock the bedroom door and went in my bed. I light a cigarette and wait for Leo to come back.

I hear him come in at midnight. He clean the floor, wash up the wares, put the food in plastic bowls and put them in the fridge. He was humming he new song.

While I wait for him to come inside, my mind drift to Colin: Colin in cassock and chasuble; Colin in jersey and khaki pants; Colin in he old school uniform in we two-room board house in Aranguez while Mammie making dhal and rice in the kitchen; Colin asking me what was the matter when I cry.

Colin was such a good boy, always – Mammie shadow in church and mine at home. He used to worship he big sister. I used to love him with my whole heart.

A small smile try to creep up on my face, but I wince instead when I try to move my lips. One side of my face was hot and swell up which part Leo slap me. The bag of ice melt long time.

Leo still crooning soft as he bathe and brush he teeth. He knock on the door. 'Babes,' he call out. I play with the idea of making him stay outside for the night, but I fraid he break down the door. I get up and unlock it and went back to lie down without opening it. I brace myself as the light from outside spill through the doorway.

'Babes.' Naked, he kneel down on the bed. I didn't move. He hand on my face was cold, but I didn't move, didn't flinch.

Under the clean smell of soap and minty toothpaste, I pick up the heavy, sweet rum on he breath. When he touch my cheek I vaguely smell something musky and fishy on he hand. He was with he other woman, then, I think to myself: soap can't wash off that smell. I turn to the wall.

Leo slide his body down mines to lie down with he belly press against my back. I was warm underneath a thin nightie. He kiss my neck. 'Babes, you does get me so vex,' he say, sounding so tender, as if I's a little child he scolding. 'You know when I cook I does like you to eat. Why you had to get on so?'

The hot, wet mouth on my neck ease the sting in the words. He move down, kissing the spot all of my lovers does find eventually. The effect always electric, like a switch throw somewhere in my brain to shut off thought and feeling except for satin skin, heat, wetness, hardness.

Leo reached around my body to cup my breast. 'Babes, you know how much I love you? I love you, babes. I never love nobody so. Why you does make me get on like that? Why you does make me hit you for?'

But he was talking into my hair, and I couldn't hear him clear. My ear, already on fire, was now ringing harder than ever from the feel of he hand skimming my belly, brushing my nightie over my thighs, holding my hip and pulling me gently at first, then harder and harder, towards him. I wouldn't turn. He settle for pushing he fingers between my thighs, prying them apart so he could get into my slippery wetness. Leo other hand went around me from underneath, holding my body to he own. He had me by the shoulders when he slip inside me from behind. I try to pull away and couldn't, but I struggle anyway.

He slipped out of me, panting. 'Babes,' he say. It had a warning in he voice, quiet thunder.

I try to scramble up from he hand. Quick like a cat, he jump on top of me and pin me to the bed, kneeling on my thighs and holding my wrists together with one hand. The other hand grab a breast and squeeze hard. I close my eyes and grit my teeth but refuse to cry out even through the pain.

'You go behave?' he growl.

I nod my head, yes.

He let me go, but he was wary. As I start to wriggle away from him, he slam me back down on the bed and punch he fist into my belly. As I wheeze, he force my legs apart and push heself back inside me, covering my whole body with he own. He mouth was at my throbbing ear, whispering. 'Take prick, cunt. You feel I don't know you was fucking your next man today. You feel I didn't see the phone. Eh? New phone? New phone?'

I try to turn my head to get away from the voice in my ear.

He tangle he hand in my hair and wrench my head to the side, staking me down to the bed with he fist. 'You's mine. You hear? You's mine.'

When he went soft, he kiss my mouth. I could taste he tears on my lips.

JANUARY 2

'Girlie, come.' Mammie was sounding just a little bit better. She had spent the night crying softly into her pillow, Alethea a shield between her and the tiny boy who had suddenly become the girl's shadow.

Mammie was in the kitchen with a baby bottle in her hand. The bottle was shaped like a cat, ginger with black stripes.

'Where they get that, Mammie?' Alethea had never seen anything like it. Her own bottle had been plain glass.

'You don't mind that. Come here.'

Colin was still asleep on the bed. He had been a comma against Alethea's belly all night; once she got up from the bed, he rolled into a ball and settled into the warm spot she left behind. Alethea still smelled like him, a bit like milk, a bit like baby powder. She was still in the vest and frilly bottomed panty she had worn under her church dress the day before. After Uncle Allan had gone, leaving Colin and a bag of clothes behind, Mammie had been silent for most of the day. The radio had been the only sound in the house, other than the occasional babble of Alethea and Colin chattering at each other.

When Alethea had had her tea that night, Colin nibbled at a piece of bake, sipping from his bottle sparingly as he watched the girl in adoration. From time to time he reached out to play with her golden-brown curls, as she giggled and danced away from his curious fingers.

Now it was morning, she was waking up to this cold, sour-faced Mammie in the kitchen.

'You have to learn to give him his bottle,' Mammie said. She handed Alethea a plaid Thermos. 'You see this? It have water in it. Careful. It hot. Put some in the bottle up to this part here. No, not there. Here,' she said, pointing to the eight-ounce mark.

Alethea couldn't read, but she could distinguish the shapes of the numbers and letters. She could see it was the line at the top of the bottle.

'Now,' Mammie held a green tin, smaller than her own yellow powdered-milk tin. 'Make sure you put in three scoops. Let me see you try.'

Alethea made a mess, pouring half the white powder on the table instead of into the bottle. Her small hand was shaking.

'Take your time, Girlie.' The milk was in the bottle, floating on top of the hot water. 'Good. Now cover it tight. Squeeze the nipple like this—' she demonstrated with one deft pinch '—and shake the bottle. You try.'

Milk squirted out between Alethea's small fingers. Mammie held her hand over the girl's, showing her what to do.

'Right. Just so.'

Mammie shook the bottle on to the inside of her wrist so that milk shot out of the brownish-yellow nipple. Mammie hissed and shook her hand. She put the bottle into an enamel cup half full of water. 'Now, Girlie, you must always remember you have to make the milk with water from this Thermos. Don't ever use the water from the bucket. Colin going get sick if you use that water. Okay?'

Alethea solemnly nodded. The enamel pail of water on the kitchen table was never for making Colin's tea. That she could remember.

'Go and bring him.' Mammie turned back to the stove where a thick bake was roasting in an iron pot. With quick fingers she flipped the disk of bread over to let the other side cook.

Alethea tiptoed into the bedroom, slipping back into the bed and curving her body around the warm, fragrant ball of boy. 'Colin,' she crooned, stroking his cheek. 'You want tea tea?'

He opened button eyes and peered at her. Then he started upward and began to scream, 'Daddy!'

'Shhhh,' she scolded. 'Daddy gone. I's Girlie. You don't remember? Girlie,' she repeated. She was holding his rigid, angry body and whispering in his ear.

'Girlie, bring him!'

'Yes, Mammie,' she said, leading the little boy out into his new life.

SIX

Jerry was leaning on the gate in front the store, he bag of carpentry tools and art supplies in a heap between he foot on the pavement. Two five-foot sheet of Styrofoam was lean up on the wall next to the gate.

'Happy New Year,' he sing out when he see me. 'I like your hair like that. Fabulous!'

I had it part on one side so that it hang over half my face. You could guess which half I was covering up.

The sun was just coming up. I couldn't deal with the crowd this early morning so I make sure and leave home before the rush. I didn't expect to see Jerry so early, and I tell him so while I was opening up the shop.

'You know me,' he say with a evil little grin, 'I accustom coming quick!'

Jerry thin like a rail, about as fat as the width of the Styrofoam boards he was working with that day. He heft he bag on he shoulder and take the boards in he hand, going straight to the window to start to work.

As I tidying up the store – putting back clothes on rack, folding up jeans and what not – and preparing to start the day, he done measuring and cutting and painting, making small talk in a high-pitch, sing-song voice.

Tamika hustle in a quarter to eight. 'Sorry, sorry, sorry!' She was breathless. 'Girl, I wake up so late! Curtis had was to drop me to work. I couldn't get no transport on the Main Road.' She drop she voice and point to Jerry with she chin. 'What you need me to do?'

'Jerry,' I call out to him, 'you ready for the clothes yet?' He was working in the window with a knife and a sheet of sandpaper, transforming the Styrofoam into a fire hose and fire engine. Naked mannequins, even paler than me, was pose up in a gaggle inside the store, just behind the window.

'Not yet. In about half hour.' He sand down the edge of a curling shape. 'And when is eight o'clock, tell me. I have to go by Samaroo's for the hats and some glitter.'

I turn back to Tamika. 'Tidy the changing rooms by the time, nah. You want a cup of tea first?' Ann and Janelle stroll in, so I tell them to open up the shop when eight o'clock reach and leave them in front to deal with any customers.

Tamika dole out the biscuit again.

'Curtis tell me we was going for ice cream last night,' she say.

'How was the ice cream?' I blow on the tea. It was so hot, steam was coming up from it. I take a quick sip.

Tamika grin. 'It wasn't no ice cream. He carry me to see a house.'

'A house!'

'He say he pay the down payment already. If you see it, girl! It nice!'

'Eh heh? Which part it is?'

Tamika stick out she tongue. 'Chaguanas.'

'Ent you run to Carenage to get away from Chaguanas?'

'He say he can't get nothing for that price in the west. Is either east – like Wallerfield or Brazil Village – or Central. Nothing on this side so cheap. Imagine me taking taxi from Chaguanas to come in town again. Travelling two hours just to get to work on a morning.'

'Pressure!' I take a next sip of tea and eat some Crix. 'How far it is from your mother house?'

If you see how Tamika face turn sour. 'Not far enough. That damn woman.'

'What happen?'

'She vex I by Curtis, nah. She say if he getting the milk for free he wouldn't bother to buy the cow. Plus, too, she never like Curtis.'

I think about Marie and the story she tell me the day before, but still I didn't say nothing.

The big clock on the wall say eight o'clock.

Jerry stick he head inside the doorway. 'You want to look at this?' He take in the scene in the kitchen. 'You have any coffee?' He settle in a chair as Tamika make a cup of instant coffee for him. Before she could ask, he chirp, 'No milk, honey. I like it strong, black and bitter.' He wink he eye at me. 'You know just what I mean, Miss Madam!'

Tamika turn she back, skin up she face for me to see, and turn again to hand him the coffee. She didn't go back in she seat. 'Allie, hear nah, give me the list and let me go get the things by Samaroo's. I'll do the dressing room when I come back.'

I glance at the clock. It was a short walk to the craft shop, just three blocks away, but I watch at Tamika vex face and tell myself that fifteen minutes away from Jerry would suit she just fine. I wave my hand at Tamika. 'Jerry, give her the list. How much money, you think?'

57

Jerry didn't mince words after Tamika gone. 'She so stiff. Like she still have that boyfriend thing up she bottom, or what?'

I nearly snort up the hot tea through my nose. 'Jerry!'

'Is true,' he say. 'She does get on like if I have germs and she will catch something if she stand up too close to me.'

I shake my shoulders. 'You know is so some people stop. You can't change they mind. My mother was just so. She did hate bullermen!'

'Who you calling bullerman?' But he was grinning. 'I am an upstanding member of society, child. Bullermen is them fellahs you does see on the corner looking for fares.'

I roll my eyes. 'Eh heh? Well, look thing.'

We laugh together, but the laughter get cut short.

'Why you let that man hit you in your face, darling?' Jerry ask the question light, as if he asking where I buy my shoes. He reach for a biscuit.

I feel my face turning red. 'Who say anybody hit me? Look, Jerry, stop talking shit, nah.'

He take a sip of coffee, looking at me over the rim of the cup. 'You feel I never get a cutass? You holding your belly like it hurting, and I never see you in so much base. That colour a little dark for you, by the way. I must take you shopping to get a nice foundation.'

I didn't say nothing, but I couldn't watch he in he face neither.

'You could tell me mind my business, but don't lie and say he didn't beat you. You could lie to the world, but don't lie to yourself.' He stop, watching my hand turning my teacup around and around on the same spot. 'Let me tell you, Allie. He not going to stop. You going to get licks until you dead if you don't leave that man.'

I finish my tea and wash me and Tamika cup in the sink. 'Why you not like every other person in this country? They could see me with two black eye and a break hand and they ent go say boo.'

'Honey, if you want me to do that, I go do that. But you with this man for five years and he beating you so? How he go beat you when is ten? He go kill you!'

'I didn't know it had a schedule for licks.'

'Hon, trust me. Look at this.' He lift up he pastel-blue linen shirt. It had a small scar, just a shiny dot, two inches from he navel. 'It don't look like nothing, but that was the tip of the ice pick the fucker try to push in my guts.' He lift up the shirt higher. The next scar was longer, about an inch. 'That was when he slash me with the kitchen knife.' Dropping the shirt hem he pull up he short sleeve. By he shoulder had a mark, wide like a schoolgirl ribbon, crisscross with stitches. 'He chop me with a cutlass. He nearly cut off my hand.' Rearranging he shirt, Jerry say, 'That was when the relationship end. He get three months for wounding with intent. And, even then,' he say, chuckling, but in a tone bitter like stout, 'is not that I done it. Is because he pick up some ho in jail and he break up with me. You believe?'

'Leo not going and chop me.'

He laugh. 'That is what you think.' He watch me, sipping he coffee with a serious face. 'Allie, girl, I not judging you. You know why you with the man. But study this: if he love you, why he must beat you? Is not like you is some two-and-six baby. Who give he the right to beat you? And I bet he does blame you for it.'

If I was red before, by then I was purple. Aubergine.

'You see? All them man is the same thing. We girls have to stick together, lady!'

The joke break the tension and I change the subject.

'Forget that, nah, Jerry. Right now I want to make sure you will finish with the window by lunchtime.'

He carry me to see what he do so far: rough Styrofoam firemen surrounding a fire truck and hose. A reel of fishing line was on the floor, waiting to hang the pieces once Jerry paint them.

I plant a kiss on Jerry cheek. 'That is what we talking about! What you think about putting some fire in it?'

'Like, little flames?'

I nod.

'Well...'

A minute later he hand me a Styrofoam cut-out paint in red, blue and gold.

'Maybe,' Jerry say, shaking he shoulders in a offhand shrug. 'Let the tight-bamsee girl bring some glitter for me, and we go see how it look.' He squint at the flame again, then turn back to me. 'And I know you change the subject, but I ent forget you, Miss Allie. You too nice to let some asshole man beat you up. Your mother wouldn't have like that.'

'My mother?' I had to laugh. But Jerry was done back in the Styrofoam, carving and cutting and sanding the little scene – a *tableau vivant* – he was making for the window.

My mother mustbe beat me every day of my life until I run away when I was seventeen. She beat me for schoolwork, for playing, for housework, for backchat, for not taking care of Colin, for the boyfriend she swear I mustbe have because you can't get pregnant without a boyfriend, ent? She beat me if I watch she in she face, and she beat me if I didn't watch she in she face. Any excuse, really. And sometimes for no reason at all.

I doubt she would have care if my man was beating me now. She probably would have say I deserve it because I like too much man.

Is true, I like plenty man.

But what not to like? I like how they does smell, how they does feel, how they does taste. I like when they hold me, when they stroke my skin and say it so smooth and so soft, when they play in my hair like I is a dolly, when they bite my neck in that place that does make me lose my mind. I like when they touch me and I like when they fuck me. I don't like when they beat me, or call me stupid, or tell me I not good for nothing but to fuck, but that come so normal to me that I just figure is the price of having a man.

That is why I like my relationship with Bobby Sharma. He does do all the things I like and none of the things I don't like. It suit me just fine.

Of course, living with a man, far less for having a next man on the side, go against everything my mother stand for when she was alive. She was the biggest Catholic in the whole island, as far as she was concern. Nobody couldn't pray more than she, go to church more than she, say novena and Rosary more than she. She feel she had a special telephone to God, more than anybody else. We didn't have a real telephone, mind you. In them days, we used to have to go by Textel in town to make a phone call; in we village, is only one family had a phone, and them wouldn't shit on we because we was poor, even though we was whitish looking. But as far as Mammie concern, she better than them because she and Jesus was on a first-name basis.

I does say 'whitish looking' because, in truth, in this island, we could pass for white. My mother was the colour of sand where the sun didn't hit her, but because she was always in the sun she was always sunburn, rough and red. Nobody didn't wear sunblock and them thing in them days – we didn't think about skin cancer – and as a poor woman raising fowl in Aranguez my mother sure didn't care about she skin. She wasn't looking for no man, so if she get sunburn, or freckles, or wrinkles it didn't matter to she. I inherit she skin colour, and she hair colour – a kind of light brown when the sun take it, and ordinary brownish black otherwise – and I suppose

I look like she, except smaller. I real short. Mammie wasn't so short as me.

Mammie mother was black like tar. I see she once in my life. Mammie never tell me nothing about she father. I figure he was white or Spanish, but she never say. You couldn't ask my mother nothing she didn't want to tell you. My father was a Spanish and he dead before I born.

People in this island does always surprise to know it have poor white people, but though we skin was light and we hair was straight we wasn't really white and we didn't have a penny to we name. If it wasn't for the little money Colin father send for Colin every month, and the barrels of groceries he used to send down once in a blue moon, we wouldn't have nothing at all.

You would never know that when Mammie, Marcia Lopez, was in church.

In church she was like a kaiser ball: sweet sweet sweet. Everybody respect Mrs Lopez, the widow, the church pillar. She didn't have money, but she clean that church every Saturday morning, cut flowers from we own garden to decorate the altar, and was in mass literally morning, noon and night. She used to clean the rectory, too. The priests used to call her their best helper. She was so proud of that. That was she widow's mite, she used to say.

Mammie had no money, but she had hands and she had knees, and she couldn't give in the collection basket, but she could give in service. So that is what she used to do.

I wonder if she went to heaven for it, in spite of everything she do me.

Mammie could have ask the priest to get me in a good school, a convent school. But she never even ask. I pass for Aranguez Junior Secondary, a three-year technical/vocational school, and is there I went, with all the other children who the Common Entrance exam say didn't have book sense.

. . .

Tamika come back with she hand full: two shopping bags, one with glitter in all colours and textures, from big round paillette to the finest gold dust, and everything in between; the next one with glue stick, and yards of shiny silver lamé, and silver-blue candyfloss fabric. She pass the bags to Jerry and went, as she promise, to tidy up the changing rooms.

By this time customers start to come in. I leave Janelle giggling with Jerry while she help he dress the mannequin and them in different outfit, and stand up near the door in case any one of the customers need help. I doesn't like to follow them around – hovering, a good word – like some stores does make their shop girls do. I find that does annoy customers too bad, the dark-skin ones especially. It does make them feel like we feel they thiefing something, and they quick to take offence and walk out the shop without buying nothing. Is not that I feel 'If they thief, they thief,' but I feel everybody should have the benefit of the doubt. Presumed innocent until proven guilty. Plus, too, I wasn't racial and I know, because of Colin, how dark-skin people does get treat in this country, even after Independence, after Black Power, after all that. Is still a kind of racial, colour-conscious place where people who look like me does get through when people who look like he doesn't get one shit.

SEVEN

By lunchtime the window finish.

'And I tell you I go finish it?' Jerry pong me when I was surprise that he done already. 'I am a woman who keeps her word, Miss Girlie,' he say.

'Ugh. That horrible name. Please, eh,' I tell him. 'Alethea. Or Allie. Or Aye You. Or Bitch. Anything except for Girlie.'

'Okay, Bitch,' he say. 'I'm going for lunch now. Bye!'

Both of we laugh but the other shop girls watch we funny. I didn't care. I know Jerry long time. I is the one who bring he by On the Town. We used to sell cloth together in Queensway, a cloth store just around the corner, years before he went and open he own decorating and event-planning business. I start off as a sales clerk when I was seventeen years, cutting cloth and walking behind customers like the supervisor used to make we do, and I work my way up to assistant branch manager by the time I was thirty.

After a couple more years, I start to knock about, working in a few different places for a little while before I come to On the Town, and everywhere I work I get them to hire Jerry to do the windows and Christmas decorations and thing. But I's a private person. I not accustom telling nobody my business, and it shock even me that I come and tell Tamika how Leo does treat me. I don't know what get into me, in truth. So the fact that Jerry only now comment on the lashing, and tell me how he used to get licks, too, not so strange at all.

Mammie always say it have outside friends and home friends, and the outside friends is for outside and the home friends is for home. I had no home friends any more, not since Jankie ups and gone America when we was seventeen.

Too, besides, man does hardly hit my face. Is like they know where to lash, where to kick, where to cuff, that I could cover it up with clothes. One time a man try to choke me; I had was to wear all kind of turtleneck and scarf and thing for weeks. Other than that, I get break hand, break ribs, a buss head once from a ashtray a man pelt behind me. When I go hospital is always the same looks I does get but always the same story I does give: is fall I fall. I doesn't like to go the same hospital neither. I would go Mt Hope, Grande, San Fernando, Arima, and even then is only when something break for sure, or bleeding bad, that I will bother to go. If is just bruise I bruise, like now, I take some tablet, put some ice and wait for the swelling to go down.

When Jerry come back from lunch he bring two painkillers. I eat half the gyro Tamika buy for me from the mall next door and take the tablets with a Diet Cokes. I wink my eye at Jerry to say thanks. It might have be my imagination, but to me like the pain in my belly and my ears ease up one time.

It wasn't one o'clock yet. Town was still busy with lunchtime traffic bumper to bumper on the road; on the pavement it had some schoolchildren in uniform walking brisk brisk, and some lahaying to reach back in school late, and bank and office workers, in their Tetrex black and maroon and navy blue uniforms, doing the same thing like the children – some hustling, some dragging; all kind of people going in and out of the mall and the stores on the street, even the one store that does open every day and doesn't actually sell nothing. Police does crack down on vendors, so is just two-three on my part of Frederick Street that day: one man sit down on a folding chair, selling cigarette, dinner mint and chewing gum from a box in he lap; the fella outside the mall selling jumbie bead necklace and bracelet and earring and making small talk with a tourist who had she long blonde hair plait in small cane row with red, yellow and green plastic beads; then a old lady, nearly as wide as I tall, selling vest, socks, bra, panty and jockey shorts at a makeshift wooden stall near the corner. A vagrant, grey and dirty like the pants he tie around he waist with a string, was wandering from side to side in between the cars, knocking on the windows to beg for money as he pass.

Me and Jerry step out on the pavement to watch the window display from outside. I put a smoke in my mouth as I was there.

It was exciting: two little firemen with a big big hose spraying candyfloss water at the mannequins, and little flames dancing around the bottom of the window. Everywhere had glitter and sequin and paillette. He little fire engine even have silver lamé for the bumpers. It was cute. Kind of tacky, too, but then, it was Carnival. Fire Fete was three weeks away and after that we would have to change it, put up some costumes with feathers and beads and what have you. The main thing was that the window was bright and colourful, and different from the hundred other shop window in town.

Me and Jerry stand up on the pavement old-talking for a while, reminiscing on the days when we used to cut cloth together in the other store, standing up whole day in a forest of bolts of cloth. I well remember him with the orange-handle cloth scissors tie on a strip of fabric around he neck, just like all the other girls, cutting yards of gabardine for school uniform, work uniform, shirt-jack suit and soft pants, and poplin and polyester-cotton for shirt and dress. When cotton bengaline come in style, and when the occasional customer could afford real silk, crêpe de Chine, jacquard, Dupioni, Shantung…chambray for work shirts and denim for jeans pants…we talk real cloth, boy. Remembering that sound of running a open scissors across the cloth weft – zrrrrrrp – a skill we had to learn because cutting cloth crooked was a crime in that store. Making bill for layaway customer months before Christmas, for who pay down on curtain and cushion cover. Nowadays everybody does buy readymade draperies, upholstery and bed linens, but when we was coming up you had to sew your own or get somebody to sew it for you – paying down on curtain lace and bed sheeting by the dozens of yards from quite in October, to make sure you have it ready in time to put away your house for Christmas.

I nearly smell the French chalk again.

'You remember how we used to sell dress pattern by the cashier in th—' Jerry start to ask me, when we hear a woman bawling for murder.

It was a bloodcurdling scream floating on the breeze from Queen Street and coming right towards we. As I say, it was lunchtime and the street was full of people, but everybody, from the vendors to the vagrant, stop and turn towards the sound. Everybody watch the woman pelting round the corner full speed, she breast hanging out of she shirt because it rip right down and she bra buss open. She hair was standing up like she see a ghost.

'What the ass…?' Jerry say.

Then we hear the gunshot.

Well, papa, if the woman screaming make we stand up still, that gunshot make we run like hell. Every zandolie find they hole, and man, woman and child was scampering, bawling out, cussing, trying to get inside, anywhere inside. The man selling cigarette throw way he box and dash inside the store behind he; the jewellery vendor forget the tourist and start to back back inside the entrance to the mall. Me and Jerry buss it inside On the Town and I pull the door behind me, lock it and hide inside a clothes rack with Jerry. One more gunshot bark. I hear glass break and watch one of my mannequin and them fly backwards, a bullet hole in she head.

Another shot. I hear a loud thud like something heavy hitting the window hard.

The woman stop screaming.

Then three-four shots fast fast fast and nothing more.

'All you, call police!' I shout out to the staff. Everybody like they freeze, bending down – crouching – behind the counter. Is Jerry who end up pulling out he cell phone and calling 999, but by that time the police did done reach already, miracle of miracles.

My cell phone start to ring. At first I didn't know what the ass that little chirp-chirp-chirp noise was, but then Tamika say is my phone. I did leave it on the counter.

'Answer it for me, nah.' I still hiding down inside the clothes rack, even though shooting stop and the police siren and them going eaaaahhh-eaaahhhh outside. I fraid to creep out. I holding Jerry hand like it would fall off if I let go.

'Is Mr Sharma,' Tamika say.

When I drop Jerry hand my fingers was stiff and cold.

I crawl out from under the clothes to find Ann and Janelle by the door watching the street like is a cinema show. I turn my eyes away. I had a mind what I would see.

'Bobby?'

'Oh my God, Alethea, I heard what happened and I ran down the road – the police won't let anybody through – are you all right, you didn't get hurt or anything?' He say that whole speech in one breath, like if he was really frighten for me in truth and not just worried about the store like I thought he might have be.

'Everybody alright, Bobby. They shoot the window, though. One of the mannequin and them dead. I mean—'

'That is nothing,' he say, quick quick. 'As long as you okay.' After a while he say, 'And nobody else was hurt? Nobody get shot? I hear was like the wild wild West—'

'Nobody get shoot, Bobby. Is just the mannequin. And the window have a bullet hole now.' I see a police in tactical clothes outside the door. He use he big gun to tap on the door for we to open it. 'Bobby, I have to go. The police want we to come.' And I hang up on he just as he was going and say something else. But I didn't want to hear Bobby and he small talk right now. I was frighten out of my mind.

Ann open the door. The police walk inside in he big, black boots, heavy navy blue wool sweater and balaclava hat. He had he submachine gun on a strap around he neck and he was holding the barrel up in one hand and the grip in he next hand.

'Everybody come outside,' he say. He didn't stop and ask if anybody get hurt, nothing. Just, 'Everybody come outside.' When I linger a little too long, he bawl, 'Now!' As if I is the criminal.

I jump. I start to shake.

Slow slow, like I make from wood or stone, I start to walk to the door. Jerry crawl out from the clothes rack and stand up and straighten he clothes like nothing happen. He give the police man one good up and down, like what he see, smile.

I was the last one out of the store.

I didn't watch the woman sprawl out on the pavement by we window. I keep my eyes down, stepping over the blood running down the concrete sidewalk. I try my best to block out the smell.

Tamika, Ann, Janelle and Jerry was standing up in a little grap on the opposite side of the street, so I walk across and huddle up with them, too.

Frederick Street was calm, the streets lonely except for the police in regular grey shirt and navy pants, and tactical police in they navy blue and black. I tell myself that was why the police man was so rough with we inside – it boiling hot outside here in the road and he in wool? He had to be damn vex. A little laugh bubble up inside me and I choke it down.

I had my back turn to the store and the woman. On the pavement next to we it had other groups of people, huddle up too. I recognise the people from the jewellery store next to we, and the girls from two-three next clothes shop on the same strip. Everybody was quiet quiet, watching the body on the road. A whisper like a wave wash over them and I see people start to point down the road, closer to Cipriani statue. I watch down, and I see a next body. A man. He was lying face down in a canal and it had blood on he white shirt, like three roses blooming.

I turn my face away and close my eye and sway a little bit. Jerry hold one side and Tamika hold the other, or I would have fall flat on the road just like the two dead people.

The police man who bawl at me before now come and ask who is the store manager. He have to go in the store and I have to come with him. I take a deep breath and say is me, and I follow him across the road to the shop. A inspector in a short sleeve khaki drill suit, black braid drape across he shoulder and a baton in he hand, walk up the road towards we and follow we inside the shop. Two of them start to pepper me with question after question.

I answer what I could and ignore the rest and it seem to go on and on forever. After a while Bobby come and they say, real polite, 'Good afternoon, Mr Sharma,' because everybody in town know who is Bobby Sharma, and nobody don't want to get on he wrong side.

'Officers, what happened?'

Was the inspector who answer, 'At around 12.55pm we got a report of a woman being pursued through the Harpe plannings by a suspect who, it seemed, was armed with a pistol. Officers on patrol in the neighbourhood responded and continued the pursuit through the plannings, across Observatory Street, down Charlotte and across Queen. At Frederick Street the officers in pursuit heard gun fire and saw the victim struck there,' he point to the window outside the shop, 'and once the perpetrator was in a clear line of sight, they fired—'

The tactical police jump in: 'The armed suspect fired upon the officers when they warned him to stop, and the officers returned fire.'

'Yes, yes,' the inspector say. 'Yes, of course.'

I count gunshots. It didn't tally up. But who is me. I consider the man with the red flowers blooming in he back, lying on he face in the gutter. He look for that, I tell myself.

'Do you know why he was shooting at the woman?' Bobby ask.

'At this time, we are not sure,' the inspector say. 'But we assume it was a domestic dispute.'

'We will be investigating further,' the tactical say.

I stop to wonder who this tactical police feel he is to be second guessing he inspector, because I know how police is and they doesn't like backchat from subordinates. But it wasn't my business. And too, besides, I was feeling faint. I lean up on the wall and close my eye and I feel the throbbing in my ear spread and spread until it was like my whole face was pulsing, beating like a heart. Bobby mustbe see what was going on and he pull a chair for me from the kitchen and put

71

me to sit down. The police keep asking me the same questions over and over, like if they ask me enough times, or in different ways, I go change my answer. But was the same answers I had every time: Yes, I see the woman running down the road. No, I didn't see the man. No, I didn't see nothing else.

When they finally tell me I could go, I grab my handbag from my locker in the kitchen and take out a cigarette one time. I light it as I hit the pavement and is a good thing, too, because the smell of the dead woman was kicking, like a butcher stall in the market when the meat stay in the sun too long. I couldn't play like I didn't smell it any more.

I turn and watch she, finally. A small woman. Not much bigger than me. She eye was close. One of them was swell up. It look like he hit she a good right hand before he start to run she down. She hair was standing up, because of how she run so far, I figure. La Cour Harpe to Frederick Street? But she was running for she life, she blouse rip and she breast hanging and she ent care because she was running for she life. And still. She didn't run fast enough.

I drag harder on my cigarette.

The police wouldn't let we go until it was after six. They move in these tents and big, bright lights, and man in white jumpsuit like alien walking up and down the road, checking this and checking that. The media come, too, right after the police, it seem, and take picture and start interviewing people. Jerry and Tamika talk to them. I didn't say nothing.

By this time I starting to worry because if I come home late it might be me making papers tomorrow right next to this poor lady. She body was still on the road, nearly five hours afterwards, and I feel sorry for she. Traffic in town was lock up tight, just because of that one block they close off, and traffic in town mean no transport, which mean I going home even later. I start to panic.

Bobby was still there with the tactical in the shop and when he come outside and see my face he offer to drop me home. I start to laugh like I mad. Imagine Leo and Bobby bounce up – one of them go dead, or me. I tell him no thanks.

The officer, standing up close to Bobby, like he hear what we say and he offer to drop me home. I hesitate and hem and haw, but eventually I give in because I see Tamika and Jerry watching me and waving their hand and shooing me like a fowl – Jerry because the man tall and nice, and Tamika because she know I wasn't in no condition to push and shove to get a maxi to go home.

It had them big metal police barrier by the corner of Frederick and Queen, and police in regular uniform was directing traffic away from we block. The tactical walk around the corner to a police jeep, a Cherokee, and help me climb in the front. I sit down on a book. I pull it from under me and put it in my lap – some textbook, it look like.

'Introduction to Criminal and Forensic Psychology,' I read off when he sit down in the driver's seat. 'You studying, or what?'

He watch me out the corner of he eye as he pull out from the side of the road. 'As a matter of fact, yes,' he say. 'I'm pursuing a bachelor's in criminology, with a minor in psychology.'

'In UWI?'

He shake he head. 'In Florida. But I have to do courses from here, and fly up for exams.'

'Police paying for that?'

He smile. 'No.'

I didn't say nothing.

After a while, he say, 'So, where to?'

'Eh?'

'Where do you live?'

'Carenage,' I say. 'L'Anse Mitan.'

He put on he siren for a little bit so he could get through the traffic by Cipriani roundabout – I raise my eyebrow but hush my mouth – and in no time we was on Wrightson Road passing the port. He watch me again. 'You disapprove?'

'Well,' I say, 'I didn't know getting me home was an emergency.'

'Isn't it?' he say. He reach out a hand, turn my face to he own, raise up my hair. 'I thought it was.'

I pull away from he hand and swing my head back, fixing my hair so it cover the swelling again.

'You realise, of course, that you could end up just like that woman in town.'

I hush my mouth again. That is your business? I say in my head. But my mouth stay shut. I make a face like I sucking a salt prunes, cross my arms and turn to watch the sea flying past my window.

'Let's start over,' he say, out of the blues. 'My name is Carl Baker. Corporal Baker. Call me Carl. What's your name?'

He want to play games.

'Alethea Lopez.'

'And you live where, Miss Lopez? Miss or Mrs, by the way?'

'Miss. L'Anse Mitan, Carenage.'

'And you live with your family?'

'With my common-law husband.'

'And his name is…?'

'Leo. Leo Naples.'

'Leo Naples,' he say, tasting the name in he mouth. 'That sounds familiar. Is he—'

'He's a singer. He was in a band named Jam. A long time ago.'

'Oh, yes!' Carl start to sing one of Leo songs in a not so bad baritone.

'Stop, please.'

He glance at me. I could see he mind working behind them dark eyes. 'Okay.'

He wait until we pass West Mall before he talk again. 'And how long has Leo been hitting you?'

'That is not your business, officer.'

'Yes, it is, actually. You're a citizen and that is assault.'

'What you know about it?' I watch him in he face and then turn my back to him.

'I know it's against the law. If you want, I could talk to him—'

'No!' I shout out. I could just imagine the level of cutass I would get if I bring police for Leo, in any shape, form or fashion. 'No, please,' I say softer. 'That would just make more trouble for me.'

Corporal Carl Baker shake he head. 'Men like that—'

'Men like what, officer? I never told you anything. You see a bruise and assume something. I never report nothing to you.'

'Fair enough,' he said. 'Fair enough. But would you promise me that if – when – you are ready to make a report, you will come to me? I'm with the Guard and Emergency Branch but I could get someone from the Carenage station to follow up right away.'

I didn't say nothing.

Sun was long gone by the time he turn in my street.

'Watch the potholes,' I tell him.

He pull up in front my yard where I tell him to stop. He go to come outside but I tell him it not necessary, and I jump out and walk around the back of the house as normal, lighting a cigarette the second I get out the van.

'You bring fucking police for me?' Leo snarl at me as soon as I come inside – breech – the kitchen door.

'No, Leo!' I duck a slap one time as I say it. The cigarette fall on the ground. He was aiming for the same ears he hit yesterday and I didn't know if I could take another lash there again, at least, not so soon. 'Is a police from in town! They shoot two people right in front the shop and they had we waiting there since one o'clock. He only drop me home, that is all.'

Leo wrap he hand in my hair and drag my head back. He come up right in my face and whisper, 'Best hads be—'

'Good evening, good evening!' Corporal Baker come walking around the house. Striding, as though he own the place. Leo let me go so fast I nearly fall down.

'Officer, how can I help you?' Leo say, all smiles.

'I just wanted to make sure Miss Lopez was safely inside,' he say, standing up in the doorway.

'She was just telling me there was a shooting?'

'Yes,' Baker say, eyeing me close as if he could see from there if Leo was misbehaving. 'Unfortunately, yes. A young lady was shot. Officers shot her attacker. They both are dead, sadly.' Turning to Leo, he say very calm, 'Domestic violence, I think. The officers didn't have a choice.'

Leo swallow hard.

'Yes, well, as long as Miss Lopez is all right, I'll be on my way. I have to get back to work. But she was a little shaky and I thought it best to bring her home.'

'Well, thank you, officer,' Leo say, pretending to be glad.

Baker turn to me and say, 'If there is anything you need, Miss Lopez, please give me a call.' He take out a little notebook from he back pocket and write down in very neat block letters he name and a cell phone number. 'Anything, anything at all.' One more hard look at Leo and he gone.

Me and Leo stand up in the kitchen like statue until we hear the van drive away. Then I run for the bedroom and he run right after me.

JANUARY 3

'What is that?'

Liloutee pointed a sharp twig at Colin. Rusty, a small rust-red pothound, panted at her heels, nosing up to sniff at the toddler through the gap in the galvanise fence.

'That is my cousin.' Alethea proudly pulled Colin forward. He stumbled and bumped gently against her side. They almost fell down but righted themselves, clinging to one another and laughing.

Liloutee eyed Colin suspiciously. 'How he so black?'

'I don't know,' Alethea said with a shrug. 'I could come by you?'

Liloutee, still contemplating Colin, asked, 'He coming?'

Alethea nodded. 'He is my cousin,' she repeated. 'Mammie say I have to mind him.'

'Come, nah,' Liloutee invited as she walked ahead. Colin had been judged acceptable.

Mammie was squatting by the back sink holding down a bucket on a flapping chicken. Its head protruded from beneath the bucket's rim, twitching frantically in the red dirt of the yard. Mammie knelt on the bucket, pushing it down hard, wielding a knife. The knife's edge gleamed silver, sharp. The chicken squawked in pain and panic.

'Mammie, I could go by Lily?' Alethea led Colin by the hand to stand a short distance from her mother. Marcia glanced up in irritation. 'Girlie, go and turn off the stove for me.'

'Then I could go by Lily?'

Mammie's warning glance sent her scurrying. Colin remained in the yard watching the strange scene. Alethea heard him exclaim in excitement just before the thrashing under the bucket increased to a frenzy. She turned off the burner under the bubbling pot of water and dashed back outside, wrenching Colin away from the scene. A spot of red dotted his white cotton vest. He hiccupped, still chattering. Pointing back to the fading noise coming from the bucket, he pulled on his cousin's hand and asked something she couldn't understand.

'It dead. Mammie kill it,' she soothed. They walked around the fence to the front of Liloutee's yard. Lush green bushes and flowering shrubs surrounded a mean shack, built of blackened board raised off the earth on a foundation of red clay bricks. Liloutee, like Colin and Alethea, wore only a jersey and underpants. Rusty lay on the low front step nipping at the fleas on his back. Liloutee idly swung her twig at the bushes, lopping off flowers as she went.

Colin's babbling trailed off. Hiccupping softly, he hid behind Alethea.

'Girlie, I didn't know you had a cousin.'

'Me neither,' she admitted with a shrug. 'He daddy bring him.'

'When?'

'Yesterday?' She screwed up her face in concentration. 'No, before yesterday. Yesterday he daddy come back. He did bring him and went home and then he come back yesterday.'

Lily nodded sagely. Another head of ixora went flying, tiny vermillion florets scattered to the wind. 'What he name?'

'Colin.'

'Colin,' Lily sang out. 'Come, baby!' No bigger than Alethea, she tried to scoop him up into her arms. He slid down into the dirt on his bottom.

'Oh, gosh, Lily!' Alethea impatiently pulled him up and beat the dust off his diaper. 'Mammie go vex if she see he clothes get nasty. We could sit down on the steps?'

Rusty dove off the step, ungently encouraged by Liloutee's bare foot to his behind. He lay in the dust and resumed his efforts.

The girls sat in the bright sunshine. A breeze took the pink and blue jhandi flying on bamboo poles planted near the gate. The flags fluttered briskly then died when the breeze dropped. Colin dug a hole in the dirt with his big toe.

'Aye, come and see this,' Lily said, breaking the silence. She trotted down the steps and crawled underneath them.

Alethea followed her, scooting on her hands and knees on the dusty earth. Over Lily's shoulder she could see a shallow depression containing four brown eggs.

'What, eggs? I done see that so much times!' Scornfully, Alethea pulled back.

'No, dummy,' Lily rejoined. 'Not that. That.' The small finger pointed at a long, papery sheath.

'What is that?'

'It look like a cobweb, eh?' She reached for it with her twig and crawled backwards from beneath the steps. Iridescent and translucent, the scaly fragment dangled like a long, thin sock from the end of the stick. They admired it in the light. 'Let we ask my mother.'

They ran around the house to the sink in the waterlogged back yard. Liloutee's mother stood bent over a concrete sink full of clothes, rubbing a shirt collar with a bar of blue soap.

'Mai, what is this?' Lily thrust the snakeskin at her mother.

The middle-aged woman started in alarm. 'Which part you get that? Throw that way, girl. That is a snakeskin. Where you get that?' She wiped her hands on her thin cotton skirt, dampening the floral pattern around her hips.

'It was under the steps, Mai. Mai, if that is a snakeskin, where the snake?'

Her mother snatched the twig from the child and flung it into the canal behind her. 'Lily, don't ask foolish question. The snake leave the skin and gone. Which part under the step, show me.'

They returned to the front, Lily pointing authoritatively to the spot where the transparent cast-off skin had been.

'Oh gorm, and is right by where the fowl laying,' the woman muttered. 'I hope it ent come back. I have to ask that man to burn some old tire to get the rid of it...' She whirled back on the girls. 'All you don't play underneath here. Find somewhere else to play.'

'But, Mai...'

'Lily, don't give me no back answer. Go and play somewhere else. Go inside.' She collected the eggs and marched the children into the small house. 'Where your dolly?'

'It inside, Mai,' Lily grumbled.

'Well, bring it and show Girlie, nah.' As Lily followed her instructions, her mother seemed to notice Colin for the first time trailing behind Alethea. 'Girlie, who is this?' Putting the eggs into vast patch pockets on her skirt, she picked Colin up and cuddled him to her chest. 'Hello, my little baby boy. Hello!'

Colin gurgled in delight.

'That is Colin, Tantie Indra. That is my cousin.'

'Hello, Colin,' Indra bounced him on her hip. 'You want some biscuit? Eh, baby boy? You want some biscuit?' She took him with her as she walked off towards the back of the house. Alethea was left standing alone in a sitting room just large enough to hold a hammock and two carefully varnished wooden sitting room chairs. The chairs' cushions were covered in deep red velvet, a luxurious fabric she had never seen used on furniture before. Although it was worn in spots and stained black in others, she didn't dare sit. Instead, she remained on her feet, looking around the room. It smelled like her house, of food and old wood, except for the fragrance of something smoky and sweet that seemed to come from the very walls.

Lily returned with her arms piled with toys. Most of them were old, but there was a brand new dolly on top of the heap. It was pink and blonde and its eyes closed when she put it to lie down. Its frilly red dress, edged with white lace, caught Alethea's eye.

'Oh, goooood,' she gushed. 'I could see it?'

Lily handed her the doll.

'How she name?'

'She is a Paula dolly. That is what my mother say. I get it for Christmas. From my tantie in Canada. She send it for me for my Christmas.'

'But I thought you doesn't have no Christmas,' Alethea asked, puzzled. She didn't know why, but her neighbours didn't make punch a crème, boiled ham, or pastelles and sorrel. They had no Christmas presents and never went to church like Mammie did. Instead, they lit string wicks in tiny clay cups full of oil and put them all over the yard once a year, and invited Mammie and Alethea to come over and eat roti and sweet, creamy parsad that night.

'Well, Mai say how Tantie Sandra send it for my Christmas. I don't know, nah,' Lily said dismissively. 'You ent like she hair?'

They stroked the soft blonde tresses. Lily produced a tiny comb and brush and they sat on the floor with the doll, undressing it, combing its hair, dressing it again, until Indra came back with Colin still on her hip. She had a plate of hot alloo pies under a folded white cloth.

'Come and eat, girls,' she sang out.

Colin held a piece of golden brown pie, putting it into his mouth and sucking at it from time to time. He gurgled something at Alethea.

'Yes,' cooed Indra. 'Tell she how it tasting nice. It tasting nice! When you done eat that it have mauby in the kitchen, you could come for some.'

The crisp, fried pies, filled with spicy mashed potato, were just the way Alethea liked them. 'I want to eat this every day,' she confessed to Lily, who made a face.

'I does eat alloo pie every day. It all right, but I rather something else.'

'Like what?'

'Like chicken and chips!' They giggled. Nobody ate chicken and chips every day. They'd have to be rich to do that.

After downing the cool cups of bittersweet mauby, they went back to the pile of toys. Lily's collection included a worn-out tennis ball, nearly bald with age and use. Alethea threw it at her, but Lily stopped the game. 'Mai say not in the house.'

Forgetting the earlier injunction, they ran outside and played catch with the rubber ball, Rusty yapping and scampering behind the ball when they failed to catch it. Lily darted behind the little red dog, chasing the ball into a clump of ginger lilies beside the fence. Rusty froze and began barking furiously at something on the ground by the base of the plants.

'Rusty! Hush your mouth,' Lily yelled, reaching for the ball. She screamed and drew back.

'What happen?' Alethea darted to her side. 'What it is?'

Lily pointed to a boa constrictor curled around the stems of the lilies. 'Look, the snake!'

As one they pelted into the kitchen, a freestanding one-room building behind the house. 'Mai! Mai! We find the snake!' Lily yelled.

Indra still had the boy on her hip as she stirred a pot on a one-burner ring stove. Hastily, she put Colin to stand and, grabbing a machete from behind the kitchen door, dashed to the front of the yard.

The children followed, Lily anxiously bawling out, 'It in the flowers, Mai! Which part Rusty barking!'

Two sharp chops later the snake squirmed in pieces in the red dirt. The girls, with Colin between them, looked in amazement at Indra, the snake and the still barking dog. There was thick blood on the blade of the knife.

'And I tell you stay in the house?' said Indra.

Marcia, chicken blood and guts speckling her old housedress, stormed into the yard. 'What is all this commotion? Girlie, you giving trouble?' She clamped a hand around Alethea's arm and wrenched her away from Lily. Alethea gasped at the pain in her arm; Colin whimpered and clung to his cousin's jersey as Marcia reeled her in towards her.

Blood dripped like syrup down the knife's blade, spattering the ground near Indra's feet as she said, 'No, no, nothing like that!' She pointed to the dead boa constrictor laid out on the ground, bloody guts seeping from its still twisting severed pieces. 'Is a macajuel they find in the flowers and them. Like it was eating the chicken egg.' Indra used the tip of the machete – a two-foot-long, flaring knife with an oiled black wooden handle – to flip over the snake's lopped-off head. In death it looked no different, Alethea thought, than it had in life. Its diamond-shaped head was about the size of her fist, and its body nearly as wide around as Colin's arm.

Mammie's fingers tightened into agonising hooks on her shoulder. 'Come from there, Girlie,' Marcia muttered.

The dead snake was at their feet, its tail whipping ever more slowly from side to side. Tan, umber and black patches on its skin blended nearly perfectly in with the withered, fallen leaves and humus heaped around the stocky, bright green stems of the flowers. Even its eyes were coloured in the same motif. Staring at the intricately patterned skin, Alethea could distinguish individual scales – they looked like small bumps on the snake's body. Indra prodded the pieces again; they still writhed but less and less vigorously with each moment that passed.

'But, neighb', it dead! It ent go do she nothing. You could cook that, you know. You want piece?' Indra, now that the reptile was no longer a threat to her eggs, her chickens or the children, was grinning at the possible treat.

Marcia, on the other hand, looked as though she would vomit. Her sallow skin turned pale and her lips thinned to a straight, disgusted line.

'When my husband come home he go clean it, yes. I go bunjay it with plenty pepper. You sure you don't want piece? Macajuel does eat good, neighb'.'

Unimpressed, Marcia marched Alethea off, dragging Colin behind them.

EIGHT

Seven o'clock next morning Jerry nice nice window was good except for the mannequin who get pass out by the shotter – it was lying down in the middle of the shop when I reach in work. It had a little glass on the floor of the window and the front of the shop from the bullet hole. That bullet fly right through the mannequin head and end up in a wall at the back. Is a good thing Tamika, Ann, Janelle, Jerry and me was stooping down or somebody other than the mannequin could have be the victim. Bobby come just after I reach and say how he arrange to put in a new window glass and for a man to come and plaster and paint back the hole in the wall. Before they reach, though, he had to bend me over the back of the chair in the kitchen and take a little thing.

The workmen had everything in a mess from the time they start, with clothes rack jam up in a corner, and everything cover down with tarpaulin.

In the meanwhile, the phone only ringing. I thought Bobby would have stay and put a hand, but he take he bull and he gone. He barely watch the workmen self.

Ann, then Janelle, call to say they feeling sick and they can't come today. That was before eight. So we go be shorthanded whole day, I tell myself. At least Tamika come.

Jankie call next, eight o'clock on the dot, when I was supposed to open the shop if it didn't have workmen fitting glass and plastering hole.

'Oh my God,' Jankie say in she Paris Hilton voice. 'You almost died!'

'That is exaggerating it a little bit, Jankie,' I tell she in a kind of dry tone.

'But what if you'd been standing up? That could have been you with the bullet in your head.'

I say, 'Well. Maybe. But I wasn't standing up, so it's what Americans would call a moot point, isn't it?'

She want to have lunch with me, she say, but I tell she is only the two of we, me and Tamika, in the shop and I couldn't take off lunch so it would have to be another day. She beg me for my cell phone number and I give she. I had to look at the sticker on the back of the phone to find the number because I didn't memorise it yet.

Next phone call was from Sita, of all people, around nine o'clock.

'Mrs Sharma!' I say, surprise for true. In all the years I work there I never hear she say more than hi-hello to me, or any of the staff. She does manage a hotel she family own down in South, a real posh boutique hotel for ex-pats working in oil and gas, so she doesn't be in town much in the first place. When she not in she hotel, she in the South branch of On the Town, down in San Fernando. I didn't like the woman much – plus I was sleeping with she husband – but to be honest you had to respect she as a businesswoman. She take that little guesthouse she nani build and make it practically a five-star place, with gourmet restaurant, spa, pool and every luxury you could think about. I never went myself, but the pictures I see in the brochures Bobby does have on he desk sometimes give me the impression is pure luxury, like something from in a magazine. They even have a valet to park the guests' cars. She had almost no taste in clothes, but my God she could run a hotel.

'Miss Lopez.'

'Please, call me Alethea,' I say.

'Al...eee...thea? I'd always thought it was Althea.'

'No, Alethea. My grandmother's name,' I explain.

'Oh, I see. Althea, I'm just calling to say I'm glad nobody was hurt yesterday. Mr Sharma told me what happened and, of course, it was on the news.'

'Yes,' I say. Is true. I doesn't watch TV but the neighbour children tell me this morning they see me in the seven o'clock news last night talking to the police man. And one of the papers Bobby walk with this morning had the poor woman picture right there on the front page, dead like a semp, with a blur over she naked nipples as if that is the obscene part of the photograph. Bobby say the papers sell out. Everybody want to see the woman who man run she down and shoot she right in the heart of town.

'And Bobby. Has he replaced the window and fixed the hole in the wall yet?'

I look around the shop to see if it suddenly had a camera that I didn't know about in a corner. She real know what happen.

'Yes, Mrs Sharma, he sent workmen. They're working on it as we speak.'

'Great. Give the rest of the staff my regards, please.' And she hang up, without another word.

I hang up the phone on my end a little slower, thinking about the woman who husband I horning she with.

I didn't know Sita to say much about she personally. I know Bobby was a weak man. I say weak because he had no self-control when it come to me – every time he see me is sex he want – and no control over the way the store manage. He might pretend he making decisions, but I know and he know is really Sita deciding everything, from what colour panty to put on the mannequin to when we have to take stock. She didn't married he for he business sense, although he wasn't a bad businessman. She married he for he colour and for he family name.

I see pictures of she when she was young – Bobby had one in he office, and one or two on he computer – she used to be a pretty Madrasi girl, with Lipton-brown skin and curly black hair. She grow up rich, even then. She family had the guesthouse and little shops all over the place, and a set of land they put up apartments on, but she was still a Chamar in the eyes of the Brahmins, so Bobby give she what he had – prestige, though he family was poor like church mouse, and living in a breakdown old mansion in Tunapuna.

Sita don't look Madrasi any more: she bleach out the skin and straighten the hair – and bleach that and all so she blonde like Cameron Diaz. And too, besides, who care about Chamar when you driving BMW and your husband have BMW to match? When you have big house in Ellerslie Park next to the French Creole and them, the colour of your skin don't matter, only the colour of your money.

I suppose I was the opposite to she: I grow up poor like hell in a two-room house, with no TV, no fridge, hardly any clothes, and more licks than food. Which part we did living in Aranguez was plenty poor people just like we, raising goat and chicken and growing tomato and bhaigan and ochro and bodi to sell in San Juan market. We neighbours was black, Indian and dougla. Everybody using latrine and everybody washing in a tub with a jooking board and bathing in a outside bathroom in the back yard, using water we full in the standpipe by the corner. The only difference between we neighbours and we was that Mammie and me had colour – she get it from she father side and I get it from she and my father, whoever he was.

Of course, thinking about that I had was to think about Colin. And speak of the devil. The phone ring again.

'Girlie?'

'Colin. It's Alethea, I told you before.'

He stay quiet for so long I figure he hang up. Then he say, 'Alethea. I was praying for you all night. Are you all right?'

'You mean the shooting?'

'Yes,' he say, sounding a little confuse. As if he was thinking, What else?

'I'm all right. Nobody was hurt here. Just one of the mannequins. A bullet hit it in the head.' I almost say, Hit her in the head. But I wasn't thinking about the mannequin. I stifle down a laugh. Not that it was jokey, but it was funny – uncanny, not humorous – talking to Colin again after all these years.

'I am so glad to hear it. Relieved. Thank God you're all right. I was so worried.' He say, ahem, and continue talking. 'I needed to talk to Tamika. For the wedding. Is she there?'

I bawl out, 'Tamika!' and tell she phone for she and went to stand up by the outside door, smoking a cigarette by the time.

Out on Frederick Street the same vendors was back in the same places; the same kind of people was hurrying up and down the road, in the same way; the same traffic back up like it was back up yesterday. Life was going on as though that woman never live and never dead. The pavement where she get shoot was cleaner than it was the day before, as if somebody bring out a power washer last night to hose down the blood and brains from where she take she last breath. Down the street where the shotter take three bullet in he back

– roses blooming on he shirt – it was spic and span too. That drain was never so clean.

As I stand up there I was rubbing my ears. All this phone conversation was irritating them, especially the ears Leo did lash. That ears wasn't so swell as the day before, and it wasn't hurting as much, but I rub it anyway, remembering last night. I close my eyes and my pores raise up. He make me feel so sweet, kissing up my whole body from toes to nose, paying special attention to the ears he did box. When he chase me from the kitchen last night I thought he was going to beat me again, but he was so soft and kind and loving when he catch me I nearly forget about how he rough me up at first when he see the police man.

Nearly.

Tamika appear and say, 'Father Colin want to talk to you, Miss Allie.'

I roll up my eye but pitch way the cigarette and went back to the phone anyway. 'Hello?'

'Gir— Alethea, I was hoping we could meet up today.'

Shaking my head as if he could see me through the telephone, I tell him not today, because we shortstaff.

'What about after work? I could take you to dinner if you meet me at mass.'

'Colin—'

'Tomorrow, then?' he jump in quick quick before I could tell him no again.

Is then I realise he not going to vanish into the sunset just because I wish.

'Okay, lunch tomorrow.'

'Will you meet me at mass?'

'Colin—'

'Please?'

I sigh, long and heavy. 'Okay. Mass and then lunch. But a quick lunch, all right? I can't stay away too long. And I can only make it if the other girls show up for work. So call me in the morning and we'll confirm it.'

He sound so happy when he say yes and thanks and see you tomorrow. It was as though he was a little boy again.

But I push Colin out of my mind because the store start to full up with people. By ten o'clock was business as usual, except that the whole place smelling like paint.

Everybody want to come and maco where the woman dead, but they shame to be so boldface, so they come inside the store instead. But if it was maco they come to maco, they was disappointed. It had nothing to see except cheap, tacky clothes and Tamika and me.

The last phone call that morning was from Corporal 'Call me Carl' Baker.

'Good morning, Miss Lopez. I trust everything was fine last night after I left?'

A little shiver went down my spine when I think about how fine it was.

'Yes,' I say. Is not he business, either way.

'He didn't attack you again?'

I didn't say nothing.

'Miss Lopez? Did he hit you again?'

'No, Corporal Baker.'

'I said, please call me Carl.'

'Well, then, no, Carl. He did not hit me.'

He was quiet for a little second and then say, 'Good. I'll be coming by the shop today to ask some more questions about the shooting.'

'But why? I told you yesterday, I don't know anything else. The woman ran around the corner, the man ran after her, he started shooting and my staff and I all hid inside the shop. We didn't see anything.'

'Perhaps. But perhaps you saw more than you remember,' Baker say.

I nearly suck my teeth long and sour for he, but then my manners stop me. 'Well, I'll be here all day. Come by if you need to.' I cut it short. 'I have to go. We're short staffed and I have customers.'

'Talk to you later, then.'

I hang up, then allow myself the luxury of the long, sour steups that I wanted to buss when I was on the phone. Blasted man.

Whole damn morning these people come in and out the shop, looking to see where the woman dead, asking questions in a casual voice that really not casual one ass. At least they buy when they come; the cash register was nice and full at one o'clock when the blasted police man reach.

He could see I was busy, but he still insist on talking to me. I give up and call for Marie to come down from the next branch to take over the register while I sit in the kitchenette with Corporal Baker. She come one time, with she cow eye taking in the police man from head to toe and apparently liking what she see because she start to bat she eye for he.

Inside the kitchenette, I offer he a cup of coffee – he take it sweet and milky, and I had to stop myself from laughing because I know exactly what Jerry would have say about that – and I make a cup of Lipton tea for myself. Crix and cheese for lunch today – nobody had time to go nowhere to get nothing; I didn't get a chance to go outside and sneak a cigarette self – and this blasted man come now to get on my nerves.

'Had you ever seen the victim before?' Baker ask me.

'Who, the woman?'

'Her name was Carol George.'

'No, I never see she before.'

'Witnesses said yesterday that she was trying to get into your shop before she was shot.'

I shake my head. 'No, no. She was just running down the street. She didn't try to come in here at all. Whoever told you that was lying. Or maybe they made a mistake.'

In my mind I see the woman – Carol George – running with she breast jumping in she rip-up shirt, she hair sticking out like she was a Looney Toons cartoon that get a electric shock. I never see she before, I was sure. And is only by chance the man shoot she in front my shop. I never see none of them before in my life.

Baker say, 'Are you sure?'

'Absolutely.'

'Do you know Harpe Place?'

La Cour Harpe. A plannings. A set of four-storey buildings choke up choke up behind the Dry River, poor and dirty. I never live there. But I live in a next plannings on Nelson Street with a man once, for two-three months. I know just what them plannings like. You up in your neighbour business and trying hard to do as though you don't hear every whisper and fart coming from next door.

The man I used to live with used to beat me bad when he drink – meaning, every night, like clockwork – and I buss it as soon as I could get a little two-by-four in Barataria. I get away. Not like Carol George.

'I said—'

'I heard you. Yes, I know the place. But not well. I lived on Nelson Street when I lived in Port of Spain some years ago.'

'You didn't know Carol George.'

'Never saw her in my life.'

'Hmmm.'

I could have see he didn't believe me. Why I go hide that? If I know the woman, I know the woman. Nothing to hide there. Blasted man.

'The Harpe is a big place, Corporal Baker. Hundreds of people live there. Am I expected to know every single person who might have been living there seven, eight years ago when I lived on Nelson Street? Besides, my memory isn't what it used to be.' I give he a little half smile.

He chuckle. 'At your age you're complaining about your bad memory?'

'I'm going on forty this month,' I tell he.

'Forty?' He do a double take and choke on he coffee. I suppose he accustom with forty-year-old woman on we island looking old and hard. I had two things to prevent that: I relentless with moisturiser and sunblock, and I don't have no children. You would be amaze at how having children does make you look old before your time.

He study me over he coffee cup, a plain black mug I buy for the shop when I start to work here. When I first start, the staff was drinking from disposable cup and I find that was disrespectful and wasteful too, besides, so I went and take my own money and buy ordinary but nice mugs on Charlotte Street, and stainless steel spoons, and a good kettle. If nobody didn't appreciate it, I didn't mind; I do it for me as much as for them.

'What about the man? Did you know him?'

'No,' I say.

'Gregory Charles? Also known as 'Killer'?'

I had to laugh at the nasty coincidence. Well, clearly not a coincidence. From the sound of he nickname, the man was a gangster, and a shotter, to boot. Not that he necessarily had to be a shotter to get a gun, anybody in a gang could borrow a gun from the gang and use it, once they pay for the bullets. I remember my ex- from Nelson Street used to threaten me and say, 'Copper cheap, you know.' Asshole.

'I didn't know anyone named Killer, Corporal Baker.'

'Carl.'

'I didn't know anyone named Killer, Carl.'

'He has other aliases, as well. Guinness? Bago?'

'Never heard of him, Carl.'

94

He pull out a picture from he notebook. A nice-looking black fella, with skin the colour of stout – that is what give he the nickname, I figure – and three teardrops tattoo on he cheeks. One for every body he drop, that is how them gangsters does do it.

'Carl, I never saw this man in my life.'

He shrug and put the picture away, drain he coffee and stand up. He go to put the mug in the sink then turn around, sit back down and ask me for another cup of coffee. I figure he going and start the small talk now. My face set up one time. You never see a beast-face until you see mines.

I make the coffee and sweeten it with condense milk from the tin in the little fridge, hand him the mug and stand up with my arms cross and my best beast-face on.

'I wanted to ask you about your relationship,' Baker say.

'I had a mind so,' I say.

'Your husband—'

'I'm not married.'

'—your boyfriend—'

'He is not a boy.'

'—your manfriend...' he stop to see if I go correct he again. I didn't say nothing. 'Your manfriend. You realise you could be in as much danger as Carol George?'

I pick a spot on the wall just to the right of he head, and raise up my eyebrow.

'Miss Lopez. Alethea. You have a choice. You don't have to stay in the relationship.'

'Corporal Baker,' I say, with ice water practically dripping from my mouth, 'that is not your business and not your concern.'

'You want to end up in the papers, too?'

'Why are you making this your problem?'

'Because too many women just like you end up dead because they don't want to leave an abusive partner. You don't have to stay with him. You have a good job, you make good money here, I presume. You're the store manager?'

I ent answer he; he damn well know I's the store manager. I tell he that already when he interview me the day before.

'Many women in your position – in an abusive relationship – don't have options. Carol George was unemployed, and she had four children for Gregory Charles. She was stuck, in a sense. But you have no children. You have your own money. You could easily find someone else to have a relationship with, if you wanted to.'

'But that,' I tell he, 'is my choice to make. I don't agree that I am in the same position as Carol George. Not at all.'

I was lying. I could see myself skin up in the road, a bullet in my head, half naked and dead on the pavement just like Carol George. I had was to stop myself from shaking.

I feel him watching me. For a little little heartbeat we eye make four. Then I look away.

He say, 'If you change your mind, you know where you can find me. I can get you help. Just say the word.'

I smoke two cigarette after I walk he outside. I couldn't get the idea out of my head: me, Alethea, dead like Carol George. I didn't even have to close my eye to see it. It was there, a ghost of a picture burning in my brain, like when you look at the sun or stare at a light too long. Carol George name keep ringing in my head.

That story somebody tell he about how she was trying to come in the shop was shit, though. Carol George happen to stop by we window and she man happen to shoot she there. It was just a coincidence.

NINE

I tell the girls I taking a long lunch Thursday.

First thing I do was pass in the library and go up to the first floor, where the adult collection is, and return the book I had before and borrow a next one. I does like to mix it up – I doesn't read Jane Eyre and thing like that, but I would read a nice book by Alice Munro, or some Caribbean writers like Colin Channer and Lakshmi Persaud, even though I like my murder mystery and Nora Roberts.

I borrow a short story book name *Drown* and a Patricia Cornwell book name *Body of Evidence* – I think I read it before but it was good, if I remember right, so is all right.

After I jook the two books and my library card back in my bag, I hustle across to the church. Mass didn't start yet. I dip my finger in the holy water by the door and kneel down in the back of the church again. This was only the second time in years I was in a church. I don't even remember when

I went to mass before that – it was with my mother before I run away from home. But it was still familiar, and kind of comfortable, in a way. Homely. Everything was just about the same as I remember.

Kneeling down there I pray for Carol George and the man who shoot she. I pray for them to find peace in heaven – although that man was a devil and a shotter and he probably went straight to hell. But I didn't say that in my prayers. One thing I remember from the Bible was 'Judge not, lest ye be judged.' I just pray that both of them would find rest.

I pray for myself, that I could figure out what the hell to do about Leo and me. I love him, I love him bad, but the licks, man. Oh gorm. He does treat me so bad sometimes, but sometimes he does treat me like a queen. The little money he does make, whatever he don't spend on rum and beers and cigarette, he does spend on me, always buying a nice dress for me or a shoes or a perfume. Maybe not always. When I stop to think about it, that was in the early days, when we was now together. Now he does only buy me nice thing when he beat me real bad, and even so, is not all the time he does buy thing for me after a beating.

But look he write the song for me, I tell myself. That was a beautiful song. I know he love me. And if I was completely honest with myself I would say the sex was the best I ever had in my life. That man know how to make love. But maybe that wasn't the ideal thing to pray about in church when I was living with a man who wasn't my husband. I had to laugh. What Jesus know about sex? He dead a virgin.

But God know and see everything, my mother used to say. Maybe she was just saying that to frighten a stupid little child. But it stick. God know and see everything.

But God, if You know and see everything, You know and see how much cutass I does get. Why you does let he beat me, Lord?

I didn't get no answer.

When I open my eye the old ladies in they office clothes was dribbling in and they start to sing 'We Three Kings'. It occur to me that that day was Epiphany. I laugh soft soft: I had a epiphany about Epiphany.

Colin come in, in white vestments, behind a middle-age acolyte carrying a crucifix on a pole and a lector carrying the altar missal with both hands, holding it high up over he head. They do their simi-dimi and Colin read the introductory rites. I take my absolution like everybody else and sing the Kyrie, just as I accustom to doing every Sunday when I was a little girl. Of course, the Gospel was about the three wise men coming to bring gifts to the baby Jesus in the manger. The crèche was still up and Colin walk over to it and point out everybody in the scene as he give the homily.

'What gifts do we bring to the infant Jesus?' he say. 'We have no frankincense, no myrrh, no gold – well, most of us, anyway,' he say. The biddies giggle. 'But what we have is our hearts. Jesus wants, more than anything, our hearts.'

To be honest, I was listening with half a ear. My belly was growling and I wanted to get up off the hard pew and go and eat some lunch. But I promise Colin I would come to the mass, so I stay. I try to listen.

He didn't talk much longer, and the rest of the mass went fairly quick. I didn't go for communion, just sit down as the old ladies was singing 'What Child is This'. A pretty hymn, and one I half remember from long time, so I sing what words I know and smile, because I remember I used to like it. I wasn't much of a singer, though. Nothing like Leo.

Before I know it, Colin was saying the final benediction. I stand up and he make the sign of the cross in the air as he say, 'May the Lord bless you and keep you. May He make His face to shine upon you and be gracious to you. May He lift up His countenance to you and give you peace.'

Amen.

'The mass is ended; go in peace to love and serve the Lord,' Colin say.

'Thanks be to God,' the old ladies reply. I find myself automatically joining in.

I slip out while they was singing the exit hymn. I went by the office door to wait for him. He change in the vestry and was done in he jeans and jersey when he come outside the church.

'Alethea,' he say, as if he had fine glass crush up in he mouth.

'Colin.'

He hug me up hard and this time I try to hug him up back.

'I have a car, if you want to go out of town—'

'Can't we just eat at the mall up the street? It's not far.' I could see he wanted to carry me somewhere but I wasn't ready for that. I set up my face.

He shrug he shoulder. 'Okay, if that's what you want.'

We walk out the Sackville Street gate and turn up Edward Street. We didn't say nothing, just walk, not too fast, in the hot January sun. I was in my usual long sleeve white shirt, properly starch and iron, and one of my black pinstripe skirt – this one was a pencil skirt, slit high up the back. I was in sensible black pumps – a Naturalizer knock-off – and no stockings. I couldn't wear them in the island heat. That stockings thing is madness. I does feel sorry for the bank girls who have to wear them as part of the uniform. My ear was still swell – although not so bad as it was at first – and a kind of brownish purple colour, so I had my hair down to cover it.

I could feel Colin sneaking peeks at me out of the corner of he eye.

Soon enough we reach the mall, a short, ugly concrete block of a building, cross the road and went inside.

The mall food court was full of people, but we lucky to find a empty seat. Colin look around a little bit.

'Creole over there, Chinese over there, roti down here and some kind of bakery there,' he say. 'Name your poison.'

'No poison for me, thanks,' I say with a straight face.

Colin look like he swallow he own tongue.

'Oh gosh, is a joke,' I say, giggling soft. To tell the truth I was kind of nervous. I ent talk to he in more than twenty years and I didn't know where to start, so I grind my back teeth and hush my mouth.

'Chinese?' he say.

I shake my shoulder. Food wasn't the big attraction in this lunch in truth.

'Do you eat pork?'

'Yes, how you mean! You forget?'

'Well, people change, you know,' he say, looking hurt.

'You still eat pork?'

'Yes, of course. Not every day, but sometimes. I try to live modestly. It's part of the whole—' he wave he hand down he side, as if to say he whole self.

'Being a priest?'

'Yes. We take a vow of poverty.'

I raise my eyebrow and make a couyon mouth, pushing up my lip as if to say, Uh huh. The priest and them I remember wasn't no pauper, and they used to well eat they belly full. Ham, lamb and jam, as Mammie would have say.

He ask, 'Char siu kai fan?'

'Sounds great.'

'Large?'

I laugh. 'Small. I watching my figure.' I make sweet eye for him, to tell him I just joking.

'And a Coke?'

I skin up my face. 'Grapefruit juice, please. Or water, if they don't have grapefruit.'

He nod. It had a little line and he join it behind some men in black suit and tie, with some small small cloth bag in their hand.

Mustbe lawyer, I say to myself. They does stuff their long black robe in this little bag and pull it out for court, ramfle up ramfle up, like cobos with rumple up feathers. If was me, I would have press it out nice, but me ent no lawyer. The one time I had was to hire one was dread enough, and the restraining order didn't work anyway. The same stupid man from Nelson Street – if he didn't get shoot in some gang thing, he might have still be in my tail. But, thank God, copper cheap.

I look around the food court and watch the Formica tables, the dingy floor. They let the place go, man. It used to be so nice when it first open. I remember me and the other girls from the cloth shop – and Jerry, and all – was real excited to come when it first open. But now it was dull and ugly, and all the tables had chips and all the paint was dirty.

The air condition was on but it wasn't blowing cold at all. I unbutton my shirt – not too much, just so I could catch some breeze – and fold up my sleeves to my elbows. I didn't self notice the bruises on my hand from where Leo hold me down – I so accustom seeing them is no big deal for me – but when Colin come back with the food he nearly drop the tray.

'What happened to your wrists?' He rest down the two Styrofoam box of food fast and reach for my hand.

I pull away. I start to blush. I was shame for he to see it. I fold back down the sleeves. 'Nothing,' I say.

'Oh, Girlie!' he say, he eye wet like if he going and cry right there.

'Alethea,' I say, soft.

'Who is doing this to you?'

Instead of answering he, I pull the smaller box of food and the cup that look like it had juice in it. I start to eat.

'You eating or you watching me?'

He shake he head and say, 'Fine.'

When we reach about half way through we food, I close mines back and drink out the juice.

'But you barely ate anything at all,' he say, sounding so concern.

'I lost my appetite,' I tell him.

He chew on that, and a piece of char siu pork, for a while. Then he say, 'I can't believe I've found you. You know how long I've looked for you?'

My eyebrow couldn't go no higher. 'Eh heh? You didn't look too good. I was right in town.'

'What do you mean?'

'When I leave home, I stay by Jankie for a while, then I get a job and come to live in town. You could have ask Jankie, she knew where I was.'

Colin look sad sad. 'She wouldn't tell me anything. You know how many times I went to see her? She and Ricky refused to talk to me. I guess they thought I'd tell Mammie or...or my father.'

I watch the peeling yellow Formica on the table, holding my hand in my lap.

'I know what he did to you, Gir— Alethea. I know everything.'

'Really?'

He nod he head.

I didn't know how to feel about that. Colin was my boy, my little baby brother. I didn't want him to know what he father do me. 'Let's talk about something else,' I say.

'We should talk about—'

'No,' I tell him. 'Let's talk about something else.'

My little Colin. I wanted to hug him up so bad. But twenty-three years and too much stories he feel he done know already was in the way.

103

'Tell me all about you,' I say.

It take him a few minutes but he eventually start to talk. He start from the start, how he finish St Mary's and get a scholarship but he went in seminary instead, first here and then in Chicago. They ordain him there and he spend a five years teaching and preaching in Philadelphia until Mammie get sick.

'They didn't want me to go, but I begged for the transfer,' Colin say. 'At first, it was more like compassionate leave, just so I could take care of her. But then the Holy Ghost Fathers offered me a job at St Mary's. I took it, and so here I am. I teach Spanish and English Literature.'

'Figures,' I say, grinning. Colin head was always in a book.

'You didn't come to her funeral.'

My smile melt away. 'Who funeral?'

'Mammie's.'

I laugh again, but it was bitter like gall. 'No. I didn't go to the funeral.'

'May I ask why?'

It take me a long time to answer he. I grab my empty cup in my hand and start pressing patterns in it with my fingernails as I talk. 'Colin, you think you know the whole story. Trust me, you don't. Let's just say Mammie...she was different with you.'

'Different? Come on, Alethea. She abused both of us. It's what people did back then. It's all she knew.'

But I shake my head and bite my lip. 'No, Colin. She was different with you. She hated me.'

'Hated you? I was the one she couldn't stand. The black one. Mammie was so colour-struck—'

'Okay, so she didn't like your skin,' I admit. 'But she had something personal against me. I don't know, boy. When I think about how she used to treat me. What she let happen to me. What she do me.' I stop talking, fus I was upset. 'She didn't like me, period.'

104

'I can't believe you're saying this. Do you know what she said on her deathbed? "Tell Girlie I love her."'

I laugh out loud for that one. 'Oh, please!'

'It's true!' Colin was picking up for Mammie. Nah. 'With her dying breath. She said, "Tell Girlie I love her."'

'She had a damn funny way of showing it,' I say.

'It wasn't all her fault,' Colin say.

'How you mean?' Finally, I watch he in he face.

'My dad. He had a lot to do with it. I know that.'

I suck my teeth. 'Colin, you don't know a damn thing.' I pick up my bag and the food and the cup. By now the cup had rings and semi-circles all around it, making a pretty pattern, the opposite of the ugly thoughts and memories jumping up inside my head. 'I have to go back to work.'

'But—'

I throw the rest of the food away in a bin by the door and didn't look back.

My handbag start to go chirp-chirp-chirp. I still ent accustom to the phone so it take me a long time to realise the noise was coming from my bag in the first place, and then to remember that is a phone I have inside there. I dig up under the two books and my purse and finally find it. It was Bobby calling.

'Like you timing me, or what? I just finished lunch. I'm on my way back to the shop now. What can I do for you?'

He start to smile, I could just hear it in he voice. 'What you could do for me, indeed...'

'Bobby!' I say. I start to blush. He out of timing but so rude and nice sometimes.

'Okay, okay,' he say, getting serious. 'I want to go up to the warehouse today, to check out the rest of the new stock. I'm sending Marie down to the branch to hold on for you. Come directly here and we'll leave one time.'

It didn't take me long to reach him. He was in he BMW – the silver to Sita gold one – idling by the pavement in front the shop. I jump in the passenger seat and we start to crawl through the traffic in town.

'So, who you went to lunch with?'

He say it casual but I shake my head because all them man is the same thing: they want to know who you with, where you going, when you coming back. Like if I's a blasted baby.

'Nobody special,' I lie and say. I never tell him I have a brother, so it would be plenty to explain now. I wasn't in the mood.

He try to push a little small talk again, but when he see I not taking him on he hush and drive. Creeping down Frederick Street take forever – well, it feel like forever – but eventually we buss out and take the turn by the Lighthouse to go east on the Beetham Highway.

The car hardly make a sound. Inside it was like a tomb, quiet and cold. All the windows was up and the air condition was on high. I put on the radio so he wouldn't try and talk during the drive.

When we pass the Beetham Estate, I look at the little houses and the barracks yards and think about Colin again. How we used to sleep like two spoon in a kitchen drawer with Mammie on the edge of the bed; when he turn, I turn, hugging up whole night because in truth it was only me he had, and he was all I had. And in the morning, dragging the pissy mattress outside to put it in the sun. We do it together, because Mammie say she don't know who pee the bed but is one of we and we better clean it up. We self didn't know sometimes, if it was he or me who do it – we wake up with both of we soaking wet and smelling bad same way.

We sleep together in that bed until the day I leave home.

He was all I ever miss.

As we drive past, I look at the houses in the housing estate, pack up close like sardine. Some of the walls had cussing or decoration paint on them. A dark-skinned little boy sucking he thumb at the edge of the shoulder catch my eye. 'Colin,' I say, soft soft.

'Eh?'

'I say commess. How these people does have to live.'

Young men was running – scuttling – across the highway like bachac, with box and bag on their head or in their hand, ducking traffic, to carry their parcels to the housing estate. If you wait long enough, you could see them scuttle back over the highway again to pounce on the rubbish truck and them going inside the landfill behind the mangrove on the other side of the highway.

'Look at them, nah,' Bobby say, sour like lime. 'Ent want no work but they digging in the rubbish for scraps. You ent see poor people deserve to stay in their shit?'

I keep my mouth shut. Bobby grow up poor, but not poor like we. Aristocrat poor people does still have nice things, maybe hand-me-down washer and dryer, fridge and stove, thing so old that it come like antique, but he still grow up in a big house, went a nice school, had shoes on he foot and food in the fridge. He don't know nothing about real poor people in this island. I hush my mouth. I was thinking about Colin, and about the little boy sucking he thumb by the side of the road.

Traffic all and a sudden stand up like a wall. Bobby start to cuss and when we reach the turnoff to Barataria he swing left to buss through the backstreets. So much change in this area since I was a little child. Where it used to have mostly house, it now had big buildings, grocery, shop, even a tall glass building with a university campus in it.

Bobby catch me craning my neck to see down a street in El Socorro.

'You want roti? Raj have the best roti in Trinidad,' he say.

'I don't eat roti.' I turn away from the window. 'My first job was in a roti shop. I hate roti.'

Cassim's Warehouse Services was a massive compound of identical concrete hangars in the middle of what used to be pure canefield. It still had cane growing all around the compound, in dark green rows, swaying in the breeze like they drunk. The pitch road going up to Cassim's was smooth like black silk compared to the dirt tracks, full of pothole and ditch, everywhere else in the cane. Driving in the BMW on that road was like floating. We roll through the steel gates in the front of the compound. Bobby flash a parking pass at the half asleep security guard in a booth by the gate. He wave we through. We park and walk a few feet to the office, a small container standing up in front the warehouse and them.

Cassim was a nashy Indian man, tall and skinny like a sugarcane stalk. 'Sharma! How things, boy? Happy New Year!' They make small chat while Cassim was getting the keys for the warehouse On the Town does share with Sita hotel. 'You bring the van?'

Bobby say, 'Nah, we just come to check the stock, we not taking nothing.'

Cassim was grinning. He look from Bobby to me and back. 'I see.'

I hit him one cut eye.

As we walk to the warehouse, I tell Bobby, 'Good, so now he can go and tell Sita we was here.'

'You forget Marie. She know we here, too. I told her we had to check stock.'

Inside the warehouse it had a couple of bales of clothes remain back from the last shipment. Bobby didn't even watch them. He grab me and pull me up to he chest as soon as he lock back the door behind he. He start to kiss all along my neck, up my jaw and the ears Leo box, across to my mouth. He bite my lip soft. I start to moan. I was done wet already.

He was tender, unbuttoning my shirt from the neck down and kissing and sucking every spot the open shirt reveal. He back me up against one of the bales, push up my tight skirt and use his face to open my legs. He slide down to he knees.

I hear a noise, like metal hitting metal. It wasn't loud, but I was sure I hear it. I freeze. 'Bobby.'

He nuzzle my panty with he nose.

'Bobby. Stop. Let's go. Something not right.'

He ent take me on, nibbling around my navel instead.

But my hackles done raise. I push he head away and he fall back, confused.

'What happen?' he say.

'I don't know. Let's go, please. Someone's watching us. I heard a noise.'

He look around the room. It was bright under halogen lights in the roof. 'I ent seeing nothing. Must be a mice or something.'

But I done button back my shirt and pull down my skirt. I leave he on he knees and walk towards the door.

'You mad, yes.' He follow me, sucking he teeth.

The motel we went, five minutes away, was behind a high wall. It had parking at the back so people passing on the road couldn't see who car was there.

'Seventy-five a hour,' the desk clerk say, sounding bored. She hand we a key on a plastic key ring and take Bobby driving permit as surety. 'The bar open if you want a drink.'

We went straight upstairs.

'I like this place better than the other one,' I say when we went in the room. I walk around looking at everything.

It was clean, even the bathroom. 'At least we get a new bar of soap. At that other place they give you an old bar they cut in two. And look, the shower head only halfway down the wall.'

Bobby wasn't interested in the furnishings or toiletries. He pull me down to the bed and whisper instructions in my ears until I was naked and spread eagle.

JANUARY 3

When Uncle Allan came to visit that afternoon, he and Mammie laughed at Tantie Indra.

'And they're going to eat that?' the radio voice purred. Colin's daddy sounded happy, except it wasn't a nice happy, but the kind of fake happy like when Mammie was talking to the neighbours, a happy that she put on to face them and took off as soon as she turned her back to walk through the rickety wooden doorway of her house. That was the kind of happy in the radio voice.

'Yes!' Mammie shrieked. There was another kind of happy in her voice, one Alethea had never heard before. This happy was sharp and dangerous and smelled funny. They were drinking something yellowish-brown from a tall bottle standing in the middle of the table, pouring little drinks into short glasses. The two of them would gulp the yellow-coloured liquid quickly, and their faces would turn red before they followed the drink with sips of water Mammie poured into the same glasses from an enamel mug. Usually it was cooking oil they kept in a bottle like that one. But this didn't smell like cooking oil. It smelled like clove and wet, rotting sugar. The scent made Alethea's nose burn and her stomach churn.

She edged back behind the curtain and crawled into the bed next to the little boy who was lying on his back with his ginger cat baby bottle in one hand, playing with his toes and cooing to himself. From here she could still hear Mammie's shrill happiness and Uncle Allan's radio voice laughing nastily about the snake Liloutee's mother had offered to share with Marcia that day. Alethea absently listened to the sound of their voices but paid no attention to the actual words, focused as she was on the small, dark toes her cousin wriggled. Every now and then he would put the bottle's teat to his mouth and suck out some milk, until he decided to try sucking his toes instead.

'Oh geed,' she scolded, yanking the little foot from his mouth. 'Oh geed, Colin. You can't suck that. You didn't bathe yet. Your foot still nasty from outside. Mammie go beat you if she catch you doing that.' The urgent whisper made the boy pause and look at Alethea with his round black eyes. Releasing his foot, he grabbed for her hair instead, tugging the light brown curls with his tiny fingers. 'Ow! It hurting!'

Colin squealed happily and pulled her hair again.

'Ow!'

'Girlie!' Mammie's sharp happiness went from her raised voice. 'What shit all you doing in there?'

'Nothing, Mammie,' she called back, extricating her hair from his damp grasp. Colin gurgled and grasped for it again but she ducked. He giggled and reached out again. She ducked again. The game went on until Colin started to yawn, his bright eyes glazing and finally closing as he put his bottle back to his lips. Milk dribbled from the side of his mouth. Alethea took the bottle from his relaxed grip and covered it before resting it upright on the floor beside the bed.

It was dark outside the board walls of the house. The kitchen lamp flared with the sound of a match being struck and threw up shadows Alethea could see on the kitchen wall over the partition between the two rooms. There was Mammie, an enormous, slow-moving black blob. And there was Uncle Allan with the radio voice, his shadow thin and spindly like a daddy-long-legs. Golden light flickered in swift, gleaming patterns in between the shadows whenever she heard liquid splash into the glasses. Alethea curled next to Colin's compact body and watched the shadows dance closer and closer to each other until her eyelids grew too heavy to stay open any more.

'Move, Girlie,' Mammie hissed at her.

Alethea didn't want to open her eyes. A wringing pinch of the skin at her waist, however, sat her bolt upright in the bed. Before she could cry out, Mammie covered her mouth with a big, rough hand.

'Hush your mouth before you wake up the boy. Go round. Your Uncle Allan sleeping here tonight. You have to squeeze up.'

Alethea, thin snot dripping from her nose and hot tears oozing from her eyes, nodded and scooted closer to Colin. Mammie settled on the bed with a sigh, her breath wafting in a sour-sweet cloud over the children before she turned her back to the girl next to her. Uncle Allan slid in beside Mammie, tucking an arm around her and his sleeping son. Alethea, still smarting from the pinch, rubbed her running nose and eyes. The house was completely dark now. She couldn't see anything, not even Colin, who was inches from her face. The darkness was warm and silent until Mammie started to snore. She listened to the silence and the snoring, inhaling the spicy, rotten sugar smell on the adults' breath and the milk, baby powder and pee of Colin's body. Uncle Allan shifted in the bed and curled his arm around the top of Colin's head. Alethea froze when his hand began to stroke her hair.

TEN

Friday evening, Tamika man – Tamika fiancé – park up outside On the Town to wait for she. He was drinking a beer, leaning up on the side of the car and listening to the soca one of the illegal CD vendors was pumping from they cart by the corner of Queen and Frederick. Every now and then, somebody he know would stop and they would talk for a while, give each other a bounce and the next man would walk on. One fella stay, though. He buy a rounds of beers and the two of them drink, talk and watch woman for about a hour until Tamika finish work. I watch them good from inside – sitting up by the cash register I had a perfect view of the two of them.

Curtis. A nice looking fella but nothing too spectacular. Not like Leo, no perfect body and perfect face, just a ordinary brown-skin man, average height. He driving B-15 like half the people on the island. Tamika tell me he working in a insurance place up the road. The friend was another story: sapodilla brown with light brown eyes and black hair cut in a flannel ball, he wasn't in no shirt and tie and soft pants like Curtis. He was wearing a basketball jersey and three-quarter jeans, with a tattoo on he neck. I could smell gangster from quite inside the shop.

Tamika barely step a foot outside before they had a beer in she hand too. They invite me to join them but I say I good, thanks, pull down the gate and lock up, smoking my cigarette like I now come out of jail.

'We going Pier One tonight,' Curtis say, in a drawl that get on my nerves one time. He feel he's a sweetman. 'Come, nah.'

'Yeah, family,' he friend say. 'I would like to get to know you better.' He had a rude little smile on he face and he skin crinkle up nice nice by the corner of he brown eyes. The eyes was sparkling in the sunset.

We might have make nice children, I tell myself, smiling on the inside but keeping my face straight like a police on the outside. 'Sorry, I have plans.'

Tamika pull me aside one time. 'What plans you have?' she whisper loud.

'Stop minding my business, please,' I say, smiling so it wouldn't sound so rough.

'Why you don't come with we? You doesn't go nowhere. Come, nah. And is Friday!'

I try to make as though I was thinking about it, but in truth it never even cross my mind to go. Mr Sapodilla was lovely – lovely, I tell you – but no way no how Leo letting me go out by myself, especially not with some man.

'I tired, girl. But let me call you later, okay?'

She put she number in my cell phone and save it and make me promise to call she.

In the maxi going home in the heavy traffic I was reading *Drown*. Junot Díaz had a funny way of writing, I find. Some parts was in English and some parts was in Spanish. I couldn't figure out if it was one book – a novel – or a set of stories almost like a novel, like *Miguel Street*. Half of *Drown* I didn't really understand too good. But I read it, and something about it I like. The boy or the boys in the stories was alone, like me; they didn't fit in nowhere. They father was real asshole man, when they had a father at all. I tell myself I go look for more of he books, even though I didn't really understand the whole thing.

Before I know it the maxi was by my corner. I cross the road and bounce right up with Leo, who look as though he was waiting for transport, dress up nice in he best shirt and pants and smelling sweet. Good, I tell myself. If he going out tonight he might go by he woman and give my poor ass a rest.

But instead of waving bye-bye he turn and walk me up the road to the house. Is a good thing, too: I nearly pass it straight because the outside paint, for the first time in the years I living there. I watch him from the corner of my eye. If I say the wrong thing I know he go get vex and I didn't want him to lash me again. I was so fed up with licks.

'Wow!' I say.

He smile, so I continue.

'Wow! You paint the house, it looking so nice!'

He still smiling. Good.

We walk around and went through the kitchen door as usual. Everything was clean and smelling nice, just like he. But still I waiting for the other shoes to drop.

'I get a gig,' he say. 'A six-months gig at the Hilton. And they pay me a advance.' He take my hand and pull me inside the bedroom. It had a bright red slip dress on the bed. A little naked for my taste, more like a nightie than something I would go out in, but it was a beautiful dress. Soft, silky crimson satin. He hold it up to me, put it near my face. I could feel the cloth slipping down my skin.

'Try it on, babes,' he say, he voice husky and sweet.

I take off my clothes and shoes and stand up there in my bra and panty.

'Well, try it on,' he say.

I reach for it but he pick it up and say, 'Put up your hand.' He slide it down over my head. It was like wearing a cloud.

'This is the wrong bra,' Leo say, and unhook my bra and pull it off me through the straps of the dress. 'And this panty showing.' He put he hand under the dress and tug down the panty, too.

'Here,' he say, reaching down by the foot of the bed for a shoebox I never see before. Red patent leather pumps with five-inch stiletto heels. 'Put on this.'

He put he hand on my shoulder and spin me around to see how I look in the mirror. My nipples was standing up like stone. The dress was short, skimming just below my bottom.

Leo, standing up behind me, kiss that spot on my neck and raise the hem of the dress. He unzip he pants.

I would have put on a strapless bra and a thong or something underneath the dress, and probably a cardigan or a pashmina, but Leo insist I wear it just so. I feel naked. A car come and pick we up and drop we right in front Hilton. I was shame that I had so much bruises on my arms, but Leo didn't care. I could see one or two people looking at me like I was some kind of ho, but nobody didn't say a word to my face.

I find the darkest corner to sit down in and Leo went to work. Hilton had a baby grand, too, and I ent go lie: I was proud of Leo when he start to play. I does have to remind myself sometimes that he have a degree in music from a American university, and that people still remember he from back in the day. Jam, the band he used to have, was local superstars long time, with girls throwing panty at them on stage and thing, as if was some kind of big artiste like Teddy

Pendergrass or Michael Jackson singing instead of just Leo. Even without the band, that night, he hold the crowd in the palm of he hand.

After he play two set I figure is time to go, but some shrivel up old white woman who pose up on the bar sending drinks for Leo whole evening come and plops sheself down by he on the piano stool to make conversation. The two of them move back to the bar and start to drink rum. She was playing with he shirt button, whispering in he ears, and I feel like a damn ass sitting down there by myself in the corner. The manager like he feel sorry for me and bring me a drink, just a glass of white wine. He stay for a minute, chatting and telling me what a great musician Leo was and how glad they was he come to play for them.

All and a sudden Leo reach by the table and put he hand on my shoulder, gripping it tight. He give the manager a big smile and shake he hand. 'Went well?'

'Yes,' the manager say. 'I look forward to much more. Same time next week?'

'Sure,' Leo say, smiling like a tiger.

The manager walk away. I stand up and Leo grab my arm like a vice. He put he hand on my bottom.

'Your dress wet. Talking to he make you get wet?' He shake me, but then remember we still inside the people place. He cool heself down and put on that tiger smile again.

The car was waiting to carry we home.

Leo was breathing rum breath in my face on top of me when the cell phone start to ring. Chirp-chirp-chirp. Chirp-chirp-chirp. I try to push him off but he spring up and reach the phone in the kitchen in record time. I stand up there in the nasty little silk dress and watch him answer.

'Alethea's phone,' he say. 'Sorry,' he tell the person calling, 'she's in bed at the moment. Can I take a message?'

He listen, then buss a big smile.

'Sure, we'd love to! I'm Leo, by the way. Her husband.'

Husband? Where that come out?

'Looking forward to meeting you. You need directions?' He tell she how to find the place and then he say, 'See you then.'

He close the flip phone snap.

'Who the ass is Jankie?' he say.

ELEVEN

Was me, Leo and Amanda in the back seat of the shiny red Jimny. Leo had he arm around my shoulder and was looking out the window, unconcerned. Amanda was only talking, talking, talking. Like nobody never tell she children must be seen and not heard, nah.

Ricky, Jankie little brother, was driving, and Jankie was in the front passenger seat. Ricky put on weight since I last see him – now he was round like he father used to be, but he had the same kind, sweet face I remember. He keep peeping at me in the rear-view mirror and I was praying for Leo not to notice.

They come and meet we by L'Anse Mitan corner Sunday morning bright and early to go Macqueripe. They had a cooler, picnic basket, folding chairs and endless towel in the back of the Jimny. Although Jankie had on makeup like if she going shopping in South Beach, she was wearing a beautiful white bikini underneath a orange floral chiffon caftan. If you see the hat, papa! Proper tourist business: a wide-brim floppy straw hat with a white chiffon scarf for a hatband. She look like she just step out from a Vogue photo shoot.

After work Saturday I did stop in the mall and buy body makeup. The sales girl swear it waterproof, rub proof, and wouldn't stain my clothes. I was hoping she wasn't lying. Without the makeup my skin look like a pretty colour wabine. But the makeup cover up everything and I just look like a normal person. My bathsuit was a plain black one-piece, and I had two yards of aqua blue ombré georgette as a beach wrap. Working in a cloth store for all them years had some benefits.

Leo, in a jersey and board shorts, shake Jankie hand like if he know she long time.

Ricky barely say a word, just blush and look down when he see me. I give he a big hug up. He was too sweet, still, even after all these years.

'So, Leo, tell me about yourself. Miss Alethea here didn't say a word about you...a well-kept secret!' Jankie say.

Leo pile on the charm. 'Nothing much to say. I'm a musician. You can catch me at the Hilton twice a week,' he say, as though he have that gig long, long time instead of just starting it yesterday.

'Really! What do you play?'

'I play piano and sing at this gig, but I also play guitar, drums, pan—'

'Ooh,' Jankie squeal. 'You play pan?'

'Yes, a bit. I arrange, as well. But I'm not arranging for any band this year. I'm taking a break,' Leo say.

I choke back a laugh. Leo was 'taking a break' from arranging from since long before I know he. The truth was that he does drink too much and nobody didn't want to hire he because he damn unreliable. I don't know how Hilton get chain up with he, nah, but at the same time I was glad we would have extra money for the next six months, unless Leo drink it out.

'So you studied music?'

'Yes, I have a bachelor's from Wisconsin.'

'Wisconsin, of all places! How did you end up there?'

Leo start to tell the long and winding story of how he was a child prodigy and how a big pan arranger take he under he wing and make sure he get a full scholarship – tuition, room and board, books, pocket money, everything – to this school nobody never hear about. At least, nobody he know. Everybody he know who want to do music was going Julliard, UCLA and Berklee, Fordham and them places. But them didn't offer Leo no full scholarship, so is Wisconsin he gone.

He spend four years up there freezing he ass off, and barely graduate – but he didn't tell Jankie that part. I myself only know because I maco some letters he had in a box in the top of the wardrobe – he was on academic probation at one time, but he manage to get through by the skin of he teeth. He come home and the plan was for he to start to teach, but he interfere with somebody girl child in the first school he went, and they hush it up and fire he quiet quiet. That was when he start the band and get famous. They had a good few hits but then the rum take over and the band break up. When I meet he, he was playing a Sunday night gig in a little bar in St James, he one and he guitar. As for the arranger, who was he maestro, he dead and gone. Leo doesn't talk about him at all.

The way Leo spin it for Jankie, he make it look like people didn't like he head when he come home, and that is why he get fire from the teaching work. It wasn't in no papers or nothing, so Ricky didn't know about the story neither. I myself only put it together because when Leo get drunk sometimes he does brag about this little sixteen-year-old he was bulling right in she mother house until the father walk in on them one day. I don't have no university degree, I never even went senior comp, but I ent no ass. I could put two and two together. If he was teaching then and the father catch them screwing, bet your bottom dollar the school would have fire Leo – unless he had money and offer to marry the girl, but that is a different story. Two months later Jam had their first hit.

The road from L'Anse Mitan to Macqueripe wasn't long. Before I know it we was driving past the bamboo and bush on that long, narrow road to the sea. We pull up and park, and Leo and Ricky hold the big blue cooler by the handles and carry it down the couple dozen steps to the beach.

I grab two plastic folding chairs, Amanda grab the other two, and Jankie load up sheself with towel and picnic basket. We follow the men down the steps.

Macqueripe that day wasn't empty, but it was early enough that we could find a good spot on the beige sand and set weself up nice. The sky was blue and clear and the water was smooth as glass, with baby-size waves washing up on the beach in no kind of hurry at all. The steep steps down – and back up – was the one reason I didn't like Macqueripe, but otherwise it was a lovely beach. You walk out past the shallows and suddenly you in so deep you can't touch the ground. It was scary but exciting, once you could swim.

I ent no big swimmer but I could tread water, float and do a decent crawl – Leo teach me when we first meet and we was all lovey-dovey. He say is a shame I from a island and never learn to swim. Sometimes we used to come here, this self same Macqueripe. More likely we went Indian Bay, just after the Alcoa station at Tembladora. Them does say the water there polluted, full of faecal matter from the yachties and them boat. We didn't study that. Leo used to hold my hand and walk me in the water and lay me on my back and put he hand under me until I could learn to let go and float. At first I fight every time I start to relax, and bitter salt water gone up in my nose, in my mouth, in my ears, but he didn't let me go. He hold me gentle like he touching a petal, and the hands underneath me finally give me the confidence to just relax and let the water keep me afloat. He turn me over and show me how to float on my belly, my hand and foot spread out like a starfish. And then, he show me how to kick, and how to move my hand over my head and through the cold water, and by the end of the lessons I was crawling, and in love with this man with he skin like satin and he voice like butter and he face like a angel.

I didn't get licks until later.

We set up the chairs and Jankie share out drinks – beers for she and the men and LLB for me and Amanda. I wanted to keep my head because I didn't want to make no mistake and make Leo get mad. I sit down on the sand and sip the LLB, cold like ice and tangy and tasting like bitters and lemon and lime, just like it suppose to. I find it nice when things is what they seem.

My old best friend hold my hand and pull me up. 'Let's take a walk?'

I still not accustom to this Paris Hilton version of she, eh. The Jankie I know from long time was pure Aranguez Indian, with long, black hair all down by she bamsee, plait in one and tie with a rubber band on the end, slick down with coconut oil and neat as a pin. She eye and them really black, and she skin was browner than it looking now. She always like fashion – I used to go by she after school behind Mammie back, and Jankie had all kind of clothes. Indian clothes – cupboards full of sari and shalwar kameez and garara in all shape and colour; western clothes, too – jeans and jersey and shirt and dress and short pants and skirt for so. She mother like she used to spend every other weekend in Miami and when she come home is only clothes and shoes for Jankie and Ricky. Not that Jankie had anywhere to wear the clothes – Raj, she father, was so protective she didn't used to go nowhere. Is no wonder she end up marrieding she PE teacher. That is the only man she get to meet outside of she family and the customers in the roti shop she father had. It didn't hurt that Mr Inalsingh look like a young Shashi Kapoor, and had some money. He wasn't no Leo.

Jankie put she arm in mine and we giggle like teenagers when we start to walk.

'That Leo! He's such a hottie! Why didn't you mention you were married?'

'I'm not.'

'But he said—'

'We've been living together five years. I suppose we have a common-law marriage by now.'

'Oh, okay,' she say.

We walk a couple more steps on the shifting, stony sand.

'It's beautiful here.'

'Yes,' I say. In truth, it was like a picture postcard. Blue blue water, green green hills, jagged black rocks sticking up from the sand. 'Imagine it used to be a submarine station.'

'Really? I didn't know that.'

'So Leo say. He know plenty things.'

'Does he?' she say soft. She watch me sideways but she didn't say nothing else.

We walk slow but it wasn't a long beach and we reach the rocks by the end and turn around to go back. Before we start back to walk, she stop and look at the water.

'I'm moving back home, Alethea. I want to start a business. And I want you to help me.'

TWELVE

'Me?' I say one time. 'What the ass I know about opening a business?' I start to laugh.

But Jankie serious like police. 'Allie, come on. You know this place better than me. And you know clothes. Obviously.' She pull my beach wrap and wink. 'Love this, by the way! I want to start a boutique. Very high end. I'll bring in the clothes, you just have to help me sell them.'

I didn't have time say boo before my girl start to talk and talk about this shop she want to open, the big diamond on she hand making sweet eye every time the sun catch it when she wave she hand to make a point. She have plenty ideas. Nothing really solid yet, but as she talk my neck start to tingle. I was getting excited, yes. Me ent say much, but I start to think.

Down by which part the cooler set up, Ricky waving at we with a plate in one hand. Lunch sharing. Ricky had a

sweet hand. The curry duck he bring was tasty and tender –
I mean bite-your-finger tasty, falling-off-the-bone tender, and
that is no easy feat when you talking duck. When I tell him
the food taste nice he only blush and rub he two foot together
in the rough sand. I could hear Leo mentally steupsing and
calling he mamapoule and soft man and all kind of thing
– that was Leo, right through – but in reality my so-called
husband just smile and say, 'Yes, this food cutting, man.' He
does cook more than me, and better than me, too, but in he
mind I sure he looking down on Ricky, not for cooking, but
for being so shy and softie.

Leo not shy at all. He bold and brash and does take what
he want – in and out of bed. And he full of charm. The idea
of Leo blushing and rubbing he foot when somebody give he
a compliment wouldn't even cross he mind. He feel he is the
froth on mauby.

In some ways, he right, too. He smart no ass, and he have
more talent in he pinky toe than most people have in they
whole body. But he is a cruel man and he like to control me
too much. And, of course, he does drink like a fish.

He there drinking beers like water, but nobody didn't say
nothing. We had a cooler full of them anyway. Ricky was
driving, Jankie was taking she time, and I was only drinking
LLB and shandy, so more beers for he. I was nervous that he
would get drunk and start to behave bad, but it was the exact
opposite. The more he drink, the more charming and nice
he get. He had little Amanda falling in love with him when
he sing a song for she, and Jankie and Ricky get completely
take in by the suave, man-of-the-world act he was putting on.
Suave. That is a good word.

He tell them all kind of funny story about when he went
on tour with Jam in England and America, how he play for
we president and all, but he manage to tell the stories in a
humble way, not making heself sound like a bigshot. I know

in my mind that that is exactly how he feel about heself, like he is the greatest musician this country ever had, but you wouldn't have guess that from the way he was talking and acting so humble that day in Macqueripe.

When Amanda say she want to go in the water, he went with she and Ricky. I watch the girl climbing up on he shoulder to dive in the cold blue sea, scaling he chest like a wall so he could flip she backwards into the water. At first I was a little worried that he might be trying a thing on she – I never hear he say, like so much man on this island, that 'after twelve is lunch', but you never know. Plus, too, I know about he and that teenage girl from the school. I watch them hard but he didn't try nothing. He was the perfect gentleman. Avuncular. Another good word.

'You don't want to go swimming?'

'I can't swim too good,' I tell Jankie. To my mind it wasn't a lie. Me ent no big swimmer. Plus too the makeup.

We watch them in the water for a while.

'He'd make a good father,' Jankie say.

The smoke from my cigarette was curling around my head before the breeze take it. We was sipping drinks by the cooler. She take off she caftan and was in the white two-piece alone. She had a body like a Barbie dolly, tight and tone and not a grain of hair anywhere, from she 36C boobs to she narrow waist and curvy hips. Jankie always had a good figure when we was girls, but I could tell this wasn't just natural – the boobs was standing up like man and I know nobody who make three children could have breast firm like that. Not that I was judging she. I couldn't afford no breast implants and liposuction to make my belly flat like a jooking board, but who's to say I wouldn't do it if I had the money?

'Do you and Leo plan on having kids?'

'Who, me? No, papa,' I say. I had to laugh. Even if I wanted to, I couldn't make children. And I sure wouldn't make none for Leo if I could. All the charming he playing that day on the beach with Jankie family, he was a nasty brute and I would fraid for any children we had. I grow up with too much licks to wish the same on any child, far more for my own. 'No,' I say again, when I done laugh. 'No.'

'Wow. That's really adamant.'

A great word, adamant. I take a drag.

'Don't you think you'd be a good mom?'

I shake my head. 'Is not just that. Well, is that too. But I can't have children.'

'Oh no!' She say it like is the end of the world. 'Why not? What happened?'

My uncle happen, is what I wanted to say. But what I really say was, 'I had a infection when I was younger. It left me infertile.'

'Did you ever think about IVF?'

Jankie mustbe living in another world, for truth. She had no idea how expensive that was.

I shake my head again, screw up my face. 'No, I good. Sometimes I wish…but, really, I had enough mothering to do when I was a little girl. Remember how I used to have to take care of Colin all the time.'

She nod, slow, remembering. 'He was like your little shadow. I guess, yeah, you really did have enough when you were a kid.' She take a sip from she beer. 'How is Colin, anyway? And what about your mom?'

I take a long time to answer she. I was still keeping my eye on Leo down there with the people girl child. Although Ricky was right next to them, it wouldn't surprise me at all to find out that Leo slip he hand in the child panty 'by accident' in all that horseplay. It happen to me when I was younger than she.

'Colin is great. I had lunch with him the other day. He's a priest now.'

'A priest! Oh my God!'

'Yes, a priest. Oh my God, indeed.'

'How did that happen?'

'The usual way, I guess. I really don't know the details. We haven't been in touch much over the years. Not since I leave home, to tell the truth.'

'He used to come by the house and ask for you. I figured if you wanted him to know where you were you'd find a way. But you stayed away from him for so long? That's a really long time, Alethea.'

Again, I take a while to answer. So much thoughts and memories, unwanted memories, hateful thoughts, was spinning in my brains.

'I just...' I stop. I try again. 'I just leave and I never went back.'

I leave it at that.

'And your mom?'

'Mammie died.' The way I say it, this time she didn't ask no more question. She could see I wasn't going and say nothing else.

Jankie finally change the subject. 'You didn't answer me about the business. What do you think?'

'Tell me again why you want to leave America and come home to this backward little island?' I making joke with she, but I was partly serious. From where I stand as a glorified shop girl, making barely enough to keep body and soul together, it didn't make no damn sense to me that Jankie would want to leave America to come here for more than a holiday.

'I just...' She shake she head. 'You don't understand.'

'Well, explain it,' I say.

She stare off in space for a good time. Waves was getting rougher, and the breeze was picking up, but Macqueripe was still fairly calm compared to further along the north coast, like Maracas Bay. There the waves could get up to ten feet high just so on a normal day. You would swear is two different sea. Maracas was green and cold and the waves would beat you like a bad lover, lift you up and smash you down and roll you in the sand until you bruise up and battered. Even now when the waves was getting choppy, Macqueripe was still so gentle, brittle old ladies and young young babies was liming in the water, easy like kissing hand.

Ricky, Leo and Amanda walk out the water, struggling through the sucking sand under the foamy waves by the shore. I see Leo pointing towards the rocks on the side of the beach and Ricky and Amanda follow him up into the bush. A few minutes later I see them again lining up on the edge of a little cliff over the deep blue water. Leo was the first to go, diving down like a Olympic swimmer and cutting the water with barely a splash. Amanda went next, in a cannonball with she legs draw up tight on she chest. Ricky went last. He try to dive but end up in belly flop that splash so hard I could hear it from the beach.

'Ouch,' I say.

Jankie didn't even notice. She still deep in she thoughts.

'Do you realise that I've lived in the States longer than I've lived here?'

'Hmm,' I say, still watching the three bodies bobbing up and down in the deep water below the ledge.

'When I left I thought I'd do so many things. I wanted to go to Princeton – Princeton! As if. Instead, I got pregnant, had three kids – wham, bam, bam – and that was my life. Rudy was my life. I did everything he wanted. I was the perfect wife. Even this,' she say, grabbing she breast like two grapefruit and squeezing, 'this was his idea. I went along because that is what a good dulahin does, right? You listen to your husband.'

'Not dulahin alone, Jankie,' I say. 'Don't be so hard on yourself.'

She snort, as if to say I talking shit. 'I've never been anybody in my adult life except Mrs Rudranath Inalsingh. I'm tired of it, Alethea. I'm tired of it. I want my own life now.'

'So you just going to leave him in Miami?'

She shrug she shoulders.

'You sure you think this through, Jankie?' I ask she, soft soft. She might think it hard to be somebody wife and somebody mother, but I could have tell she the alternative much worse. People does look at you like something wrong with you when you tell them you don't have no children. Like if that is all a woman could do. Worse yet when you tell them you is forty and you never married. Is like a crime in this island to be a woman on your own.

Not that I was ever really on my own. I went from my mother house to Jankie house, and even when I was living in my own place I always had a man. I went one man to the next, for most of my life. Not all of them beat me, is true, but they make me feel like I stupid, like I don't know my ass from my elbow, like I wasn't nothing without them. But people does get on like if you, as a woman who have no man, you not good enough, like you's not a real woman. So if is either stay with a asshole or have no man at all, I rather stay with a asshole.

But Jankie don't know nothing about that. She married we junior sec PE teacher when she was seventeen years – is either she married him or Raj would have kill the both of them – and she never know what it is to be a single woman, or a woman living in sin, or a woman without children. To she, living in that marriage come like a cage. Call me dotish if you want, but if being married to a man with money, who treating me good and not beating me, who minding the children and not beating them, who buying me diamond and breast implants and designer clothes – if that is a cage, lock me to ass up.

Leo, Amanda and Ricky swim up to the beach and climb up the rocks again. When Ricky come out the water so, he belly red red red from the belly flop. Poor soul. Next time he do better, but not much.

'The kids are grown,' Jankie suddenly say. 'They're all in college. I don't have anything to do any more. No soccer practice, no homework, no cheerleading, no "Mom-would-you-take-me-to-the-mall." Rudy...well, let's just say Rudy wouldn't mind if I moved back home.'

'You guys having trouble?'

'Oh, no, nothing like that,' Jankie say. She still staring off into space, sounding dreamy dreamy. 'It's just that, after twenty-three years, it's not the same any more. I could move here part time. Spend time in Miami and time at home.' She grin and watch me with a sly look. 'Remember Mai and Papa? I get it. After all this time, I get it.'

'You mean why she was in Miami every other weekend and he was here?'

'It's just that you get tired of seeing that face every day, you know? It's not that Rudy is bad. And it's not that I'm with anybody else—' she say that quick quick '—it's just... dull. And I would like to think that I could be something else, something other than just a wife and mother.'

We life real different for true, yes, I say to myself. I would love to be in your shoes.

Amanda fall asleep in the Jimny on the drive home that afternoon. She lean on me and snuggle up, smelling like salt and sunblock and sweat and curry. Ricky smile at me in the rear-view. I do like I didn't see nothing.

They drop we off in front we house. I was so glad Leo paint it the Friday, because I would have be too shame for Jankie to see what a state the place really was in. The little coat of paint brighten up the house, and from the front you would never know it was falling apart.

Jankie and Ricky wouldn't come inside – Ricky didn't want

to wake up Amanda. I thank God for small mercies and wave bye-bye from the front yard.

When the car gone, Leo had the tiger smile on again. 'I like your friends. And I could tell that Ricky really like you.'

I suck my teeth and walk off.

Leo follow me inside the kitchen, already starting to bother my tail about Ricky.

'First time I see he in over twenty years, and you feel we have something going on?' I tell Leo, sucking my teeth. I strip off my clothes and head for the bathroom. I had to take off the body makeup with a special cleanser, so I start doing that in front the bathroom mirror while Leo just watch me.

The makeup come off with every stroke of the cleansing wipe, showing the bruises underneath.

'You look like a Etch A Sketch.'

We eye make four in the mirror. I didn't say nothing. I went back to taking off the makeup.

'Babes,' he say, cosying up behind me. 'Babes, I sorry.'

I just keep on doing what I was doing. When that wipe get too brown with makeup, I take a next one out of the pack and continue.

Finally I stand up in front the mirror, stark naked and black and blue and brown and red where he kick me, cuff me, slap me, grab me. I watch he in he eye in the mirror just a little bit, then went in the shower.

He strip and follow me there, too.

I turn on the water and he take the fluffy plastic shower pouf hanging from a hook on the wall, throw some body wash on it and start to make suds on my skin. He turn off the shower. He start by my neck, wash right down my back, my bottom, my arms. He was so tender. He turn me around and wash my breasts, my belly, my thighs. Stooping down he wash my legs, then my foot. He stand up, drop the pouf on the ground. With he hand, he wash between my legs.

135

Leo turn back on the tap and use he whole body to guide me under the falling water. The water was cold but we was hot. He hard cock was pressing up on my belly, slipping from side to side in the suds and water. We stand up under the water for the longest time before he turn it off again.

He wrap he hand around me, soft soft, like if I's a little child. 'Babes, I sorry. I so sorry.'

He sound like he mean it.

Lying in bed afterwards, he ask what me and Jankie was talking about so long. I tell he what she say about coming home and starting a business, and how she ask me to help she.

'You?' he say, laughing loud loud. 'Stupidee like you could start any business?'

He laughing, I burning. My face turn red but he couldn't see it in the dark.

I didn't argue with he, because we was having a nice day and a nice night, and I didn't want to get him vex. But in my heart I know he was wrong.

He get up and put on he clothes – soft pants and a shirt I never see before.

'Where you going?'

'Work. I didn't tell you the gig is twice a week?'

He doesn't tell me nothing. He could be going on the moon for all I know – when he leave the house he doesn't say a word about where he going or who he going with. Me, on the other hand, I lock down here like I in jail. I can't go nowhere but to work and back. If I going anywhere, I have to tell him where I going, when I coming back, who I going with and what I going to do. That is partly why I doesn't go nowhere. The other reason is that sometimes it just not worth it because even if I going to the grocery, when I come back is like a interrogation about who I see and what man I have.

I not saying I innocent. Of course I know I have a next man. But that is my business. As far as I concern, I not married, no matter what Leo tell people. I could take man if I want – I just can't let Leo find out.

He kiss me on the lips soft and sweet, still laughing at the idea that I could start a business, and tell me he go see me later.

When I hear he pass the window, I get up and put on a duster.

I look out through the jalousies in the drawing room to make sure he gone – he travel this time, no taxi come and pick him up – and when I see he gone for truth I pick up the phone and call back Jankie again.

'Girl, I was thinking about your idea,' I tell she. 'I feel it's a good idea. Let's talk about it tomorrow. Lunch?'

We make we date and I went back in my bed. I pick up the book again, and read some more. This Diaz fella had a way about he, boy. It wasn't just the characters, but the way he would describe things. It was like poetry somehow. I can't explain it. But it make something inside my chest get big and hollow and before I know it I was crying.

I wasn't crying about the book – at least, not the book alone. I was crying over my whole miserable life. The licks. How Leo don't have no faith in me. How he think I stupid. How I have to go behind he back with Bobby just to feel like somebody really love me. And even Bobby. How I could call that love when he have he wife and he self can't make a move without she? Two of we like two sides of the same coin.

I put the book down and wipe my face with the sheet.

My mind start to wander. I think about Jankie and Ricky and gradually a little smile creep up my face. It wasn't always terrible. I had a friend. When we was in junior sec Jankie and me was like bim and bam. And Ricky did like me too bad, ever since. The three of we was always liming together in school, inside the hall every day. We was on morning shift, and when we walking back after school I used to go by them sometimes for lunch. Not every every day, but often. I used to eat roti till my belly buss.

That is why, when I finally decide to leave home, is by Jankie I went. I stay by she for a couple months well.

By then I was out of school long time – Mammie say she didn't care whether I went senior comprehensive or not – so after I leave junior sec at fourteen I get a work in the self-same roti shop and was cooking, cashing, cleaning, everything, from five in the morning until five in the evening. The pay wasn't much, but it was more than I ever had in my life. Mammie take almost all when I get my little brown envelope at the end of the week, but at least I had a little bit for myself, a little bit to give Colin pocket money for school. He was bright, brighter than me. He pass for a good school after Common Entrance, a big name college, St Mary's. Mammie didn't have to beg no priest for Colin to go a good school. Even then, I know he would grow up to be somebody. Not like me.

Colin was my whole heart. From the time I lay eyes on him when he was a little baby, just learning to walk, I was in love. Them shiny black eyes, that smiling face, them white teeth just coming up. He was a chubby little boy, but when he reach about eight, nine, he shoot up and then he was taller than me. At home, we do everything together. As Jankie say, he was my shadow. I used to feed him and bathe him and dress him when he was a baby, even though I was hardly more than a baby myself. As we grow up, everything I do, Colin want to do; everywhere I go, Colin want to go. At first when I went by Jankie I couldn't even sleep without him.

But, eventually, I learn how.

THIRTEEN

Bright and early Monday morning Tamika come with one set of *Brides* magazine and a notebook.

'You know everything about clothes and accessories,' she say. She slam down the magazine and them on the kitchenette table. It sound like a bricks falling.

Like we had a new routine. I make the tea and she put out the Crix and cheese. We sit down and start to go through the magazine one by one.

'Well, I never plan no wedding,' I tell she francomen.

'Even still. You know clothes, Allie. You's a boss with cloth and accessories, don't mind you does dress like that.' She screw up she face.

'Dress like what? What that suppose to mean?'

She watch me in my eye then watch my clothes. She point to them with a couyon mouth. 'Like that. Like a schoolteacher. Like you have no shape. Like you hiding. Every blasted day is the same thing: white shirt and black skirt. The skirt could be pinstripe, chalk stripe, plain black, or charcoal, but is the same thing. Flare, pencil and straight: black skirt. Same thing with the shirt and them. I don't know who you trying to fool, dressing like that. Like you fraid colours or something. But I see you with customers, and I know you know plenty about clothes, Allie. You can't fool me up.' She cross she arms.

I had to laugh. Tamika look so vex.

'Okay, okay. I give up. You make me out,' I tell she. 'It just easier to have a uniform. And I not wearing no polo and jeans.' It was my turn to skin up my face. No way, no how they catching me in a orange jersey and a jeans pants every day. I rather dictate my own pace, at least when it come to my clothes.

'So, tell the truth.'

'About?'

'How you know so much about clothes?'

'You feel is you alone could buy magazine, or what?' I give she a grin. I did forget how much fun it is to have a friend you could make mischief with.

'Uh huh. And…?'

'And what?'

'You didn't learn about all that from no magazine, Miss Allie.'

'Okay, okay. I work in Queensway a good while. Since I was a little girl, you could say. I was seventeen when I start, and I leave there as a assistant manager.' I pause. 'In the bridal department.'

She go to pelt a magazine behind me. I duck and run so fast my tea throw down and the cup shatter on the ground.

'Oh, gosh, Allie, is joke I making!'

I was shaking, in a small ball squeeze up by the sink. Tamika come and pick me up and put me to sit down in the chair again. She mop up the tea on the table with the J Cloth from the sink, wring it out and reach for some paper towels to mop up the floor. She pull out the hand broom and dustpan to sweep up the shards of the mug what break.

All this time I sitting down and trembling like a leaf. I don't even know why. The amount of thing people pelt at me in my life, you would think I accustom by now. But somehow just seeing Tamika raise that magazine and go to throw it at me, I feel like I was going and get another cutass. No, that is not true. I didn't think, I didn't feel. I just move. Is only when I was kneeling down on the ground, with one hand wrap around my belly and the other hand wrap around my head, that I realise what I was doing. That is what had me really frighten.

'You okay?' Tamika say. 'Let me make a next cup of tea for you.' She fixing up by the electric kettle, pulling out another mug from the tiny tiny cupboard over the sink, when she say, 'I didn't mean to frighten you, Allie. I really, really sorry.'

I laugh, but it sound like the mug when it break on the tiles.

The kettle boil again quick quick and she make the tea with extra sugar.

'Ent sugar good for shock?'

'Shock?' I say. 'Who in shock?'

'Girl, you whiter than white. You looking like you see a ghost. And your hand shaking. I think you in shock.'

I make a effort to pull myself together, paste a smile on my face and take a sip of tea. It was scalding hot. The Crix and cheese taste like cardboard when I take a bite, trying to act normal. I nearly couldn't swallow. But I smile and do as if I was okay. I hide my hand in my lap.

'Miss Allie. Alethea. I know we's not friends friends. I would like to be. But you so... thing.'

'Thing?'

'Yes, thing. Like you fraid to talk to anybody. Nobody know nothing about you. Even that big maco, the cow, Marie, who know everything about everybody working On the Town – she and all don't know nothing about you. But, Allie, I like you. I want to…'

'What.'

'I want to be your friend.' Tamika giggle. 'Oh gorm, I sounding so stupid. Like a TV show or something. Sesame Street. "I want to be your friend."'

I smile. Yes, it was dotish. But this was the first woman I was even a little bit close to since Jankie ups and leave me. Before that, was just Liloutee, and I never see she since she leave by we.

I doesn't have woman friends. Woman deceitful, my mother used to say. You can't trust them. And every man I ever had discourage me from making too much friend – not with words but with their attitude. If I suggest we go out with some girl I meet in work, or with a neighbour, they roll up their eye and do as if I asking them to drink poison. A time I bring a girlfriend home a evening, my man behave so rude and out of timing, I never bring none back. Them men always happy to keep me lock up in the house, just like Leo does do now. So is home and work, home and work. I hardly ever went out by myself. Whatever man I had, is he I going out with, not no girlfriend.

I think about all of that but I didn't say it.

'Okay,' I tell Tamika. 'Now we have to sing 'Wind Beneath My Wings'?'

Both of we buss out laughing. When we cool down weself, she take a sip of she tea and watch me in my face. 'So, you want to talk about it?'

I know she was asking about how I duck and cover.

I shake my head. I would have to really think about how this could work: friendship. 'Let we just look at the magazine and them. You could tell me what you want to feel like on your wedding day. We could start from there.'

Before I know it, lunchtime reach and Jankie breeze in the store on a cloud of Light Blue. I tell Tamika I going in the mall next door and to hold on for me at the register. Jankie in a sheer black net vest appliqué with panels of alligator leather, and a black drill blazer over black drill cigarette pants and red patent ballet flats. She had the same hobo bag as last week.

'Wow!' Tamika whisper. 'She so glamorous.'

'Ent?' I whisper back, before I pick up my purse and walk out with Jankie.

'We're not going to the mall,' Jankie announce.

'What? Where we going?'

'I want to take you somewhere nice. How about the Normandie? Do you recommend it?'

'Me? What I know about glamorous— I mean, nice?'

Jankie laugh. 'Okay. This is my treat, too, so don't worry about it.'

'All right, Mrs Inalsingh,' I say, teasing she. But it was a cruel joke and she know it.

We take taxi. Jankie didn't bring no car because she didn't want to park in town. Walking next to she to reach the taxi stand I feel frumpy and old, boring and plain. She was wearing nice clothes and I was just in my regular 'uniform' – today a ankle-length, four-gore flared dark charcoal poplin skirt. The only pop of colour I had on was a sheer coral lipstick. My skin was glowing from the beach the day before and even though my outfit was boring, I know my face look nice.

Jankie hire a taxi by the stand to carry we St Ann's and drop we in front the Normandie. The restaurant was dim and elegant. Crystal glass and shiny steel knife and fork – flatware, I tell myself – was sparkling under the spotlights hide away in the corners of the restaurant. A hostess in black and white carry we to we table. Jankie did order ahead so we wouldn't have to wait so long. Considerate.

With the linen napkin on my lap, sipping ice water from the glass in front of me, I was a little nervous and out of place. Only Friday I was in Hilton lounge in a skimpy skimpy dress, feeling like a whore; three days later, Monday, I was the opposite, in this long skirt and long-sleeve shirt button right up.

'I hope you don't mind the Parmesan chicken,' Jankie say.

'Nope,' I tell she. 'Sounds great.'

She order a glass of white wine when the drinks waiter come around. I take the same. Ordinarily I doesn't drink, but I say what the hell. How often somebody does carry me Normandie for lunch?

'Can I tell you something?' She lean forward and hold my hand. 'I like what you've made of yourself.'

I ent go lie: it sting a little. I feel like she was talking down to me. We come from the same place, after all. I mean, she was rich and I was poor, but is nearly the same place both of we born and grow. She wasn't rich rich like Sita family, but rich by Aranguez and El Socorro standards – Jankie had a inside toilet, a TV, a electric stove in the house over the roti shop. Middle-class, I suppose. But Raj still talking as if he living El Socorro, bet your bottom dollar. Ricky running the roti shop – shops, actually, since they have it franchise all over the country now – but he and all ent no big shot.

I try to pull away my hand, but Jankie hold it hard. 'I'm serious. I'm proud of you. You didn't even finish high school and here you are, managing a store on Frederick Street. Looking great. Talking like…I don't know, talking like a lady. I'm really proud of you.'

I get vex. But then I say to myself, you know, Jankie never put water in she mouth. She mean well. If she say it, is because she believe it, and she think is a compliment.

'Jankie, I could very well say the same about you,' I say, instead of cussing she black is white.

She buss out laughing in the people place. A few other customers turn to watch we, then turn back to their food. 'I guess you could. We were wild!'

I give she a grudging smile. Is true, though. Not that we was wild – between Mammie and Raj we was under heavy manners – but that we come from far. I couldn't see the old Jankie in this perfect, polish woman sitting down in she couture clothes and salon hair. She couldn't see the nashy, hungry child in me, either. I figure we was still there, though, underneath.

'Anyway, let's forget about that. I want to tell you my ideas, bounce them off of you to see what you think.'

'Okay. Shoot.'

She say how she find the island have room for a couture boutique. Not local designers – we have that already, like Meiling shop in Kapok Hotel and The Cloth, in this self-same Normandie. What she wanted to do was bring in high-end prêt-à-porter fashion from Armani, Dolce and Gabbana, Dior and Chanel, and sell it in a posh boutique. It would be small and personalised, probably in one of the big malls in the west. She was already thinking about two-three spots, she say.

'And the best part is that we'd have personal stylists there. So it's not like you come in and just buy a blouse or trousers. You'd come in to get a look. We would give you a palette, advise you on hair, makeup, even foundation garments. The works.'

The waiter bring the wine.

'What do you think?'

I take up my glass and say, 'Cheers.'

After that I had a whole set – a cascade – of ideas and suggestions, about where it could be, how it could work, who

145

we could hire, all them thing. It was flowing so sweet, I was shock when we finish eat and the bill come.

Jankie pay with she Visa Platinum and I went to the ladies' to thief a smoke and fix back my lipstick before we went back out in the road.

As I rounds the corner from the bathroom, who I should bounce up but Colin. He was in a white shirt jack and a khaki pants, looking cute and boyish, and chatting with one pretty woman. Poverty and chastity, eh? If this is the kind of place he does normally go, no wonder I never see him in twenty-three years. My kind of man was more Smokey and Bunty than the Normandie, and I doesn't go out nowhere unless is with my man.

Colin face light up when he see me.

'Alethea! It's so wonderful that you're here. Please. I want you to meet my friend...'

Friend, my ass. But I smile and shake she hand and say something nice about she ugly black gabardine pants and white shirt. Then Colin ask the woman to excuse we, and he pull me aside.

'Alethea, I really want to meet with you. Please don't give me the brush off again. I have important things to discuss with you. It's about—'

'Mammie? Your father?'

'Yes, that too. But it's more about our grandmother. Your namesake, Alethea. It's important. Please.'

He look like a puppy, with them big, shiny black eyes, so hopeful and so open. How I could say no?

'Can we meet after work? I go to evening mass and it ends at seven.'

I shake my head. No way Leo go let me stay in town that hour without throwing a fit.

'What about before work? You do eat breakfast, don't you? Can't we meet up before eight?'

'You don't have morning mass?'

He shake he head this time. 'I do lunchtime mass on this rotation. The deacon takes the morning communion service. We only have one priest at the moment and I can't say more than one mass in a day. We're not allowed.'

'Oh,' I say. 'Well, in that case, yes, a morning would be fine.'

'Tomorrow? Seven o'clock?'

'Okay. But you come to my shop. I have things to do so I can't be long. Bring your breakfast. You know where the shop is?'

The 'friend' was watching we very funny while we shoo-shooing to one side. When we done make we arrangement, Colin was beaming. The woman raise she eyebrow high like the sky.

'Remember I told you about Girlie, my sister?' he tell she, as they walk to the tea room at the back of the hotel atrium. I went back to the restaurant to find Jankie ordering a taxi to carry we back in town.

Colin was true to he word and seven o'clock on the dot he was tapping on the glass door of the shop. I did come in early that morning, just to tidy away the shop and put on the kettle before he reach. Although I doing as if I don't want to know about what he have to say, it was really burning me inside. What he had to tell me that was so important, and about we granny to boot?

He was holding two paper bag with doubles. He hand me one. 'Slight pepper?'

I laugh. I couldn't believe he remember all these years how I love doubles. In we days it was singles. A man on a bicycle with a big box in front used to ride around selling them every lunchtime. All the children in we junior sec used to crowd up where the man park up outside the school – we on one side of the BRC fence and the vendor on the next side, passing twenty-five cents through the wire. He would pass the singles – one barra and some channa, piping hot in a sheet of brown paper – back through the fence, steaming and smelling like coconut oil, delicious. Like ambrosia: doubles, the food of the gods. On a Sunday, if she was in a good mood and if she sell enough egg, Mammie would buy doubles for we in San Juan market. Doubles was just the same thing as singles, with two barra instead of one.

Of course, doubles was Mr Doubles now; is two dollars for one, sometimes two-fifty. And nobody doesn't ride around selling doubles on no bike no more. It have doubles vendors set up under big umbrella by every corner in town.

I lead Colin to the kitchenette, seeing it through he eyes. A tiny, narrow table in a six-by-six square, four plastic chairs and a card table, a counter with a sink and a cupboard above and below, and a row of grey steel lockers to one side. The white Oster kettle was boiling. It had a automatic shut-off switch and the click it make when it turn itself off was loud. The kitchenette had a microwave in it, too.

It wasn't much but I was proud of the kitchenette. Most shops like this didn't have nothing so. Is I who insist Bobby put in a break room, because these girls on they foot whole day, from eight to four, and longer if they making overtime, which most of them does do every day anyway, because the shop closing six in the evening to catch the workers going home. In most other shops, the girls would eat in a dressing room, or the stock room.

'You want tea?'

'Yes, please.'

I give him a plate for he doubles and eat mines from the bag. They was still hot. We eat first, then talk when we drinking we tea.

'So.'

148

'So.' He wipe he mouth on the napkin from inside the paper bag. 'You have a house in Valencia.'

'Excuse me?' I put down my tea and watch him with confusion in my face.

'When she died, she left us the house in Valencia.'

'Who "she"?'

'Our granny. Ma. She left us the house in Valencia. I can't take it. I don't want it and I wouldn't have any time to maintain it. So it's all yours, Girlie. Alethea. A house and twenty acres of land under citrus cultivation. You could sell it, or you could fix it up and live there. It's mostly overgrown, but you could rehabilitate it. There's government money available for that, if you want.'

I didn't know what the ass to say. Twenty acres? I didn't even know how much land that was.

'I...' You know the expression, words fail me? That was exactly it. Twenty acres and a house. Wildly, I start to giggle. 'I thought it was supposed to be a forty acres and a mule?'

Colin laugh, but I could see he didn't find it all that funny. 'The house isn't in great condition,' Colin say. 'Ma was very old and it was a lot to manage at her age. But I checked with a contractor after the probate and he said it was structurally sound—'

'Wait. Please. Please start from the start. I have no idea what you're talking about.'

Colin take a deep breath and let it out slow slow slow.

'Ma died just before Mammie. Her lawyer contacted me. Ma left the house and the land to us, in her will. I had the will probated. We couldn't find you, Alethea. You just...vanished.'

I suppose it kind of true. I wasn't hiding, really, but I never went back to that house in Aranguez, never went by Ma in Valencia, never keep in touch with nobody from that part of my life. Mammie never look for me. She see me once in the cloth store and never say a word; she never come back, neither.

When Mammie dead I see she picture in the papers – in a obituary in *The Express* that I didn't self read – but I wouldn't have go that funeral if you pay me. She ruin my life. As for Uncle Allan, I wouldn't piss on he if he was on fire, so worse yet. I had to walk away from Colin, from Jankie family, the only people I had who really care about me, but I had to walk away from them. I had to do like they was dead to save my life.

'I know why you left,' Colin was saying.

'You don't know nothing,' I tell he again.

'Yes, Alethea. I know everything. Mammie told me everything. On her deathbed. She told me what my father did to you. I kind of knew. Sort of. I mean, I was a little kid, but I would have had to be blind not to see that every Christmas when he came you kind of…shrivelled up inside yourself. When he was there…every year…you would look so frail. Like a petal in the wind. I knew something was wrong, but I was too young to understand. Mammie knew all along. She finally told me when she was dying. She told me.'

He start to cry. I don't mean quiet-tears-dripping-down-he-face cry. I talking loud bawl-like-a-cow cry, with snat running out he nose and spit hanging from he mouth.

'I'm so sorry, Girlie. I couldn't help you. I didn't know. I didn't know…'

I get up and stand up behind he chair and hug him up, rocking from side to side with he head resting on my belly like he's a little baby again. 'Shhhhhh,' I say. 'Don't cry, Colin. Don't cry. It wasn't your fault.'

'Yes, it was my fault…'

'But how it could be your fault, Colin? You didn't even know it was going on.'

'It's my fault,' he say, and he keen like a old woman catching power in a Baptist church. Keen, yes. Keen. 'If he hadn't brought me to live with Mammie, he never would have molested you the first time. And if I hadn't been living there, he never would have continued to rape you, again and again, every year when he came to visit me, until you ran away.'

'Shhhhhhh, Colin,' I say. 'Shhhhhhhh.'

FOURTEEN

Colin finish cry. Just in time, too, because Tamika knock on the shop door and rush in when I open for she, apologising for reaching late again. I wave it off and tell she never mind, come and see who here. Colin had enough time to catch heself. When Tamika come in the kitchenette he was looking almost normal.

'Father Colin,' she say, 'what a nice surprise! Good morning.' She looking from me to Colin and back again as though she don't know what to do.

I laugh at she and say, 'Just tidy up, nah. He just come to give me some information. He going just now.'

Colin take the hint and get up. He eye was red and wet looking, but other than that he was okay. He hug me up and say he go be in touch. This time I hug him up back.

'Wait,' I say, and dig in my bag for my cell phone. 'Take my number. You must call me, okay?'

Tamika was dying to know what Colin had to tell me so. I say, 'Girl, you wouldn't believe it.' I tell she how we grandmother leave a house for Colin and me, but Colin ent want it. So the house is mines.

She jaw drop. 'Serious? A house? A whole house?'

'Girl! Tell me this thing, nah. And land, to boot.'

'Way sah!' Tamika face bright bright and happy for me. She practically jumping up and down, fus she excited. 'So what you going to do with it?'

I shrug my shoulders. I didn't even think about that yet. I still amaze, studying the house and land. Mines?

My whole life I never had nothing of my own. I never had a house, only renting here, there and everywhere – semi-furnish apartment only. A little more expensive but at least I don't have to be paying Courts every month and I could pick up and go, just so, whenever I want. I living in Leo house, yes, but is not mines. I come there and meet fridge, stove, washing machine, furnitures. All I had to my name was one chrome kettle, my clothes, some books and my toiletries.

Some people who grow up poor like me does want to buy things, plenty things, to make a home for theyself like they never had when they was coming up. I never had that feeling. Ever since I leave home when I was seventeen years, I never want to have nothing to hold me down. Fridge and stove and furnitures is weight. I don't want no weight. I want to be able to get up and is gone I gone.

The idea that I have a whole house now just hit me for six. What the ass I going to do with a house and twenty acres of citrus in Valencia, of all places?

I didn't have too much time to study it that day because all and a sudden the shop was busy busy busy. From the time the door open, foreign and local and freshwater Yankee coming in by the dozen to buy party clothes for that weekend. I didn't even self have time to go for lunch, fus it busy. Then, as we go to close up that evening, Ann, Janelle and Tamika corner me and insist we talk about plans for Fire Fete.

'On the Town going to have a big posse,' Tamika say. 'Everybody coming. Well, except Mr Sharma.'

'Of course.'

'We getting the jerseys print this week. What size you want, small?'

'Medium…'

'Nah, Miss Allie,' Ann jump in. 'You go be swimming in a medium. Take the small.'

'And Leo, what size for he?' Tamika ask.

I was dumbfounded. Leo?

'A large? How he does wear he clothes? Tight or loose fitting?'

'Loose, I suppose…'

'Well, a XL, then,' she say.

Janelle chime in with a uh huh – she was making notes.

'You have a black short pants?'

'Black—'

'All of we wearing black short pants,' Tamika say. 'The men and them wearing black jeans.'

'No, I—'

'Well, you could take one from the shop. Janelle, put that down. Ann, find a pants for Miss Allie.'

Ann gone by the shelf of black shorts and come back with what my mother would have call a 'piece of pants', and that nowadays we does call a 'battyriders' or 'pumpum shorts'. I shake my head one time. 'No, that too short.'

Tamika roll she eye and send Ann back.

The girl come back this time with a Bermuda shorts. 'Bettter?'

I skin up my face. 'I can't just wear jeans?'

Tamika cross she arms and look like she want to cuss. 'No. You have to wear short pants. All of we go be in short pants. Come, nah, Allie.'

'Okay, okay,' I say. 'Give me the battyriders.'

The girls cheer, yes.

Leo was cool cool when I tell he about the Fire Fete plan. 'Is work,' I say. 'Everybody going. It go look bad if I stay home. You will come?'

'I have to work that night,' he say.

'I thought you was playing Friday and Sunday?'

He didn't say nothing.

'Oh gosh, Leo, please,' I say. 'We carrying a cooler, and food and everything. I go buy the tickets. All you have to do is come.'

'I don't have nothing to wear,' he say.

'Or hor,' I say. 'That is the next thing. They want we to wear a jersey and jeans. They getting the jerseys print up. I tell them you does take a extra-large. And you have a black jeans, ent?'

'Yes, babes, I have a black jeans. But I don't want to go.' He was pouting like a baby.

'Why not?'

He give me one cut eye. I start to back off.

'Well, it was just a idea. I go tell the girls...'

Just so, he change he mind. 'Okay. We go go. Let me see what these so-called singers doing these days. What does pass for music in this place is a shame...' He went off quarrelling – off on a tangent, I thought – about how soca music is shit, how it have no real music in it, how these artistes getting so much money for doing so little bit of work and blah blah blah.

I tune he out, killing myself not to turn over the book I holding in my lap. That murder story was going good. I glance down at the cover.

'I talking, babes,' he say soft soft. 'You find the book more important?'

Before I could say anything he wring the book from my hand and fling it in a corner of the bedroom. I dash off the bed but he make a grab for me and I hear my nightie ripping. It remind me of the sound the cloth used to make when I was working in the cloth store, that same sound when you tear it with the open scissors.

It wasn't the first time I wake up with my bottom and nanny sore after Leo get on so. He does like to take things out on me, humiliate me, hurt me.

I doesn't always know what does make he get vex. Sometimes is me, something I say or do. But other times like he just mad for everything and it don't matter what I say or do, he go cut my ass anyway, and then bull me in my bottom, hold me down and skin me up all how like I's a dolly he have instead of a real woman. He favourite thing is to hold my hair in he hand, make a fist and wrap my hair around it until I pin down on the bed and can't move. He like to see the look in my eye when he do that. When I close my eye he does tell me to watch him in he face. 'I want you to see who fucking you, babes. You love me? You love me? Tell me you love me.'

The week fly by. The shop was full every day and I barely had time to study Leo, Valencia, Colin or Jankie. All I could do was keep ringing up sales and keeping the books. Friday morning, Bobby call me to take a next drive with him. I figure, why not? It go be nice to take a little break from the shop, to get a little loving up for a change.

We went back in that same hotel we went the week before. This time, Bobby bring a box of strawberries and a bottle of chocolate syrup.

When we finish the sheet and them was brown and red. I feel shame, but then I figure that is what the place for, so what I feeling shame about?

I was putting on my clothes when my phone ring.

'Hello?'

Nobody answer. They hang up.

'Wrong number?' Bobby ask.

'Must be.' I start to feel cold and all my pores raise up.

When we reach back in town, the cow Marie take special pleasure in telling me how my man come to look for me in the shop while I was gone. She had a malicious glitter in she eye, the bitch. Good thing I come back with a bale of stock from the warehouse, or she would have had more to say, I bet. Bobby unload the bale from the trunk of he BMW and wave as he drive off.

'Marie,' I say, 'please help Ann and Janelle unpack this before you go up to the other branch.'

I went in the kitchenette and get a glass of water. Chocolate does make me thirsty. Is Tamika who tell me I had a strawberry stem in my hair. I blush, but I didn't say nothing. Just take it out and went back in the shop.

When evening come, Curtis and he brown-skin friend was liming by the door again, drinking Carib and talking shit and watching woman.

'Family,' the friend say when we come to lock up outside, 'you coming to lime with we today?'

'Doux doux, I sure you have plenty woman to lime with. Why you only asking me every Friday to come and lime with you?' Well, who tell me say that.

He take it as a invitation to chat. He rest the beer on the roof of Curtis car and he take my hand, cosying up to me like if I's he good friend. 'Family, my name is Luke.'

'Luke?' Tamika buss out. 'That is your name? I never hear nobody call you that, Sugars,' she say.

He come up to whisper in my ears, 'They does call me "Sugars" because—'

I pull away. I didn't want to know why they does call he Sugars. Or, rather, I wanted to find out for myself, but not right at that moment. I had to go home or Leo would get on again. I had about enough of that for the week. Sugars would have to wait for another time.

Tamika clear she throat loud loud. 'Curtis say he could drop you home. You want a drop?'

I consider it. A drop home would be nice – I wouldn't have to stand up by the maxi stand and push for transportation. But to spend a hour in traffic with the lovely, golden-brown Sugars might be too much temptation.

Shit that. 'Yes, thanks!'

I jump in the back seat.

Sugars jump in next to me.

'So, family,' he say, oozing charm and sweetness, 'your name is Allie? Short for Allison?'

'No,' I say.

'What it short for?'

'Alethea.'

'Wha—? Alicia?'

'Just call me Allie.'

He take my hand and look at it. 'Allie, you have nice fingers.'

'Thank you.'

'Sugars, stop harassing the woman,' Curtis say from the driver seat. 'She have a man.'

'Eh heh, family?'

'Yup,' I say.

'So which part your man is?'

'He home.'

'He not working nowhere?'

'Yes,' I say. 'He's a musician. He does do gigs in different places.'

'Eh heh?' he say again. 'So, how all you meet?' All this time he still holding my hand and playing with my fingers, eh.

'In a bar in St James,' I tell him. 'He was playing 'Lady in Red'. He sing it for me.'

'Eh heh,' Sugars say. He start to make circles on my palm.

'Yup.'

'That is how you meet in truth?' Tamika ask. 'That sound so romantic.'

'It was. It was,' I say. 'Was.'

Me and Sugars' eye make four. He slide he hand under my skirt.

The Sunny pull up in front the house and I take my time, making a big scene of hugging up Tamika when I come out the car. Sugars didn't get a second look.

But Leo wasn't even home. Like he did gone he gig already. I bathe and put on a nightie and make a cup of tea. I sit down in the kitchen and reading my book when the blasted cell phone ring again.

'You finally reach home, eh?'

It was Leo. He sound drunk, all he words slurring and lazy.

'Leo! You at work already?'

He do like he didn't hear me. 'Where you was today, eh, babes? Where you went with your boss?'

'We went to the warehouse in Central, Leo. It was work.'

'Work, eh?'

'Yes, work—'

But he hang up.

If he was drunk so in the people lounge he might lost that work already, a week after he get it. I close my eyes and try not to cry.

He come home about four in the morning and pass out on the couch.

. . .

159

I leave Leo sleeping and went to work Saturday, my mind heavy. I know when next I see him it would be a big fight.

Tamika was there before me, waiting for me to open up.

'Sugars like you,' she tease me. 'I give him your number.'

'You what?'

'Calm down,' she say. 'I tell him only call you when you in work. I go show you how to delete the number from your phone. He's a nice fella, Allie. He doesn't lash.'

I still uneasy in my mind, but at least Tamika was distracting me.

'So,' she say, as we drinking we tea, 'tell me something.'

'Like what?'

'Tell me about you. How you and Colin grow up? Ent them is the kind of thing friends does talk about?'

I laugh. 'I guess so.' Thinking about it, I never really tell nobody my life story as such. I does keep myself to myself, like Mammie always wanted me to do. I didn't know where to start. I figure I would just tell she the basics. 'I born and grow up Aranguez with my mother, and when I was about five Colin come and live with we. I never know my father. Mammie say he dead before I born.

'I went San Juan Girls' RC and pass Common Entrance for Aranguez Junior Sec. Jankie – you remember my friend who come in the store last week? – Jankie and me went junior sec together. After junior sec I leave school and went to work in she family roti shop.'

It had plenty I could say about that time in my life. That is when I get pregnant for my uncle and my mother beat me and make me loss the child, saying is some man I have. That is when I get the gonorrhoea that make me barren. But I skip them thing out.

'I leave home when I was seventeen years and went and work Queensway, selling cloth. As you know.' I give she a little mischievous smile.

She didn't try and pelt nothing behind me this time. She smile back.

'I was living in a tiny little bachie in town, with just a mattress on the ground. As soon as I could afford, I rent a nicer place. Semi-furnish. I meet one or two fellas,' I say, shrugging my shoulders. One or two? More like ten or twenty. Before Leo, I never stay with nobody too long, and plenty fellas just get a one-night stand and that was it. 'Some nice, some not so nice. I live with some but nothing permanent. Until Leo. I living with he five years now.' She didn't say nothing to that but she make a real sour face. 'I work in Queensway for a long time, until about eight years ago. I get fed up with the work and I went to a next place, a boutique. Then I work a couple more places until I see On the Town was looking for a manager and I apply and I get it. That is about it,' I say.

'Huh,' Tamika say. 'So you work in the cloth store almost your whole life?'

I nod.

'That is where you learn to—'

'That is where I learn nearly everything. It had a Syrian man there, we boss son. He used to give we etiquette lessons, diction lessons, fashion lessons, management lessons. He was very particular with the workers. He wanted we to have style and class. You could ask Jerry when you see him. Jerry used to work with me for years.'

Tamika skin up she face. She didn't like Jerry head.

'What about you?' I ask.

'Me? Well, you know I's twenty-six. You know I was a dancer – Best Village, then modern and a little bit of soca – I dance for a band one year…but I break my foot.'

'For true?' I never know that.

'Yeah. I had was to stop dancing. I still love it but my ankle never heal right and I does can't dance too much now. Even the standing up in the shop does be pressure.'

'Or hor,' I say. 'But you never tell me that.'

She move she hand as if to say that is nothing. 'I does miss the dancing, but is okay. What don't kill you does make you stronger.

'I know Curtis since we small. We families was neighbours before they move to La Horquette. He mother don't like me, but she can't really say nothing. And my mother find he should have married me long time, so she vex too. Sometimes I feel the only people happy with this wedding is me and Curtis.'

I feel guilty about what Marie tell me, about Curtis and Tiny. All the time I was saying it wasn't my business, but ent that is what friends for?

'Tamika,' I say. 'Curtis does have woman outside?'

She face set up, a thundercloud ready to buss. 'How you mean?' she ask, flat flat flat.

'Marie say—'

'Marie is a old gossip. You believe anything she say?'

'As I buy it, so I sell it, Tamika. I don't mean nothing by it.'

She play with the mug in she hand for a little while. 'What Marie say?' She still watching the mug, eh. She not watching me at all at all.

'She say Curtis was with Tiny. She see them by Smokey and Bunty a night. Tiny was in Curtis lap.'

'Tiny who?'

'The gold teeth girl who used to work up by Marie and them. She leave and went to work Hadeed's.'

Tamika suck she teeth long and hard, so sour that I fraid for the milk in the tea. 'That kiss-me-ass gossip. Marie could lie!'

'What you mean?'

'I was there with them that night, Allie. I know what she talking about. Tiny was in Curtis lap, yes. But I was standing up right next to them. It was just joke Tiny was making.'

I didn't know what to feel. I wasn't sure if Tamika was just playing as if, or if she really and truly believe that she man was faithful to she. I never meet a man yet who wouldn't horn you if you give he a chance, but maybe that was just me. I is a bad-man magnet, I does tell myself sometimes.

But if Tamika say she know and is nothing to worry about, who is me to say otherwise?

We chat about the wedding and drink we tea and then it was time to open the shop. We didn't say nothing more about Curtis, Tiny or Marie for the rest of the morning.

Jankie and Ricky and Amanda pick me up at lunch and carry me West Mall.

West Mall is probably the most bougie mall in Trinidad. The area have plenty rich people, and plenty white people, so is mostly them you seeing in the clean, chilly corridor and them. The place big, shiny, and expensive. We walk around looking at the potential competition – it had one or two real nice boutiques, selling some local but mostly foreign garments. The prices was hot for so.

'This is one of the spots I was thinking about,' Jankie say, showing me a empty shop downstairs next to a shoe store. It was kind of chook up. I try to picture myself working there and selling prêt-a-porter couture stuff. I couldn't see it. Somehow the mall was too cold, too impersonal.

We went by Long Circular Mall, too, but it was the same thing. And all I keep hearing in my head was Leo laughing at me, saying how I couldn't do nothing. I drown he out.

'Jankie, girl, I don't think we should look at a mall. We want something more intimate, something with some character. What do you think?'

Jankie eye get bright. 'Allie, you know what? You're right!' She put one of the French tips in she mouth and start to think as she suck it. When she pull it out she say,

'A house? Somewhere chic, a good neighbourhood...but a house. Yeah?'

'It would have to have somewhere customers could park. Maybe not a residential area necessarily. What about some one of the houses they renovate in Woodbrook, or St Clair? And we could make it really sexy, like a lounge, with music and low lighting. We could give the customers chocolates and champagne when they come inside. Treat them.'

The bright eyes get tears in them. 'You get it, exactly. Leave it to me.' She give me a high five. 'Partner!'

JANUARY 5

The Hillman Minx bumped down the narrow, muddy lane. Alethea, in her good church dress, pressed her face against the window and bounced on the red vinyl seat as the car turned on to Boundary Road and headed for the main road. Uncle Allan sat in the front next to the driver, a man who had already smoked two Anchor cigarettes since he had picked them up only minutes ago. Mammie was at the other end of the back seat, again wearing the dress she had worn to church on New Year's day, once again smelling like perfume and My Fair Lady dusting powder. She had on glossy red lipstick the same colour as the kiss mark on Uncle Allan's mouth. Alethea could see the mark when he turned and draped his arm over the back of his seat. His hand rested on the shiny silver jacket he'd thrown there when he'd sat in the car. Colin was sleeping already, his head on Mammie's lap. Alethea didn't want to sleep. She had never gone on a trip like this before and she was more excited than she had ever been. They were going to see Ma.

'You sure they go be home?' Mammie asked, fussing with the decorations on her pillbox hat. The hat was a present from Uncle Allan. It was a deep, rich blue, the colour of the sky when the moon was fat and round. The flimsy net at the front was attached to the crown of the hat by a richly patterned blue and green feather – both came down to Mammie's nose. The feather bobbed up and down whenever Mammie moved her head.

'My dear, you look fine. Stop interfering with the fascinator or the feather will fall off.'

'But you sure she go be home?'

'Yes, Marcia.'

'What if we go quite up there and the house empty?'

Allan sucked his teeth. 'Look nah, man. Big Sunday afternoon. When they come from church, what country people does do on a Sunday? Not one ass. She go be home, Marcia.' He tapped his own pack of cigarettes and plucked out one. 'Gimmie a light, Dave.' Wordlessly the driver handed over a golden object that Allan flicked open with his thumb. Click! Flame burst from the top of the open box. He put the flame to the cigarette and drew in, exhaling a plume of smoke. With another flick of his thumb, Allan closed the mysterious object.

'Uncle Allan! I could see it?' begged Alethea from the back, clambering to her feet.

'Sure thing, sweet cheeks.'

But Mammie snatched it from her fingers before she could make it click and flare to light. 'You mad, or what? Take care she burn up the whole car.'

'Gosh, Marcia. It's a Zippo, not a flamethrower. She's completely safe.'

But Mammie put on a sour face and Allan took the treasure and handed it to the driver, who slid it back into his pocket. Alethea knew better than to complain. She sat and stared out the window again.

'What if the old woman don't want to give we the land?' Mammie asked.

'Good God, Marcia. Would you please shut your damn mouth.'

Mammie was once again fidgeting with the hat.

'For God's sake, leave the hat alone. At this rate, the peacock is going to come to take back his feather—'

'Uncle Allan, who is the peacock? That is who give you the hat to give Mammie?'

He laughed loud and long. Even the sour-looking driver cracked a smile. Mammie only rolled her eyes. Alethea didn't understand the joke.

Gasping for breath and rubbing tears from his eyes, Allan sputtered, 'Not who, Girlie. What. A peacock's a kind of bird. It's got these pretty feathers on its tail, just like the one on your mammie's hat there. Ever heard anybody say, "As pretty as a peacock"?'

'No, Uncle Allan.'

'Marcia, what the hell are you teaching this kid? She doesn't know what a peacock is?'

Mammie rolled her eyes again, sucking her teeth too this time.

'Honey,' he promised, looking down at her sincerely, 'I'll send you some books when I get back to New York. You're too pretty to be so dumb.'

'Oh gosh, Allan, she's only four.'

'I's nearly five! My birthday is just now, ent, Mammie?'

'Hush your mouth, Girlie. Nobody not talking to you.'

'But Uncle Allan was talking to me!'

A sharp crack across Alethea's face stopped her words.

'Don't back chat me, you hear!'

Rolling along the pitch road to Valencia took hours.

Trapped in the fog of Mammie's glare, it seemed like forever to Alethea. Colin woke up, fussed, kicked Alethea in the face when she tried to comfort him, and suffered a swift slap from Mammie for his trouble. His full diaper began to stink and he cried even harder. Mammie grumbled continuously as she took a folded cloth diaper from her purse and changed him, releasing the potent smell into the hot air in the car. The driver, previously silent, muttered, 'Oh geed,' to which Allan replied, 'Well, shit is not roses, eh?' Alethea herself badly wanted to number one, but she knew better than to say so. She wriggled and bounced on the seat now to distract herself from the fullness of her bladder.

Finally, the white car turned into a long, rutted road lined with dusty, short trees, and stopped in front of a big wooden house. Alethea hardly dared to move, lest she wet her good dress, but she managed to slide out without embarrassing herself when Uncle Allan opened her door. Standing with her legs tightly crossed, she waited while the men unpacked a box from the trunk. Mammie held Colin's hand to stop the small boy from darting into the trees. Alethea tugged her mother's dress. 'Mammie.'

'What?' Marcia snapped.

'Mammie, I have to peepee.'

'You can't wait?'

Alethea shook her head quickly. Talking about it made it worse.

Marcia sucked in a long breath and exhaled harshly. 'Why you wait till now to say anything? Damn stupid.' She fixed a smile on her face and marched the children up the front steps into the front porch, calling out, 'Good afternoon! Good afternoon!'

Someone peeped through the jalousies beside the door. 'Who is that?' The voice was small and old.

'Is Marcia and Allan, Ma.'

'Allan? Marcia?' The creaking door was thrown open by a tiny old woman, her skin as dark as Colin's. 'Look who!'

Before anything else was said, Alethea tugged Marcia's dress again. 'Mammie, I have to—'

'Hush up!' Marcia hissed.

Alethea scrunched up her face and tried very hard to hold it in. It wasn't enough. As Marcia bent to kiss the old woman's leathery cheek, the hot urine ran down Alethea's legs right there on the front porch.

The old woman tut-tutted and led the crying girl around the house into the back yard to the tune of Marcia's scolding. An enamel wash sink stood on a blackened wooden stand behind the house. A rusty copper vat, like an enormous upside-down hat, held the water from which the old woman dipped a bucket to wash Alethea off. Alethea's shiny black shoes the old woman simply put in the sun to dry. Cool air blew against her skin, caressing her naked bottom while the woman washed her soaking panties and socks.

Ma's hands smelled of the strong yellow Sunlight soap with which she had washed the clothes and bathed Alethea.

Alethea trailed her up the back steps into the house and waited next to a large four-poster bed in a room that smelled like camphor and lavender while Ma searched a tall chest of drawers for a suitable garment. She found a white camisole, embroidered with white anglaise, and handed it to the child.

'Go on,' Ma chided, when Alethea made no move to change into the vest. 'Chut.' Withered, bent hands slid the garment over Alethea's head. 'Nice. See?' She turned the child around to see herself in a standing mirror.

Marcia came in, fanning her face with her hands. 'That child is a trial, Ma. Always making trouble for me.'

Ma ignored her daughter and took Alethea by the hand. 'So, is how you name?'

Alethea was tongue tied and only stood there in the borrowed camisole, saying nothing.

'I know you not no dummy,' Ma said seriously. 'What is your name?'

'She name—' Marcia said, but Ma shushed her.

'Is the child I ask, not you.'

'I name Girlie,' Alethea whispered.

'Girlie? That is your name?' Her raised eyebrows made Marcia fidget.

'Is Alethea, really. But we does call she Girlie.'

'Alethea? You name the child that long-time thing?' The crone sucked her toothless gums.

Marcia's face turned as red as if her mother had slapped her. 'I thought you would of like it if I name she after you.'

'Why, boy? I don't know why you keep the child in the first place.' The old woman gave Marcia a long, hard look. Marcia looked away, turning a deeper red. Ma gently tugged Alethea outside to the drawing room – a dark, high-ceilinged room furnished with Morris chairs scattered with white crocheted doilies. 'Come in, sit down, sit down,' she called to the two men and the boy still on the porch.

Colin, babbling excitedly, charged in and ran straight to Alethea.

'And who is this little one?'

'That is my boy. Colin,' Allan said. 'Marcia minding he for me.'

'Eh heh?' Ma made no further comment but watched the boy with keen interest.

Jolly and loud, Allan remarked, 'But the old place looking good, Ma. How you does keep up all this cleaning plus the land and everything?'

'If you did really want to know your ass would have be here instead of in America,' Ma casually replied.

It was Allan's turn to go red.

'But where my manners? I could offer you something to drink? All you drive very far to reach here.' She toddled off to the back of the house again, calling for Marcia to come help her. They returned shortly, Marcia bearing a waiter with three glasses of mauby and two of orange juice.

'I tell she he can't drink in no glass yet but she doesn't listen,' Marcia groused.

Ma pretended not to hear her, passing through to the porch with a pitcher of water in her hand. Alethea heard it splash on the boards and knew the old woman was washing down the mess she had made. Mammie's lips thinned to invisibility.

'Marcia, you go ask she?' Allan whispered.

'You is she favourite, you ask she,' came the hissed reply.

Ma re-entered and put the pitcher on the sideboard. She perched herself in a rocking chair and sat serenely, gazing at the little children. 'All you, sit down, sit down,' she admonished with a laugh. Alethea looked to Mammie, waiting for a nod before she sat with Colin in her lap. 'Give she the juice to give him, Marcia. See how she make out with it.'

His little fingers enfolded Alethea's hand when she put the glass to his mouth. Some of the juice dribbled on to Alethea, but he got most of it where it belonged.

'She like a little mother, eh?' A toothless grin beamed satisfaction at the two children. 'A perfect little mother.'

'So, Ma, how everything?' Marcia ventured.

'*Comme ci, comme ça.* So you see me, so I is.'

'Ma!'

'What you want me to tell you, Marcia? I never see hide nor hair of you or your brother for all these years and suddenly you show up and you want me to skin and grin? Is not so, my dear. Is not so at all.' She rocked slowly, never changing the creaking chair's rhythm. 'Is what you want?

Best you come out and tell me one time. Don't beat around the bush.'

Allan and Marcia looked at each other with wide-open mouths. Dave excused himself and went out to the porch. Soon Alethea smelled cigarette smoke.

'Ah...'

'Spit it out, Allan. I know you is the ringmaster here and whatever it is, is you want it, not she.'

Allan's narrow face was like thunder.

'Is exactly why nobody doesn't come here and look for your old ass,' Marcia muttered below her breath. 'You ent have no respect.'

'I? Disrespectful?' Ma laughed out loud. 'Well, look me crosses! As a matter of fact, look my crosses right there. Cross One—' she pointed to Allan '—and Cross Two,' she said, pointing at Marcia. She cackled again.

Allan straightened the lapels of his sharkskin suit and forced a smile. 'Very funny, Ma. Look, I'll come straight to the point. What's going on with the land?'

'What land?'

'Dupigny's land.' He spread his arms, encompassing the house and its surroundings. 'All this.'

'This land? You never once wanted to know how a flower on this land grow, so what the ass you want to know about it now? "Father, give me the share of the property that falls to me?" But me ent no saint. Haul your ass back where you come from, Allan. That is what going on with the land.' She continued to rock, smiling at the children.

'I tell you she wouldn't give we nothing,' Marcia wailed.

'Hush your mouth!' barked Allan at his sister, who flinched from his voice. Turning back to his mother, he wheedled, 'Ma, you're not young any more. This land, this house—'

'Not one ass,' the crone repeated.

'My dear, you think you're going to live forever?'

'No, but long enough. Too besides, you asking the wrong question.'

'What you mean?'

A sly grin lit the weathered face. 'You think this is my own? No! That old bitch make sure it not in my name. She dead and leave the man there, and I mind he, cleaning he bottom until he pass, but she make sure he didn't leave one penny for neither me nor the two red-skin bastards she husband make with the maid. Vindictive bitch. All this—' she mocked her son with the same sweeping gesture '—belong to the church when I dead, my dear.'

'But—'

'But what?'

'How she could do that? Ent she dead now?'

'Long years. But the law is the law, my dear. Your father make he will before she dead and that is what it say. I could live here until I dead, but Alethea Reece don't own nothing but she own black ass – and even that belong to God, so is not really mine either. All I could give you is advice: God don't sleep. If the two of all you don't stop all you nastiness, you go eat the bread the devil knead.'

And that was that. Anything else they asked on the subject, she blandly ignored. But to Colin and Alethea she was charming, clucking over them and stuffing them with pawpaw balls, toolum and sugar cake. Neither did she let them leave empty handed. The trunk, emptied of the trinkets Allan had brought in vain from America to pacify his mother, went back full of juicy navel oranges, the biggest ones nearly as large as Colin's head.

FIFTEEN

Sunday morning I take the opportunity to sleep late. I didn't have nothing to do except some washing, but that could wait for later. I stretch out in bed and snuggle up with Leo, playing with he smooth chest and trying to instigate some loving. He wasn't taking me on. He roll over and start to snore.

Is a good thing the stupid cell phone ring. Ordinarily I would have be cussing, because I doesn't give up so easy when I want a good bull, but in this case I give Leo a bligh and get up and answer the phone. It was in the kitchen where I does leave my handbag.

'Alethea,' Colin say. 'How are you?'

'I good. Sleepy.'

He laugh. 'It's nearly eleven! You're still in bed?'

'Not like I have anything better to do.'

'Well, you do now. I want to take you to see the house in Valencia. You game?'

'Ahm...' I study Leo and how he sleeping hard and whether to wake him up to tell him come let we go Valencia. 'Hold on, okay, Colin?'

I put down the phone and tiptoe inside the bedroom. I shake Leo shoulder, calling he name soft. He wasn't sleeping one ass. He eye open big big one time.

'Who on the phone? Is it Jankie?'

I tell him no. 'Long story, but you want to go for a drive?'

'Drive where? With who?'

'Valencia. I go explain. But the person on the phone...'

He sigh heavy heavy, like I asking he to carry the weight of the world. 'Okay, babes.' Leo swing he legs off the bed and went in the toilet to pee.

I trot back to the phone in the kitchen.

'Okay, Colin. Yes. What time?'

'Where are you?'

'L'Anse Mitan, in Carenage. You know where that is?'

'Sure,' he say. 'Give me about half an hour or less. I'll call you when I get to the corner, you can give me directions from there.'

I jump in the shower and wash off my skin quick quick. The laundry could wait until tomorrow.

Just as I come out the bathroom and looking to get ready, Leo come up behind me and want to make love. All the time he didn't have no time for me, but as soon as I have something to do, he in the mood. I push him away, but he lock my neck from behind and take what he want. It was fast. I went back and wash off, and ent say nothing.

'So, who we going with now?' Leo say, from outside the shower.

'I tell you is a long story. He name Colin. He is my brother.'

'But you never tell me you had no brother,' Leo say. You could hear it in he voice: he feel I lie.

'It have plenty things I never tell you, Leo. And you never ask.' I come out the shower again to see he face looking like a cutass waiting to happen. I bite my tongue and run – scurry – like a mouse to pick out my clothes.

'So where this brother come out?'

I choose out a little sundress in peach broderie anglaise cotton, with cap sleeves and a elasticated bodice. It does make me feel like a little girl. Is a dress I does hardly get to wear, seeing as how I doesn't go nowhere. I pick up tan mules with a little wedge heel for my foot and rest the dress on the bed and the shoes on the floor. Leo lean up by the bedroom door watching me.

'You not going and bathe? He coming just now,' I say.

'You didn't answer me. Where this so-called brother come out? You never tell me you had a brother.'

'Well, I have a brother. Adopted. He is my cousin, but we grow up together. My mother mind he from small. He name Colin. He is a priest now.'

'A priest?'

'Yes, a priest.'

'So how come I never meet he, or even self hear about he before?' Leo was still leaning up by the door, as though he had no intention of moving, even to let me pass. I had to squeeze through the small gap between he body and the doorframe to get to go and put on my lotion and perfume, brush my teeth and comb my hair.

'Oh gorm, just go and bathe, nah!'

He move quick like a cobra and wring my hand behind my back as if he want to wrench it out of the socket. 'Who the fuck you think you talking to so, babes?' He was so quiet, he could have be asking the time of day.

'I sorry, Leo. I sorry. I just…you hurting me.'

He didn't ease up one time. But eventually he let me go. I rub my hand and my shoulder.

'I run away from home when I was young. I never went back. Is only last week I see he again, for the first time in years.'

'So what it have in Valencia?'

I get excited, although he just nearly break my hand. As if the lancing pain in my wrist, elbow and shoulder would let me forget so fast. 'He say we granny leave a house for we! I only went there once. I mustbe was four or five.'

'So this man, who you say is your brother, who you say is a priest, want to carry you Valencia to a house you say your grandmother leave for you?'

I could feel the excitement drain out of me like if I pull a plug from a sink. 'We, Leo. He want to carry we to see the house.'

Leo eyes was flat and cold. He turn without saying nothing and went to bathe.

Of course, when Colin drive up, fifteen minutes later, Leo was all smiles and sweet like paradise plum. He shake Colin hand and give him one of them half hug up that men does do, and say he didn't know he had a brother and he was glad to finally meet him.

Colin was smiling until he see the red mark on my wrist and the panicky look in my eye. He go to say something but I stand up behind Leo and shake my head so hard I nearly get dizzy. Colin hush he mouth and force a smile. He still had them small white teeth.

The three of we get in Colin Corolla and gone Valencia.

The drive was shorter than I remember. The onliest time I was there was when Mammie and Uncle Allan and some friend of he own carry we in a big, black car with red leather seats. I remember the trip because Mammie didn't have no car and it come like a adventure to go for a drive in them days.

But now it only take a hour to reach Valencia, even though Colin wasn't driving all that fast. He and Leo keep up a stream of chatter in the front seat about all kind of thing, including the church, being a priest, being a musician, life for a black man in this country, whether Black Power fail or not. I could see that Leo like him, even in spite of he own self. Colin was always a smart boy, and I was proud of him again, listening to how he debate with Leo and answer back every single point with facts and figures.

In Valencia, we drive down a track that was full of pothole, with long long razor grass and tall tall ti-marie growing by the side. All around it had old, bend-up citrus trees. I could see orange on one side and grapefruit on the next – full, ripe fruits just sitting on the tree and them, or falling to rotten on the ground.

After a while, we drive into a clearing and I see the house. A big, old gingerbread house, it had tapia walls and wooden beams making a gallery right around the sides. It paint either a fadey cornflower or a bright baby blue, with the beams and lacy trimming – fretwork, I tell myself, fretwork – in dingy white. A pretty house, but real old.

Colin park the car and the minute I get out I smell country: fresh air, manure, the citrus trees, dirt and grass. I smile. The porch was empty but I could almost see Ma standing there, a small, hard, dry woman in a old headtie, she skin the same black like Colin own. I never know she. Mammie didn't like she, and she didn't like Mammie – or so Mammie used to say, every time I ask when next we going and visit she in the country.

We unlock the front door and went inside. It was cool and quiet. A Morris chair set, with crochet doilies on every cushion, was in the drawing room and I could see, through a next doorway, a mahogany dining table. The doors to other rooms was closed. Inside, the house was paint cream, and all the mouldings and doorframes was dirty white. Everything had a layer of dust on it, as though nobody wasn't in the house for a long time. The room smell like lavender water, soft candle, Radian-B and camphor.

'This is it,' Colin say. 'I had a contractor come and take a look. Some of the flooring needs changing, and the roof ought to be replaced. But you'd be surprised at how well the walls and everything have held up. Trinidad teak and Guyanese purpleheart, he said. All the beams are solid, and the fretwork, mouldings, everything, is in great shape considering that the house is about ninety years old.' Colin wink at me. 'And it's all yours.'

I take a deep breath. I could smell the little old lady in the boards of the house.

'I thought Mammie always used to say the house was the white people own,' I say to Colin. I explain to Leo, 'Ma used to work for the white people who own the house.'

'Owned,' Colin correct me. 'They died without any heirs. Well, except for us.'

'Eh?'

'Oh, come on. You must have guessed that the old man was your grandfather.'

I couldn't be more shock.

'Close your mouth. You look like a wabine,' Colin say.

I shut it with a snap.

'What the ass is this I hearing. Mammie never say a word.'

'Didn't you ever wonder how come Ma was so dark and Allan and Mammie were so fair?'

I shrug my shoulders. Leo was by the door taking in everything Colin say. He eye open big. He open he mouth to talk but close it again. He turn around and went on the porch. I smell he cigarette smoke drifting in.

'Of course Marcia – Mammie – didn't tell you that. She was too ashamed.'

179

'Of what?' I was so confuse. I walk out the house and went to stand up in the gallery, next to Leo, leaning on the old teak banister and breathing deep so I wouldn't fall down.

Colin follow me outside and put he hand on my shoulder.

'It's a lot to take in.'

'You telling me!'

He laugh, but it was a uncomfortable laugh. 'I couldn't really believe it myself. So, this is what happened: Ma, Alethea – the first Alethea – worked for Mr and Mrs Cyril Dupigny. She was the housekeeper. Mrs Dupigny fell ill. He and Ma…had an affair, I guess. But it was more than that. She took care of the old woman, even though everybody knew Ma had these two children for Mr Dupigny. He had two children with Ma and none with his wife.

'Mammie told me the old lady, Mrs Dupigny, was very fond of my father. But she was also very cruel to him, Mammie said. I don't know. She said he would come out of the old woman's bedroom shaking with terror, but with gifts: candy, books, clothes. She treated him like a pet. She ignored Mammie. At least, that is what Mammie said.'

All this was news to me. I never know none of that. The most Mammie ever say about she mother was that Ma was a evil old lady and that Ma didn't like Mammie head at all. Mammie never once mention that the old white man Ma used to work for was she father.

Colin continue to talk. 'When Cyril Dupigny died, he left the house to Ma. She refused to give it to my father and Mammie. Mammie was very bitter about that. She was ashamed that she had to mind chickens to make a living when her mother had a big old house in Valencia and all this land. But Ma wouldn't budge. She wouldn't let Marcia or Allan live here, not ever.'

Colin take me by the shoulders and turn me around to watch him in he face.

'There's something else…'

I close my eyes. I didn't want to hear nothing else. This was too much already.

'Mammie never had a husband. I'm not your adopted brother, Alethea.'

I vomit over the banister.

The first question I ask when we get back in the car was how to sell the house and land. 'You don't want any of it?' I ask Colin again.

He shake he head. 'I really have all I need. I may not look it,' he say, laughing and patting he flat belly, 'but I get three squares, a house and a car. I don't need a house and land.'

I watch the shops and houses in Valencia slipping past the windows as we drive along the road back towards town.

'How she do it?' I ask.

'What?'

'All of it. Lie to me my whole life. She sex with she brother – she make a child for she own brother!'

Colin stay quiet and drive. Leo didn't say nothing, either.

'Answer me, nah! How she do it?' I was feeling like I was going to explode, or fly away, something. Like I was floating or dying. My whole insides was churning up, even though I vomit up the bile I had in my belly until I lean over that banister just retching and retching and nothing coming up but my own bitter spit.

'She said she found a man, a panyol, she called him, to put his name on your birth certificate. Alethea, you don't know how ashamed she was, how desperately ashamed. And it wasn't an option for her to have an abortion. She was a Catholic. And it was the sixties. She had no choice. Ma certainly wouldn't have taken you – she tried to get Mammie to put you up for adoption.

'I don't know why Mammie kept you with her. I think that's partly why Mammie treated you so badly. You must have represented everything she was ashamed of in her life.'

Badly is joke. She beat me every day God send. She beat me with she hand, with belt, with guava whip, with cocoyea broom, with pot spoon, mop stick, chair foot, anything and everything, until I used to pray for she to dead so I could get away from she. And that man. Every year he come for Christmas and force heself on me I used to want to kill he, kill myself. My uncle. My father. No wonder Mammie beat the baby out of my belly.

I wanted to scrub myself with a Brillo pad, inside and out. I never feel so nasty, so disgusting in my life. Now I wanted to dead for truth.

Leo sit down quiet for the whole ride home. By that time I was lying down on the back seat of the car, my eyes dry but my mind turning and turning like a barrel rolling down a hill. They practically carry me inside and put me in the bed. Leo make some Maggi soup and bring it for me, but I couldn't eat. I was feeling so sick, so shame.

Evening come and Leo tell Colin he had was to go to work and if Colin could stay with me. All this time I ent say nothing, just lie down in the bed, roll up in a little ball, and stare into space. Colin sit down on the bed next to me, holding my hand and stroking my head.

All kind of thing was going through my brain.

I spend my whole life in a lie. My father was my own uncle. My grandfather was some white man I never know. My cousin was my brother. My life was a fucking *Young and Restless* episode without the hot tubs and champagne.

I remember and remember every time Allan put he thing in me, make me do him all kind of disgusting thing, force me to sex with he every time Mammie was out of the house, from the time I had five years until I was seventeen.

And Mammie know. She did know all along.

At least I never had no children. The nastiness in we family would dead with me.

What eventually get me out of bed was that I was thirsty and I wanted to pee.

Colin walk me to the toilet – I was dizzy and faint. He bring a cup of soup and some bread for me and I try to take something hot.

'Marcia know everything,' I say. It wasn't a question.

'Yes,' Colin say. He was walking around the bedroom, looking at the clothes in the cupboard, the books on the bed head. 'You read a lot?'

'I read a lot. It does remind me of you.'

He flash a little shy smile at me. But I wasn't finish with Marcia and Allan yet.

'If she know what was going on, why she didn't say nothing? Why she do as though I was taking man, when all the time she know is she own brother who was—' I couldn't say it again.

Colin look so sad. He open he mouth three-four times, like a guppy underwater, before he finally find the right words. 'Alethea,' he say, hesitating as though he still not sure what he have to say. 'My father was a bastard. Actually, he was,' as though he only just notice is true: he father and Marcia, both of them was bastards. 'What I mean is that he was an evil man. Something was wrong with him. After you left he would take it out on Mammie, hitting her, shouting at her, making her feel so small.

'Don't you remember how he would come at Christmas with a suitcase full of things, with a pocket full of money? He had Mammie under his thumb, Alethea. I'm not trying to make excuses for her, but she depended on him for money, and also, I think, in a very sick way...for love. She never had anybody but him. He was her only friend, her only family, because she cut herself off from Ma and felt she was better than the neighbours because she was half white.'

'Half black, too.'

'Yes, but she never rated the black half, only the white. It was a long time ago, Alethea. Things were different then.'

'Eh heh? Things not different one ass, Colin. People still don't rate black. You know how much thing I get because I look like this? How much people willing to give me a pass because I kind of whitish? How much man does run me down because I fair-skin? You feel I would be anything in this place with no education, no family background, no money, no nothing, if I didn't have colour?'

Colin laugh but it wasn't a happy laugh. 'I take your point, but Alethea, everything you have, you have achieved through work, not because of the colour of your skin. Tamika talks about you like you're the second coming. She really admires you, you know. She thinks you're a brilliant manager – a brilliant person. Education isn't intelligence.'

Sound like bullshit to me.

Colin try again. 'Look at what you've done, Alethea. You've come from nothing. From the worst poverty. The worst abuse. I know how Mammie made you feel. I heard how she tore you down, made you feel like you could never be anything at all. And I can only imagine what my father did to you.'

I laugh. He couldn't imagine that.

'I did a lot of research on child abuse, you know. After Mammie told me. After she died. There are people…they're helping me. They can help you, Alethea.'

But he wrong. Nobody can't help me.

JANUARY 6

Alethea stooped behind the galvanized fence, peeping through the holes in the metal at the two men who were standing at the back door talking to Uncle Allan. The men were in old clothes, shirts that were ragged at the sleeves and hems, and pants with patched bottoms and huge holes at the knees. One of them had a big red pencil behind his ear. The other had a silver and yellow cube in his hand. He kept pulling out a yellow strip that looked like a hard ribbon, and letting it snap back into the silver and yellow box.

Uncle Allan was inside the kitchen, leaning over the bottom of the Dutch doors and pointing to the space behind the latrine. The one with the silver thing in his hand shook his head again and again, but Uncle Allan kept pointing at the space and raising his voice louder and louder. The man with the pencil pointed to the other side of the house, the front yard. It was Uncle Allan's turn to shake his head.

'What they quarrelling for?' Liloutee whispered loudly, crouching beside her and jockeying for a good view through the small holes.

'Me ent know!' Alethea whispered back. Looking down, she noticed Colin dragging a stick through the dust and putting the tip into his mouth. 'No, Colin. Nasty,' she said, and took the stick from him.

He plucked a leaf from a low bush at their feet and began to chew it instead.

'Who is them men?'

'Uncle Allan say them is carpenter. He say they going and make a coop.'

'What is a coop?'

Alethea shrugged.

'Girlie, look Colin eating bush!'

'That is all right,' Alethea said. 'I does eat that. It does taste like pumpkin.'

The girls picked leaves of their own, and the little bush was soon stripped naked. They walked around the yard looking for other plants to eat, followed by Colin who was now crawling on his hands and knees. Rusty lay on Liloutee's front step, his long red tongue hanging out and his lazy glance flicking over the children as they wandered around. Then Colin started to cry.

The little boy was frantically rubbing his mouth and his eyes. As Alethea watched, little clear bumps raised there and Colin cried harder. Soon, he was screaming. Rusty jumped up and started to bark, angry, sharp yips that made Colin cry even more.

'What happen, what happen?' Alethea asked, seizing his hands and struggling to keep him from rubbing his face.

Liloutee gasped. 'Ooh goooood, is stinging nettle, yes.' The distinctive dark green hairy leaves of a shrub next to Colin were crushed and torn. 'Mai! Mai!'

Indra ran out of the house. 'What happen?' She scooped up Colin and rocked him, murmuring soothingly, 'Nice boy, petit popo, hush baby...' She noticed the rash on his face. 'What is that?'

'Stinging nettle, Mai.'

Indra made an unhappy face, screwing up her mouth and squinting her eyes. 'Ah, Lord! Well, go and get some shining bush for he, then! Do quick. This must be burning like fire. Poor baby.'

The girls hunted around looking for the small, heart-shaped, glossy leaves of the shining bush plant.

'I find it!' Alethea yelled, yanking up a whole plant by the roots from a sandy bed next to the fence and dashing back to Indra.

Liloutee's mother broke off a handful, crushed the delicate leaves and thick, juicy stems in her fist, and rubbed the juice on Colin's blistered skin. 'Give me your hand, baby,' she coaxed in a low, tender voice. Colin was still crying and she had to put him to stand up so she could unfold his clenched fingers and rub the squashed leaves and stems on his little hands. In seconds his wails eased. He stood with his arms outstretched for Indra to pick him back up. She gently wiped his wet face, careful not to touch the blistered parts, and raised him back into her embrace. 'You feeling better, baby? Eh? You all right now? Eh, baby?' Clucking and cooing at him, Indra looked at Alethea. 'Where your mammie, Girlie? She not home?'

'No, Tantie Indra. She gone by Ibrahim's to buy some chicks.'

'Oho. All you getting more fowl?'

'Yes, Tantie.'

'So them men come to build the coop, then?'

'Yes, Tantie. Mammie didn't tell me nothing about the men and them. I only see them when I was playing with Lily just now. Uncle Allan say they making a coop.'

Indra turned back to the house. 'All you stay out the stinging nettle. And mind you don't cut yourself on that galvanize. When your mammie come home, Girlie, tell she I have Colin.' She disappeared into the back yard, heading towards the kitchen. Colin's hitched breaths faded as they turned the corner.

'Girlie, you see how he face get them buttons? So quick!' Liloutee's eyes widened. 'You ever see that?'

Alethea shook her head. She was glad Colin was better. Seeing him hurt like that had frightened and confused her. The idea of what Mammie would do to her if he were injured… She didn't even want to think about it. 'I never see nobody rub stinging nettle on they own face. It does hurt!'

'Colin real stupid, boy.'

'No, he not stupid. He's just a baby, that's all. Babies just don't know nothing.'

'A time, I get stinging nettle on my bamsee,' Lily confessed. 'I was in a panty and a vest and I sit down on it by accident. My whole bamsee was burning me. Mai rub the shining bush on it and it stop hurting.'

'I never get no stinging nettle,' Alethea said. 'But it had so much bumps on he face. All by he eye. All by he mouth,' she said with a shudder. 'I glad Tantie Indra was here. I wouldn't have know what to do. I sure Mammie would have beat me.'

'Why she would have beat you? You didn't do nothing.'

'But was me who was watching he. And if he get in trouble is my fault.'

Lily twisted her mouth doubtfully and grunted, but said nothing else about it. She changed the subject. 'My pa home today.'

'Oh, yeah? How come he home?'

'He say we have to move.'

'Move what?'

188

'I don't know. That is what he say. We have to move.' Lily took Alethea's hand and the two girls went to sit on the step, shoving Rusty off to make room. 'Whole day Pa taking up everything inside the house and putting it in box. Even the bed, and all, he mashing up.'

'He mash up your toys, too?'

'No.'

'Well, then, bring your dolly, nah.'

'Mai done put that in a box already. Since yesterday when all you did went out. Where all you went?'

'We went by my granny. Mammie mammie. It was far! We drive whole day and when we was coming back we drive whole night.'

'Whole night! It must be was real far in truth. So who is your granny?'

'She nice! She name Ma. She small small, smaller than Mammie, and she look just like Colin. She give we sugar cake and toolum and orange and a thing name pawpaw ball. I never see that before. Is a ball, like toolum, but instead of black, it green. It soft soft and it had white sugar on it.' She looked slyly at her friend. 'It still have some. You want me bring for you?'

'Yes, yes!' Liloutee jumped up, clapping her little hands together in glee.

'I go bring it if you bring the dolly…'

'It done pack up, I tell you.'

'You can't ask Tantie Indra? Please! I never get no nice dolly so. My dolly not so clean.'

Liloutee knew her friend's bald, dirty doll, wearing its patched and ragged dress. 'Okay. I go ask Mai. You go and bring the toolum and thing. I go get the dolly.'

Alethea dashed to the fence and ducked through it to her house. Allan and the men were still in the back yard. She ran to the kitchen and grabbed the brown paper bag of treats from the table before bolting back to Liloutee's house. Liloutee was nowhere in sight but she could hear a man's voice rumbling inside the house. In a moment, Liloutee appeared at the door. Her eyes were red and her hands, empty.

'What happen? You didn't find the dolly? You want the pawpaw ball?' From the bag Alethea drew the sticky, squashed candy, which had begun to melt. Bits of shredded coconut, crumbs from the white sugar cake in the bag, coated one side of it. She dusted off the coconut and held the green ball out to Lily.

'Pa say no. He say he too busy to look for no dolly for me.' Tears brimmed from her eyes and her arms remained hanging at her sides. 'He say we not going and live here no more. He say we leaving today and a big truck going and take all we thing and carry it in a new house.'

'So how I go play with you, then?'

'We not going and play no more. Pa say I go make new friends which part we going.' Her face was wet now. Her lower lip trembled. 'I don't want no new friends. I want you to come with we.'

Alethea thought of going with them. It would be wonderful to live with Lily and Tantie Indra and Lily's Pa. They would eat alloo pie every day and play with Rusty and they would make new friends together. Maybe a boy their age lived where Lily's new house was. It would be exciting, an adventure – like her trip to Ma's house, except she wouldn't pee herself down, she promised herself.

But then she remembered Colin. If she left, Colin would be by himself with Mammie. Mammie would beat him and make him make his own tea. He would miss her. She couldn't leave him.

'We could bring Colin?'

Lily bit her wobbling lip. 'I don't know. Let me ask Pa.' She vanished inside the house again. Alethea dropped the pawpaw ball back into the grease-stained bag and licked her sugary palm. She sat down on the step, again hearing the deep masculine voice coming from inside the house. Lily reappeared. 'He say we can't take you and Colin with we. It ent go have no room for all you.' Lily sat next to Alethea.

A heavy, hot feeling came into Alethea's chest. She put the bag of candy down next to her and draped her arm over her friend's drooping shoulders. It was sad to think Lily would not be there any more. But maybe she could come back, she whispered to Lily. Maybe they could still be friends. Lily could come with Rusty. She and Rusty could take the bus with Aunty Indra and walk up the track together and come by Alethea and they could run about in the yard with Colin running behind them. They could pick yellow buttercups and put them in their hair and pretend to be dressed up; they could squeeze the purple juice from the hibiscus and rub it on their cheeks and lips and pretend to be big women wearing makeup. They could throw leaves into an enamel bowl and stir them with a stick, playing they were cooking, and serve their dollies tea made with mud and water. They could—

'Girlie! Where the ass that child gone?'

Mammie was home. Alethea scrambled to her feet. She squeezed Lily's hand urgently, then ran home, leaving the brown paper bag of treats on the step.

Mammie was shorter than Uncle Allan, but much taller than Alethea. She towered over her, gripping the neckline of Alethea's thin, ragged vest in her fist and shaking the small girl hard until the cloth ripped.

Alethea sobbed. 'Oh, God, Mammie! I sorry, Mammie! I sorry!'

Mammie slapped her face. Mammie's hands were flat and hard and Alethea's head snapped back on her neck like a rubber band stretched far and let go with a twang. 'How you could make the child eat stinging nettle? I leave you

191

with he for five minutes. Five minutes! And you make he eat stinging nettle!'

'No, Mammie! I sorry! I sorry!'

'Sorry, my ass. You nearly kill the child!' She drew back a fist and started to bear down on the little girl, but Allan held her from behind and dragged her hand down to her side. He pushed her and she bounced her hip on the kitchen table, rattling a pile of dirty plates stacked there.

'That's enough, Marcia. A little stinging nettle won't kill him. Look at what you're doing to the girl.'

Snot and tears mixed on Alethea's cheeks, fiery red where the slap had hit, the baby fat quivering with each piercing wail. Her thin hair was tangled and hung in clumps around her face.

Marcia sucked her back teeth and shoved the bawling child away. 'Go and wash your face,' she growled. 'And stop that shitting crying before I give you something to cry for, you ungrateful little bitch.'

Alethea skittered away, stifling her cries until the only sound she made was a small hitching in her throat. She ran out the door and knelt next to the bucket of slimy water Mammie kept in the yard. Black mildew coated the rim of the chipped blue enamel.

White sawdust floated on top of the water in a fine film. The workmen were gone, leaving piles of the stuff around the yard.

Alethea dipped her hand in the bucket and splashed tepid water on her stinging cheek. Water ran down her neck and soaked her torn vest. She kept dipping and splashing, dipping and splashing, until the stinging eased. Then she rubbed at her eyes and nose until they felt clean.

'Marcia, I hope you don't plan on treating my son like that when I'm gone,' Uncle Allan said. His radio voice was low.

Alethea felt he was saying something bad, because Mammie's voice went up very high when she answered him. 'Me, papa? Not me. Not your precious little nigger baby—'

Smack! 'I tell you already, Marcia. I warn you, my dear.' The radio voice was gone and he sounded just like Mammie again.

Mammie didn't say anything this time.

Alethea remained by the bucket, sitting on her heels and dabbling her fingers in the mud and sawdust on the ground. She found a perfect curl of wood shavings and put it in the bucket to use it as a boat, blowing on it so it went around in lazy circles. Lily going. Lily going, was all she thought. She wanted to cry again but remembered the slap, the violent shaking. She kept her tears inside.

The house was quiet for a long time.

The chicks Mammie had brought home were in a big white box with holes the size of pennies in its sides. The box was by the kitchen door. Alethea heard scritch-scratching, soft cheeping and the fluttering of wings coming from inside. She put her face close to the box; it smelled dusty and fishy.

Alethea could hear Marcia moving around in the bedroom. There was the creak of the old press door opening, and the squeak of rusty bedsprings when she sat on the bed. Colin babbled happily, squealing with laughter from time to time, and then they came outside and he was dressed in a little sailor suit, white long pants and a white long-sleeved tunic with blue stripes around a big, floppy collar. Mammie had greased and brushed his fluffy hair until it lay in oiled waves on his small head.

'Girlie, I going back in town. Don't let me see you in them nasty clothes when I come back, you hear?'

'Yes, Mammie.' She watched them moving down the track, Colin slung on Mammie's hip and still babbling as they disappeared.

Uncle Allan scared her when he snuck up behind her and yelled, 'Boo!' in her ear. She fell on her bottom in the mud. It was cold and wet, as slippery as her snot, and she could feel it creeping in under her panties as she sat in the puddle.

'Oh gosh, Girlie! Look at what you did,' he said, but it wasn't like Mammie would say it. He was smiling, laughing, even, and he held her arm lightly and pulled her to her feet. 'My dear! You need a bath in the worst way. Covered in mud. And sawdust, too,' he said, tenderly pulling another wood shaving from her tangled hair. 'Now, how did this get here?' The radio voice was deep and warm. It sounded the way cocoa tea tasted, she thought.

He stood her on her feet and pulled off her vest and panties, tossing them in the bucket.

'That is not for clothes, Uncle,' Alethea corrected him, but he didn't pay any attention. He took her by the hand and walked her to the small room with no roof where they bathed. The walls were planks of warped, mossy wood. Another enamel bucket was there, also full of water, this cleaner than the water in the other bucket but covered in soap scum.

'You want hot water?'

She shook her head. Mammie hardly ever put hot water for her to bathe with. Mammie always said that pitch oil was too expensive to waste.

'Don't shake your head like a dummy. Say, "Yes, Uncle Allan."'

'Yes, Uncle Allan.'

'So you want the hot water?'

'No, Uncle Allan.'

'So why'd you just say yes?'

The question confused her, but she saw the twinkle of laughter in his eyes and she knew he wasn't mad at her. He took the bar of yellow soap balanced on top of a corner of the wall and lathered it up in both hands, rubbing the bubbles softly on her back and chest and over her round belly. 'Close your eyes,' he whispered. 'Say, "Yes, Uncle Allan."'

'Yes, Uncle Allan.'

Warm, large hands slid over her eyes and cheeks. He wasn't rough like Mammie. He took his time and went very slowly and very softly. She kept her eyes squeezed tightly closed as he lathered more soap and rubbed her hair, her arms. The large hands stopped moving when they reached her thighs.

'Spread your legs, Girlie.'

'Yes, Uncle Allan.'

He washed between her legs very quickly, then her bottom, her thighs, her calves. She had to stand on one foot, resting her soapy hands on his shoulder to keep from falling when he washed her feet one at a time.

He dipped water out with the little enamel bowl they kept in the bathroom, and poured it over her head. She rubbed her eyes. 'Soap burning you?' he asked. The radio voice was gone again. He sounded hoarse, like he couldn't breathe.

'No, Uncle Allan.'

'Good.'

He picked her up, holding her under her armpits and swinging her around in the air. She giggled at first, because it was nice to see the colours of the yard blurring faster and faster as they went around. But he kept spinning her and spinning her and spinning her until she felt to vomit and that wasn't very nice. She wanted to cry, but she was afraid of what he would do if she did.

Finally he stopped spinning. He cradled her like a baby with her head on his chest and took her inside, locking the back door behind them. She could hear his heart thumping fast in his chest. She looked up at his face. He was smiling, with all his teeth showing, but it wasn't a nice smile. It was frightening: the look Rusty had when he was snarling at the snake in the flowers.

He put her to lie on the bed. Drops of water ran down her skin, leaving the sheet damp. The bed began to smell. She was embarrassed because she knew he could smell the pee where she had sometimes wet the bed. He whipped a towel up from a nail beside the doorframe and used it to pat her dry. It was an old bath towel, its dull red and brown floral pattern still showing even though it was thin and worn through in spots. Then he stretched it on the bed and made her lie on it. Her fingertips played with one fraying end.

'Where your mammie does keep your clothes?'

She pointed to the top drawer of a chest of drawers, its pitted surface black with the stains of years.

He opened the drawer, shook his head. 'This is all your clothes?'

She shook her head, no, then remembered to say quickly, 'No, Uncle Allan.'

'Well?'

'Well what, Uncle Allan?'

'Where the rest of them? Your nice dress, your frilly panty?' He was angry now. He sounded like Rusty just before he dashed towards another dog and started to bite it.

'In the press, Uncle Allan. In a brown bag in the press.'

The door creaked when he opened it. She sat up to get a look inside. On top of a dusty blue chenille bedspread, there inside the brown paper shopping bag was her organdie dress with the white lace collar. White nylon panties, satiny smooth, with circles of frills of white lace sewn on the back, were neatly folded beneath the dress. When Allan noticed her sitting up, he sighed and shoved her back down with pointed fingertips.

He took out the dress and panties and laid them flat on the bed next to her. Picking up the circular puff and the tin of My Fair Lady talcum powder that Marcia kept on the chest of drawers, he sprinkled sweet white powder on the puff and dusted her chest and back with it. The long, pale fibres of the puff tickled her skin.

Slowly, slowly, he put one of her feet then the other into the panty, drawing it up her legs while she still lay on her back. 'Up,' he said. She stood on the bed. 'What do you say?'

'Yes, Uncle Allan.'

Old and sagging, the soft mattress and the bed's loose springs surged under her slight weight and she shifted to keep standing up.

'Keep quiet,' he said.

'Yes, Uncle Allan.'

'Raise up your hand.'

Again, slowly, slowly, he put one of her arms at a time into the sleeves of the dress, then pulled it down over her head. When he straightened the lace collar, his hands shook.

'Where the brush?'

'The brush?'

'For your hair.'

Mammie used a tan wooden hairbrush with white roses painted on the back, and Alethea pointed to it on the top of the chest of drawers. Its bristles were clumped with Mammie's curly brown and grey strands. He dug out the clumped strands with his fingertips and threw them under the bed. The soft white bristles smelled like coconut oil and Mammie when he pulled the brush through Alethea's hair.

'Who looking so nice?' he growled.

She didn't say anything.

He lightly slapped her cheek with his flattened palm. It didn't hurt but it shocked her and tears came to her eyes.

'I say, who looking so nice?'

'Me, Uncle Allan.'

The room was a little dark. All the windows were closed and only a few slanting rays of light came in through the gap between the roof and the walls. His eyes were shiny bright points in the dim light.

'Come. Come here.'

She took a small step towards him. She was scared of the rough, uneven sound of his breathing, the smell of rum and cigarettes on his breath as he bent towards her and picked her up. He held her upright against his chest with one arm wrapped around her thighs, so their foreheads touched.

'Give me a kiss, Girlie.'

She puckered her rosebud mouth and planted a shy kiss on his cheek. The skin of his cheek was prickly and dry. She hid her face in the crook of his neck. He squeezed her cheeks and dragged her face back up. His mouth loomed, large and strange, open, when she looked at him. He was panting now. She shut her eyes. He put his mouth on hers and wriggled his tongue between her lips. She twisted her head away but he slapped her again. 'You don't want me kiss you?'

'No, Uncle Allan.'

Another light but firm slap. Now she was crying, her little coughing moans stifled in her tight throat as tears ran down her chubby pink cheeks.

'You want me to tell your mammie you's a bad girl and you don't want to listen to your Uncle Allan?' It was a warning and a threat. 'You don't want me kiss you?'

'Yes, Uncle Allan.'

His tongue was bitter, clammy, pointed, muscular. She couldn't get it out of her mouth. He was holding her too tight, pressing her whole frail body against his chest with an arm as stiff as a wooden post.

He sat on the bed and put her to sit on his lap with her back to his chest. She remembered the feel of his big hand stroking her leg the night before, and now he did it again. When he slid his hand under the panties and touched her private part she jumped. 'Shhhh, shhhh,' he crooned. His fingertip was cold and it hurt her, so she cried out. 'Shhhh, shhhh,' he repeated.

'It hurting, Uncle Allan!'

'Hush, I say.'

He removed his hand and it stopped hurting for a moment. He fumbled with his belt and the buttons of his fly. He held her thigh hard with one hand and with the other dragged her panties off.

And then she felt pain searing and searing in her private part, like a wash of hot oil or a burning stick or a hot iron was being forced inside of her. He covered her mouth with his palm and held her down with the other hand, an arm as hard as the iron bed wrapped around her waist, and she couldn't move and she couldn't get away and it was hurting so much and she felt like she would split in two and he wouldn't let her go. She screamed and screamed, her open mouth against his hand, her teeth pressing into the fleshy part just under his thumb, her lips crushed flat against the rubbery skin, but she knew nobody could hear her screaming because he had covered her mouth and she could only hear the loud high wails inside her head.

When Mammie came home she found Alethea curled up under a cover in the bed, her hair neatly brushed. She was in a clean panty and vest, her skin dusted with talcum powder. Mammie sniffed. 'Allan, you use my good powder on this child?'

'Oh, God, Marcia. It's just some cheap dusting powder. I'll bring you plenty when I come back next Christmas, okay?'

Mammie didn't answer him. She put Colin to lie down next to Alethea. He was asleep. Red, sweet-smelling spots covered the front of his sailor blouse, and his mouth looked sticky. As Mammie bent over the bed, she looked more closely at Alethea. She picked up her limbs, observing the blue bruises on her legs and arms, and squeezed her cheeks between her hands as she looked at her mouth, raw and swollen. Mammie released her and looked away.

'Look, Girlie. Your Uncle Allan give me money to buy a special dolly for you.' Mammie held up a white-skinned dolly with long, brown hair.

Uncle Allan came into the room and stood by the bed, stroking Alethea's hair. Alethea flinched when he touched her head.

'Don't you like the dolly?' he asked in the radio voice.

'Yes, Uncle Allan.'

Marcia put the dolly in Alethea's hand, folding her fingers around the plastic body. Alethea stared into her mother's eyes. There was no expression there. Marcia's eyes were as dark and empty as the space under the bed when it was night and everything was quiet.

'What you have to say?' Mammie asked.

'Thank you, Uncle Allan,' Alethea whispered.

'Any time, Girlie. Any time,' he said.

Colin moaned and shifted restlessly.

'Let's let these two have a nap,' Allan said. He and Marcia went to the kitchen. Alethea soon heard the sounds of a pot spoon ringing on the rim of an iron pot, and then plates and spoons clicking and clacking. Nobody spoke.

She climbed off the bed and put the dolly on the chest of drawers. Colin awoke when she rocked the bed as she got up. Sitting, he yawned and reached for her with both arms. She picked him up. He smelled like guava sweeties. She wet her thumb and scrubbed the stains from his mouth, rocking him from side to side as she did it. 'Nice baby,' she cooed.

SIXTEEN

I take the next day off. Leo was with me whole day, making breakfast, lunch and evening supper, and just generally minding me. He didn't say nothing about the story he hear the day before, just treat me like a piece of glass that he fraid to break. When Bobby call that morning to find out which part I is, Leo just tell him I feeling sick. I sure Bobby feel is beat Leo beat me, but I honestly couldn't bring myself to talk to nobody on the phone. I didn't want to see nobody, neither. I feel as though anybody who see me would see my whole disgusting family history write on my face clear as day.

I don't know what fly up in Bobby head, but around lunchtime he drive up in he BMW to see if I all right. He pull me square right in front Leo face and ask me francomen if somebody hurt me. I say no. He watch me hard, but he had was to drive away because I didn't tell him nothing else and he could see I was standing up: no break hand, no break foot.

'You tell he something?' Leo say. He sound suspicious – but, as though he still didn't want to upset me, he take it easy and didn't rough me up.

I tell he no, and went back in my bed.

After work, Tamika, Curtis and Sugars pull up in front the house. Leo know Tamika from the shop and he smile up with she. He watch Curtis and Sugars a little hard, but Tamika insist all of them must come inside to talk to me. Just when I wanted to hide away, like every Peter, Dick and Harry want to come in my house and see me. I peep out in the gallery and tell them I just feeling sick, nothing serious. When me and Tamika eye make four, I say, 'Is nothing, Tamika. I just feeling sick. That is all.'

'You sure? Because you don't have to stay here, you know,' she whisper in my ears.

I shake my head. 'Is nothing like that, Tamika,' I whisper back. 'I really just feeling sick. Okay?'

I don't know what exactly Tamika tell Sugars and Curtis, but Sugars like he sizing up Leo, to decide if he could take him. Leo ent no badman, and I know that – he does rough me up because I small and weak, but he not like some of them drunks who does get in fight and tussle all over the place. Underneath everything, Leo was a middle-class boy. He parents had good civil service work – he father in the Government Printery and he mother in the Ministry of Education. He grow up soft. If Sugars had a mind to take him, he could knock him out clean.

Tamika insist she must stay with me, so I went back in my bed and Tamika come and lime with me. I talk a little bit – idleness, nothing to do with what happen the day before, nothing to do with Leo – but mostly I just close my eye and listen to she. A hour later, Curtis and Sugars swing back and pick she up. I roll over in my bed and try to sleep.

. . .

It was the Tuesday before Fire Fete. I didn't want to go to work but I feel like I had no choice. I couldn't take all them people coming to see if I okay again. I feel I wasn't worth it, and they was just wasting their time.

I bathe, dress, slouch down the hill and crawl inside a maxi. I open up the shop and went inside, looking around at the place like I never see it before. I make some tea, but I couldn't drink it and end up throwing it down the drain.

Tamika, Ann and Janelle come in and only asking me if I okay, if I need anything. Lunchtime, Tamika want me to come to church with she, but I couldn't bear to see Colin again, at least not yet. I was sick to my stomach at the thought of the whole dirty story.

Even Jankie couldn't pull me out of the mood I was in. She call a few times and I didn't take the calls. Finally, she come by the shop and try to get me to talk to she. I just shake she off and tell she I go talk to she next week.

Bobby and all try to get me to go Central with he again. I was tempted, eh, I wouldn't lie. Good sex is one of the few things that does make me feel better when I upset, but this time the idea of anybody putting their hand on me just remind me of Allan and I wanted to vomit again. I tell Bobby no, and I mean it, for the first time since he know me. He do like if the world going and end.

That is how the whole week went.

Friday I drag myself home and just went straight in my bed, in my shoes and all. Leo wasn't home. I was lying down there when I start to hear voices coming inside the house.

Tamika stick she head around the corner and say, 'Surprise! Happy birthday!'

It was such a shitty week I even forget it was my birthday.

She take my hand and pull me out of the bed. She tie a cotton bandana around my eye and lead me through the house.

For somebody who start the New Year without a friend in the world, I was suddenly full of friends. Curtis, Sugars, Jankie and Ricky crowd up in the grungy living room. Leo come out of the kitchen singing 'Happy Birthday', with Colin walking behind him holding a birthday cake blazing with candles.

I cry like a baby.

It was the first birthday party I ever had in my life.

In a little while, Leo carry me back inside the bedroom, unbuttoning my shirt and kissing up my neck.

I say, 'Leo, not now! All them people outside...'

'Don't worry, I just want you to change. We could do that later. Remember, I still have to go to work tonight. I want you to come with me.'

I don't remember Leo ever asking me to do anything before. I was shock. But I put on a scoop-neck black chiffon dress, cut in a A-line and tie with a band under the breasts, with a silk shell underneath, and long kimono sleeves. It was completely cover up, but sexy because the chiffon was sheer, showing my skin glowing pale underneath it. I mustbe wear the dress once since I had it – where I does go to put on black silk chiffon gown?

When I step outside in my strappy silver sandals and a little bit of makeup, everybody make a big scene. Next thing I know is Hilton, every man jack gone Hilton, yes.

Me and Leo ride in Colin car.

I say, 'But, Colin, I thought you had to go to evening mass?'

'I thought this was more important.'

Me more important than mass? Impossible.

'Hmm,' I say. Then I realise I didn't even know how this whole thing come about. 'Wait, nah – is you who organise this?'

He buss a big laugh. 'You got me! Yes. I thought it would be nice for you to celebrate your fortieth birthday with your friends. Leo and Tamika helped.' He pause. 'And I thought it would help you get out of the funk you've been in.'

I watch out the window.

Leo say, 'It was a good idea, man. Thanks.'

We split up when we reach the hotel lounge, with Leo going to talk to the manager before he start he set, and me and Colin waiting by the door for Tamika and Jankie and them to catch up with we.

Them order cutters and drinks when they reach and for dinner we end up having buffalo wings, sweet potato fries, sushi and something name ceviche. A strange mix of food I never eat before, but it was all right.

Leo do he first half and come and spend a five with we, slipping he hand in my drawers under the table and making me blush. He didn't know that Sugars would be doing the exact same thing a few minutes later.

Leo finish he second set with 'Lady in Red', and dedicate it to me.

'But you're wearing black,' Colin say.

Tamika jump in, 'That was the song he sang for her when they first meet. Shhh.'

Next thing you know is because Leo get up from the piano bench and singing a cappella, walking over to we table. When he get down on one knee and reach in he pocket I didn't know what to do.

What else I could say but, 'Yes'?

Even Tamika, who was ready to fight Leo just a few days before, get take in by the 'romance'. She had tears in she eye. Like everybody in the whole place start to clap and cheer. Everybody except for Sugars, who face look like the opposite of he name, and Colin, who couldn't even muster up a smile. I figure he was thinking about the bruises on my hand what he see the other day. He look downright vex. But both of them bite they tongue and keep quiet. Leo force a diamond ring on my finger. It was tight. When he finally get it on my hand he kiss me long and hard.

After that, gifts start to share. Colin give me a book, Jankie give me a fat envelope with a card in it. I figure it was one of them real expensive card with a set of flap to fold out. Ricky give me a pretty lilac pashmina, and Tamika hand me a bag with two red jersey in it.

'For tomorrow,' she say. 'Your first Fire Fete. We buy the tickets for you and Leo. No excuses. You have to come.'

We barely reach inside the house before Leo rip down my drawers and bull me on the kitchen table.

The second rounds, he take he time. He put the soft, creamy cake icing on my nipples and eat it off.

I was still feeling a little weird about having sex and so I ask him if he wasn't disgusted by what he hear Colin tell me.

'No, babes,' he say. 'You is still my woman. And I want to married you.'

I stay quiet in the bed for a long while.

'You want to hear the whole story?'

'No,' he say. 'That is the past. It don't matter any more.' He hold me and pull me close to him so I was lying down with my head on he chest. He hand was on my bottom, drawing little lines down the side of it. It was tickling.

'Leo,' I try one more time. 'You know I can't make children.'

'Can't, or won't?'

'Can't. Because of—'

'Shhhhh,' he say. 'I don't want to know. Is all right. We don't have to have no children. It go be just you and me. Together forever.'

All and a sudden I remember Jerry with them scars all over he body. My pores raise up. Leo take that as a sign that I was ready for a next rounds.

As he fall asleep, I went by the sink, soap up my hand good and try to get the ring off. My finger was swell up around it and I couldn't get it off for nothing, all how I try. The diamond keep winking up at me.

SEVENTEEN

Short shorts. I tugging and tugging at the hem of the black pants riding up between my bottom. 'You sure, girl? I feeling like one skettel,' I tell Tamika. We was in my bedroom; Leo done in the car waiting with Curtis and Sugars.

Tamika toss she new weave and grin at sheself in the wardrobe mirror. 'Who say is only skettel could wear battyriders?' she bawl out loud loud loud.

I skin up my face for Tamika and pull at my pants again.

Tamika say, 'Here, let me fix that jersey.'

Both of we was in we red On the Town jersey, the red the same colour as the fireman in Jerry store window. The jersey print say *On the Town Crew*, with a tiny mannequin silhouette next to the words. The whole crew was suppose to wear them tonight – even Marie, the old cow, and Leo and Curtis and Sugars. The jersey barely skim the waistband of my tiny, tight pants.

Curtis blow the car horn.

'Oh, gorm. We coming,' Tamika shout out. She had on sneakers on her foot, and pumpum shorts on she bottom. She was ready.

Me, I wasn't so sure. I ent know how Leo allow me to wear this outfit. Normally he does like to see me cover up, unless he decide he want me in something skimpy. But he watch me in the jersey and pants and he watch Tamika face set up and just went outside without complaining. It make me nervous; he wasn't he normal self.

'One last thing.' Tamika hand me a red and white bandana. She had one just like it and tuck it into she back pocket so the end trail nearly to the back of she knee.

'What this for?'

Tamika shake she head like I asking something ridiculous. 'You ent know? Don't worry, you go see.'

It had a solid block of traffic in all directions, coming and going, for about half a mile around Fire Services Headquarters. People done park they car on the side of the road, riding the pavement and blocking everybody driveway. Pedestrians line up like bachac by the temporary gateway they put up in the small road going around the side of the main firehouse. I could see spotlights waving in the smoky air behind the building.

Tamika jump out the car and the rest of we follow she, leaving Curtis to go and find a park. 'You have the tickets?' he ask everybody before he drive on. Everybody check their pocket. Yes, we had them.

'Family...' a boy passing murmured to me. The hem of he jeans was dragging on the ground, the pants belt under his hips so he red boxer shorts was showing. He smile, flashing a diamond in he front teeth. 'You looking sweet, girl.'

I flash my own diamond back at he.

'That don't mean nothing, family,' he say, before Leo step in front of me and give he one look. The boy scuttle away like a crab, grabbing he pants so he wouldn't trip.

Tamika suck she teeth. 'Oh gorm, he ent go bite she. Besides,' she tell me with a naughty look on she face, 'he was kind of cute.'

'He's a little boy!' Leo bawl.

'You feel he studying that?' She suck she teeth again and turn to the crowd. 'Right, let we go.'

We join the line behind a fat woman all in white. 'Lady, you brave to wear that, yes,' Tamika joke under she breath.

The woman glance over she shoulder, scoffing. Excellent word. 'You feel I ent have soap and water home or what?'

A neat looking Rasta, he hair wrap up in a two-foot tall turban, walk past the line, chanting, 'Cigarette, tringum, cigarette, tringum.' He had a transparent plastic messenger bag strap to he chest – bulging with packs of cigarettes and chewing gum in red, green and blue paper.

'Bobo!' Tamika bawl out. 'You want chewing gum? Cigarette?' Tamika ask we, plucking a roll of hundreds from she bra. 'I could get a pack of Du Maurier?' she ask the Rasta. 'And a lighter. A red one. Yeah. That. And some tringum. Doublemint.' He hand she the pack of cigarette and she pass it to me along with the lighter. She tear open the mint-green pack of gum, unwrap a stick and slide it between she red lips before cramming the rest in she small small fob pocket.

The fat woman in white lean over by me. 'Darling, lend me a cigarette there, nah.'

'Lend you? You go pay she back?' Tamika start to laugh.

The fat woman screw up she face, suck she teeth and turn she back one time. I pluck a cigarette from the pack and tap the woman shoulder.

She face suddenly turn sweet with a radiant smile. 'Thank you, darling. At least some people still have manners.' She cut she eye at Tamika. Tamika ent take she on. She there chewing she gum noisy noisy, with a blank expression and innocent wide eyes, popping a little bubble inside she mouth.

Me and Leo light two cigarette from the pack and smoke as we stand up in the line.

The line was moving forward slow slow slow through steel scaffolds by the gate. The scaffolds was so narrow, it was one person at a time, Indian file. As we come up near the front of the line, I hear people cussing and shouting behind me just as I feel Leo hard body slam into my back. In turn, I tip forward, jamming up against Tamika, who end up getting crush between me and the fat woman in white.

'Oh God, all you take it easy, nah!' the fat woman shout. 'All you go squeeze out the baby!'

Even Tamika laugh at that while pushing back with she hips, forcing me to push back too. 'You okay?' She turn around to check me out, putting she hand on my shoulder.

I nod my head. Leo slip he hand around my waist. I couldn't help but skin up my face a little bit.

Tamika say, 'You sure you okay?'

The fat woman say, without turning around, 'Oh God, if she say she okay, she okay! You is she mother, or what?'

Tamika nose flare and she eye bug out. It was my turn to put a hand on she, not to comfort but to hold she back. 'Tamika, no,' I tell she under my breath.

It take a minute before Tamika relax the steel hard muscles she coil to spring like a mapepire snake. The fat woman keep she back rigid, as if she expect Tamika to start a fight, and when none come she peep over one shoulder to look at Tamika.

'Some people does be begging for a cutass, yes,' Tamika drawl out loud, kissing she teeth in a long, wet noise of disgust.

Leo hand tighten around my waist.

Edging forward, we finally reach the front of the line and give we tickets to a woman sitting down by the gate.

A middle-age man with one enormous handlebar moustache leer at Tamika and me as we pass him, one by one. 'Ladies,' he ooze, 'this way, this way...' He point towards two female security guards. Bored-looking, they was waving metal detector wands over the women in the line ahead of we. The men was in a next line, with a male guard, going through the same thing.

The fat woman in white spread she hand and foot as she stand up for she inspection; the guard wand start to go mad, beep-beep-beep-beep-beep, when it pass over she breasts. They was so big they was spilling over the top of she Spandex bodice. As the guard pat she down, she say, 'I don't like women, eh, miss. Try not to feel me up so, please. Thank you very much.' Finally, the guard let she pass. I went next, and then Tamika.

We walk in, joining up with the edge of a massive crowd. The training buildings of the Fire Services Headquarters make a square and it had a stage down towards the back of the space. Between we and the stage it had thousands of people. I never see so much people on one spot before in my life, but then again, I never went a Carnival fete before.

A man in baggy jeans, yellow like egg yolk and reaching to just above he ankle, stumble with five big plastic cup of ice in he hand and one cup bite between he teeth. A chattering group of girls, like me and Tamika in some crew uniform, was blocking him until he tip icy water over one girl foot. She scream, 'Whatthemothercuntwrongwithyou!'

She friends and them hold she back from rushing the man, but they cuss him stink as he walk away, drifting from side to side as he went.

'Don't worry 'bout them,' Tamika say, leading we towards the corner the man just come from. It had a bar set up under a tent. The tent remind me of the woman who get shoot, but I shake off the memory. People – mostly men – was in a crowd around this tent, waving hundred-dollar bills in the air trying to get the attention of the two over-busy bartenders. Leo and Sugars squeeze in by the bar. Me and Tamika stand up there for a long time, waiting, while the two of them bawl out for beers and rum every time a bartender pass them.

Curtis come walking up to we from behind.

'You mean I had time find a park, line up and come inside and all you still ent get drinks yet? Nah, man.' He angle heself in between Leo and Sugars and start to make one set of noise until a bartender give he two bottle of rum and six beers. Leo and Sugars take the tins and Curtis come out with the two bottle of Black Label rum chook under he armpit. 'I hope them have chaser,' he say.

Tamika was scanning the crowd all this time. 'Look them over there!' She point towards a red flag, big like a tablecloth, floating over the crowd at the top of a length of PVC pipe. It had On the Town logo stencil on it, with the same design as what we had on we jersey. With Tamika in front like a tall, thin bulldozer, we jostle through the crowd to go and stand up under the flag.

All the people from the next branches of the shop was already there, standing up next to a six-foot long cooler. It had some faces I didn't recognise and I figure them was new people from the South branch. Marie was like the mother hen, guarding the cooler, taking out drinks, passing sandwiches from a big plastic Tupperware box. Mark was wining on Ann, with Janelle press up behind him wining too; the only people I didn't see was the Sharmas. But I figure them was in some posh all-inclusive fete, not in the old-nigger fete like we. I introduce myself to the South people; the uptown branch people, especially Marie, was watching Leo hard hard hard, so I introduce he too.

'This is Leo, my—'

'Fiancé,' he jump in. 'We just got engaged yesterday.' And he hug me up tighter than ever.

Of course, Marie was first in line to pull up my hand and turn it from side to side to maco the ring that was squeezing my finger. The diamond wasn't nothing to speak of, in truth, and I could see she laughing at it even while she saying, 'Congrats!' But she good eye up Leo and at least he pass – you could say what you want about how he does behave and how he does drink and how he does beat me, but the man damn good looking. Marie had a hot, greedy look in she eye as she scope he out.

Curtis start to lash the rum hard, and pour out drinks for he friend and Leo. Tamika take a shot sheself, and chase it with beer. I help myself to a shandy from the cooler. Leo come back and stand up behind me, holding he cup of rum and Cokes in one hand and holding me around my waist with the other, as though he fraid I run away. The place was getting more and more ram out, and we was a circle of about twenty people in the middle of a crowd thick like a forest. Pretty soon it had people bouncing Leo from behind. He tighten he grip on me and drink out the rum before it throw away. Curtis didn't stick at all – he hit him with a next drink one time.

Sugars was flirting with a chubby dougla girl from South on the other side of the circle, but every time I watch in he direction, he watching me, not she.

All this time music pounding hard hard from the direction of the stage. It had speakers stack up about two storey high and fifteen foot wide on either side of it, cover on top with a blue tarpaulin, with scaffolds holding up the speakers and the stage. The stage itself had no lights on, but you could see people in black clothes walking around, and then the band come on in the dark and start to sound check.

A man from the crowd, bareback and in a short pants and sneakers, climb up the scaffolds and hold on to them with one hand, wining like a madman to the sound of the soca the DJ playing.

As I watching that, I see a woman come flying up in the sky out of nowhere. When I look, is because she on some kind of cloth, like a blanket or something, and six strongman around she flinging she up in the air and catching she back. I start to look around at the crowd. It had all kind of people. Young, old, dress up, dress down, man, woman and child – well, not exactly children, but it had some teenagers in there for sure. Most of them was standing up facing in the direction of the stage, drinking and chatting with one another, but some of them was drunk already, sitting down on the grass with their head between their knee.

Plenty people was dancing. It had a girl just next to we, facing a man, with one ankle up on he shoulder and jooking she nanny against he pants zipper. She was wearing a thongs; you could see she liver and all from that angle. Tamika sheself had she two hand on the ground, bend over double and wining back on Curtis crotch. I feel like a old granny, forty years and in my first and only soca fete, doing a polite social wine, barely twitching my waist from side to side. Some of the things I see the people doing – the women, especially – was things I would do in the bedroom but not out in public. Me, do that? You mad or what? Couples was on the grass, practically making love, but really just wining. It had a man lying down between a woman legs, and she on she back with she two foot up in the air like a dead semp. Man had woman riding on they shoulder, as if they playing cockfight. One woman was even sitting with she crotch in the man face, wining up there as though is nothing unusual.

Curtis and Sugars walk up by we and tell Leo, 'We going and take a little pull. You coming?'

Leo hesitate. He didn't want to leave me in the crowd but he couldn't refuse to go off with them. He would look like he is a soft man.

'Babes, you go be okay?'

'Yeah, man,' Curtis say. 'She go be right here when you come back, don't frighten.'

Leo let me go as if he would never see me again, giving my hand a squeeze and kissing me on the lips.

As they walk off into the crowd away from the stage, Tamika say, 'Well, finally! I thought he would never let you go. That man like a tick in your ass! How you could stand that, boy?'

I shrug my shoulders, drinking my shandy and lighting a cigarette.

Without warning I feel somebody come and pressing their hips against my bottom. I swing around one time.

'Take it easy, Miss Allie,' Mark say. 'I just thiefing a wine!'

'Eh eh,' I tell him, shaking my finger. 'Go back by Ann and them. If my man catch you wining on me he go cut both of we ass.' I was grinning. He didn't know I was serious like Gramoxone.

'But, Miss Allie, you in a fete! How you expect to stand up there and nobody would wine on you?'

Tamika say, 'Is true, Allie. You can't fight them off.' She self had some man wining on she bottom already, just minutes after Curtis walk off. She wine back as though is the most natural thing in the world.

'Who is that?' I ask Tamika.

She turn she head to watch the man face. She shrug. 'Me ent know.'

Mark laugh. 'You does get accustom.'

'Well, I not accustom, okay?'

He grin at me and went back by Ann and Janelle. They put him back in a sandwich, eventually falling down on the ground with Janelle on the grass, Mark on top of she, and Ann riding both of them like a cowboy.

Up on stage the lights come on and a man in a sharp white suit come on and start to talk like a circus ringmaster. 'Ladies and gentlemen...are you ready for...Roy Cape and the Kaiso All Stars!'

'Is Roy Cape coming on now,' Tamika say, as though she had was to translate for me. The music from the band rise up in dramatic opening notes – like a rock anthem. 'Them people going and push. Get ready.'

The man behind Tamika brace he legs wide and bend he knees to keep heself upright against the crowd.

I didn't know what to do. All I feel was a surge, a wave of hot, sweating flesh shoving me forward along with it. I try to resist at first, on my toes and struggling to keep my footing as people push me left and right, bumping my body, but then I was literally off my feet. I didn't weigh much, and is like I get suspended between sweaty hips, waving arms, thrusting chests. I start to panic when I see the flag vanish, and I try to claw my way backwards but my foot wasn't touching the ground at all. I had nothing to keep me upright and I start to sink.

I just make a grab for the nearest thing to hold on to, and that turn out to be a shoulder. My fingers curl around it and dig in, hard. The man who shoulder it was turn to watch me, see me like I drowning in people, and angle through the heaving crowd. He manage to wedge heself under me so that I was prop up on he hip like a baby. I cling to him. If you see the size of the man.

At first I was rigid, sitting down on he hard hip bone.

'Relax, family,' the man say, 'it going and settle down just now. Just hold on.'

My fingers was a anchor, but I still feel myself slipping down, so I wrap my foot around he waist.

I was watching he face out of the corner of my eye. But he didn't spare me a glance. I could have be a dolly for all he care – he focus was on the stage where the band was playing their first song.

The pushing and shoving cool down. When I realise he stop moving, and nobody wasn't going and trample me, I relax and let myself slide down from off of he. I stand up next to this man. He mustbe was six-foot-five, build like a ox, a big wall of a red man.

I look around, trying to spot the flag again, but it was way back and it didn't have no way I could get through that crowd by myself. It was a sea of people, shoulder to shoulder, hip to hip, surging up and down in time to the soca.

The man look back, following my gaze.

'That is your people? Don't worry, family. When Roy Cape done I go carry you back by the flag. Just enjoy yourself, all right?'

People come up closer around we, like waves rolling on the sea. The air was thick and hot, and I couldn't hear nothing but the music washing over we, and the crowd around we singing along to every word. Somebody shove me from the side and push me towards the man and he catch me against he chest.

I stiffen up, fraid again, but he start to laugh at me, watching me in my face. 'I not going and eat you, little girl.'

I blush and I laugh back, still a little nervous but relaxing a little bit more. He had a kind face.

Feeling like a castaway, I turn slow slow slow to watch the show.

He bend his knees and sway he hips and I start to sway mines too. Nothing like Tamika, or the woman with she foot cock up on the man neck, but it was something. This wasn't like Leo crushing me – the man hold me loose enough so I could pull away if I want, but hard enough so that the endless people rocking around we wouldn't separate we when we wine.

The music start to seep into my skin, my muscle, my bones. I start to sweat. It wasn't just the movement or the body heat, it was like a fever sweat, and in a little while I was soaking wet from my head to my foot.

I look around and didn't see nothing familiar, no face I know. The man big, rock hard body was all I could recognise. He rhythm was my rhythm, he dance was my dance. In a timing, we start to move together like if we doing it long time, without talking, drifting with the crowd until we merge into it. I don't even know the exact moment when I stop thinking at all. It only had this music and this wine, this man and this moment.

When the music stop it jolt me. I look around wild wild wild to see what happen. But it was only a guest performer coming on stage to join the band. When the ringmaster call the name, the crowd surge up again, dragging even the man along with it like flotsam on a wave. I hear a voice on the speaker say: 'Who ready to blaze the fi-yahhh?' A roar buss out from the audience. Cup, kerchief, flag, jersey, hand fly up in the air. I only see some of it – I was small, and the crowd was tall and thick. All I know is that suddenly I get soak down in beer, and was even wetter than I was before. It didn't get me vex. Something fly up in my head like a madness. I was melting, a drop in the ocean, one with the water. All and a sudden I remember the rag Tamika give me. I pull it from my pocket and I was waving, too.

It feel to me like the song went on for an hour. Every time it seem to stop, the band start up again, the crowd roar again and we get push forward again.

I ent say word one to the man since he tell me we go go back by the flag when the band finish play, but it didn't matter. I didn't know he name, in fact, I didn't know nothing about him, but that didn't matter either. He was. I was. We was wining to this music in this fete at this moment, and all I could do was wine and wine and wine.

Then, braps, the band done. Like a wave drawing back from the sand, the crowd pull away from the stage, seeping back to where they was before, or going by the bar or the toilet or wherever. The man looked down at me with a grin. 'You see, family? Let we go and find your people now. The red flag there?'

Tamika grin when she see me stumbling back through the crowd with this big wall of a man behind me. She teeth shine bright in the light from the distant stage. 'Eh eh! Look who pick up!'

Leo face was blue vex.

'No, nothing like that,' I say, real quick. 'He just help me, that's all.' The man done gone already.

'I could see that! He help you wine!' Cackling like a old witch, Tamika take a shot from the cup in she hand. 'I go drink to that! Girl, you don't want some rum? Take a drink.' She scoop up a bottle of rum from by the cooler and try to pour some in my mouth. Leo knock she hand back and the bottle fall, throwing rum on the ground. Marie scramble to pick it up. I duck down behind the big, maco cooler.

Curtis square off with Leo and push he hand in he face. 'You fucking mad, or what? You could beat your woman but don't fucking touch mines, you hear?'

Leo had two rum in he head and the weed he smoke make him brave. He push he own hand back in Curtis face. 'Boy, haul your ass, nah. Why you don't control your fucking woman?'

Before I know what happen Sugars was parting fight. Curtis and Leo was tangle up in the dusty grass, pelting cuff and slap. Sugars aim a kick at Leo – of course he have he boy back – and drag Leo from off of Curtis, but Curtis keep coming and Leo keep struggling. All three of them was push up against one another. Next thing I hear is a gunshot and the crowd scatter, screaming.

The music cut.

Curtis was on the ground, screaming, bleeding from he shoulder. Tamika fling she self down on top of him, bawling as though he dead.

Police rush in, barging through the crowd in a long line of navy blue wool sweater, with big machine gun strap on their chest. Sugars back off one time and put he hand in the air.

A small black gun was in Leo hand. He stand up by heself, watching around as though he now waking from a dream. He see me hiding behind the cooler and raise he hand, with the gun in it, in my direction. I didn't think he was going to shoot me.

'Babes?' he say.

'Drop it! Drop it!' I hear the police shouting.

Leo like he confuse. He just stand up there watching me.

I hear another shot.

EIGHTEEN

Fete done one time.

A tactical police hold Sugars, who was standing up there stupid stupid looking at Leo. If you see how fast Fire Services ambulance drive on the field and pick up Curtis and carry him hospital. Tamika went too in the ambulance, crying and screaming like she mother dead. I watch the grey colour bus drive off through the crowd. Leo was lying down on the grass. It had blood everywhere around him. The tactical police make a space around the body and all the staff was standing up in a grap shoo-shooing and pointing at Leo. Nobody wasn't looking at me. I only there like a mumu, still stooping down behind the six-foot cooler which part I dive down when the bacchanal start. I ent make a peep. I feel the black hole start to suck me down inside it, slow like molasses, sticky like pitch.

The ringmaster come on stage and tell the audience that it had a tragic incident and the police shutting down the fete.

Some people boo but the niggergram spread fast and by the time they announce that, everybody done know already that police shoot and kill a man in the fete. The crowd start to drain away, except for the people choke up around by we.

Through the dark, I see a face watch me from the circle of police around Leo.

'Miss Lopez!' It was Corporal Baker. He in the wool sweater again and I suddenly feeling sorry for he. Hot wool does real scratch. 'Miss Lopez,' he say. 'Are you all right?'

I only watching he – one big gun strap on he chest. He had a hand on the butt and the other hand on the barrel. He wasn't aiming it at nobody but the black steel make me cold. I couldn't say boo. Only Leo running through my mind, the confuse look on he face when he say, 'Babes?' The gun in Leo hand, pointing at me.

Corporal Baker pull me up from behind the cooler. I was like a statue, or a mannequin.

A police in ordinary uniform, grey shirt and navy blue pants, grab Sugars from the tactical who was holding him hard by the collar. He hold one of Sugars hand and twist it behind he back and march he off with a next police towards the gate. Sugars throw a desperate glance back at me, but I still ent say nothing. I see he talking to the police. They stop, and one of them walk over, tell Baker something in he ears, and went back to escorting Sugars to wherever they was carrying he.

Baker watch Sugars, then watch Leo on the field. 'Well,' Baker say.

As the people dribble away from the fete the place start to get cold. My skin, wet from beer and sweat, now getting goose pimples and I start to shiver. My teeth was chattering. Baker put me to sit down on top of the cooler. I wish he did give me he sweater.

Marie tell Baker how is she cooler and if she could get it please. Baker hit she a cut eye and she pull back like he slap

223

she face. She say – no, she *mutter* – 'I could get it later, yes,' and melt back into the grap of On the Town workers who was standing just off to the side of where we was.

After a while, somebody put a blanket on my shoulder. I don't know where they get it from, or who put it on me. It smell dusty. I start wondering if Leo wasn't feeling chilly, too. I rather they put the blanket on he, but I couldn't open my mouth to say that because my words and all was down in the black hole.

Baker went by Leo and stoop down and examine him without touching him, and then some other police come and Baker stand up and stay talking to them for a long while. Somebody give me a cup of hot tea, sweet, with plenty milk. I hold it in my hand until it get cold. Finally, a officer rest a cover over Leo – a grey wool blanket. It was too short to cover Leo foot. He sneakers was sticking out.

Baker come back. He tell me, 'We need a statement from you, Miss Lopez. Do you understand?'

I watch he in he face and for the life of me I couldn't figure out what he was talking about. Everything was dark, hard to see, hard to hear, hard to understand.

'Miss Lopez,' he say again, 'we need your statement. What happened here?'

That was a question I couldn't self answer. What happen? One minute we was good. Next minute, Leo dead, Curtis in hospital, Sugars in jail. And I here by myself in a ridiculous short pants showing my whole bamsee and sitting down on this cooler big like a coffin.

Marie come over again. She stare at me when she was coming but she never say word one to me. Instead, she turn them eyes on Baker and say, 'Officer, I see what happen.'

'Yes?'

'Yes. She man, Leo, and Tamika man, Curtis, get in a fight because she man slap Tamika.'

'She man...'

'Yes, she man. Leo. He.' She point she finger at the sneakers showing under the blanket. 'They start to scuffle and Curtis friend try and part the fight.'

'Curtis friend?' Baker listen without taking notes. He still hugging up the semi-automatic in he hand. He glance at me once or twice but he mostly keep focus on Marie.

'Yes, that's the guy all you hold.' Baker nodded. Marie continued, 'Then Leo pull a gun from he waist—'

'Whose waist?'

'Ahmm...' she say, looking up in the sky like if she watching a video replay in she head. 'Leo. Leo pull a gun from he own waist. And shoot Curtis. Curtis fall down and then Leo go to shoot Miss Allie.'

That is not true, I wanted to say. *She lie. Leo wasn't no going and shoot me.*

He turn to me. 'Miss Lopez, did Leo come into the party with a gun?'

And all of we get scan when we come in? How he could have any gun? How anybody could have any gun? But like I freeze. Words just couldn't come out my mouth.

I sit down there on the cooler in the middle of the empty field. It could have be hours for all I know. Then somebody walk me and Marie to a police car and carry we down in the station.

Corporal Baker keep asking me the same questions over and over and I still ent answer he. Because all how I look at it, Leo didn't have, *couldn't* have no gun. Leo was a musician. He wasn't no gangster. Things was so fuzzy in my head and I couldn't think straight no more. I feel the black hole coming up, opening in front of me wide wide. I sink down inside it. No matter what Baker do, I wasn't moving. Eventually he leave me alone. 'I will contact you later, Miss Lopez,' he promise. Or threaten.

The next thing I remember is that Bobby Sharma was calling my name. Nobody know who was my next of kin other than Leo, so Marie tell the police call my boss instead. Bobby reach in the station looking like he now come out he bed, in a long-sleeve shirt he drag over a jersey and short pants. He hair sticking up like a madman and he eye puffy puffy. He jiggling he keys in he hand, rubbing he head and watching from me to Marie, Marie to me. He didn't know what to do.

Outside, it was now coming on daylight. Bobby go to put me in the front seat of the silver BMW, but Marie move swift and plant she big backside down as the door swing open. I would have shake my head if I did care. Instead, I slide in the backseat. Bobby try all how to catch my eye but I don't want to see nobody. The car cold cold, as usual. I wasn't wrap up in the blanket no more – somebody take that from me since we reach in the station – and I start to shake.

'You feeling cold? Look—' Bobby take off he shirt and put it on my shoulder. 'You want me carry you in a hotel? Carry you home?' He fussing with the shirt, jooking it down behind me, all under my bottom until I wrap up like a roti. I sit down quiet and didn't help him. 'Allie? You hear? You want me carry you home?'

Marie, in the front seat of the car, swing around to watch we with she eye open big big big, as though she getting confirmation of what she suspect all along: that me and Bobby in thing. But I ent studying she. Home? Where that was? El Socorro? Aranguez? Nelson Street? Barataria? A million places I live in my life and none of them was home. The last place I wanted to be was in L'Anse Mitan Road, in Leo house, in Leo bed. It was early Sunday morning. I look up. My brother church was by the next corner. 'I want to go by the church.'

Both of them watch me funny. Under Bobby shirt I was in a battyrider short pants, with dust and grass all over my body, my hair tangle up and my face white with shock.

'Which church?' Marie say.

I point.

She say, 'Mr Sharma, she could walk that.'

Bobby help me come out the car and we leave Marie in the BMW. He hold my hand and wrap he arm around my waist and I lean on him a little bit, but then I straighten up. Nothing wasn't wrong with my foot. I could walk by myself. I let go he hand.

We reach by the gate. He hug me up and say in my ears, 'Take all the time off you need, Allie. Marie will hold on for you. Just let us...let me know if you need anything.'

I know he wanted to say something more. I could feel he breathing on my neck. He stop talking and start again twice. But he didn't say nothing else and is a good thing, because I didn't want to hear it. Bobby Sharma couldn't give me more than he done give me already. When he walk off I didn't turn to watch him go. I just went inside.

I sit in the back of and wait for mass to finish. Colin see me when he was sharing communion. He nearly jump out he skin, but he collect heself and carry on as normal until the mass done. Then he hurry down to where I was sitting and say one time, 'What happen?'

All the parishioners who see start to shoo-shoo. Them mustbe scandalise he talking to this dirty looking whitish woman in the pumpum shorts and red jersey under a big big long-sleeve shirt, looking like she just come out a fete. But Colin didn't even study that. He hold me by the arm and walk me to the presbytery. He put me to lie down on the couch and bring a sheet and a pillow. 'Go and sleep,' he say when he hand me the sheet to cover with. 'We will talk when you wake up.'

Colin make bake and butter and cocoa tea and fry sausage. I sit down to eat in he kitchen in one of he jersey and football pants, smelling like soap and shampoo, not beer and sweat.

First thing he do when I wake up was carry me in the shower. It was clean and nice, not like how mine by Leo was. I check out the shiny tiles. He mustbe have a church woman just like Mammie who does come and clean for him. She widow's mite.

When I come out the bathroom, he give me the clothes and point me to he bedroom to change. It clean and tidy, but *monastic*. He does sleep on a single divan with no headboard and he clothes in a old-fashion press like we had in Aranguez. It had a desk and a straight-back chair and a bookcase full of books, but no curtain, no pictures, no decorations, no nothing. Like he in jail.

The kitchen was just big enough for a table. He sit down on one side with he breakfast, waiting for me to reach. It had a plate waiting by a empty chair on the other side, so I sit down, too. I didn't mention the room, and I didn't mention the widow who I feel does clean it.

The bake was hot and salty with the butter running down it. I shock to find out I actually hungry. I sink down in the fragrance, the smell of that hot, fresh bread, and bite that bake like is the first bake I ever eat, feeling fullness move down into my belly and reach all down by my toes. Colin hand was sweet – the sausage melt on my tongue and the cocoa tea was silky, full of spice and not too sugary.

I look around at Colin kitchen. It nice, just like the shower. 'Nice' is a useless word. The kitchen *understated, modern, minimalist,* I force myself to think. Green accent tiles over the white backsplash, white cupboards and new white fridge; everything spic and span. A woman like Mammie does clean here, too, I think. But maybe not – he make the bake for heself, so he not helpless like some of them old white priest they use to send from Ireland who Mammie had to do everything for, wipe their bottom and all.

'Sometimes people throw things over the walls at these fetes, you know,' Colin say.

He surprise me. I there busy with the bake and thinking about Mammie and I ent studying he. I look up from the food.

'Guns, knives, drugs. Then they walk around and collect them once they're inside. Or sometimes they come in to the venue early and they hide things away, to fish them out later. It isn't unusual. That's why there are so many police at these events, because no matter how many scanners you put at the gate, people always find a way to bring weapons inside.'

How he, a priest, know all that?

Is years he never see me but he could still read my face like when we was young and he know what it mean when I raise my eyebrows. 'It's an urban parish,' he say, shrugging he shoulder. 'You learn things.'

'But still,' I say. 'Leo?'

'Maybe it wasn't Leo's gun,' he say. 'That guy Sugars, he looked like a gangster to me.'

I couldn't argue with that. I and all had that feeling when I meet him. Gangster. I shiver. But out loud I tell Colin, 'Judge not.'

He blush. 'Sorry. You're right. I shouldn't judge by appearances. But that puts us right back to square one. Where did Leo get the gun?'

Colin take a week of compassionate leave and went with me all where I had was to go, from Forensics Centre to funeral home to police station and back. Everywhere we went it had a set of reporter pushing their recorder and microphone them up in my face. He block me from the cameras and carry me through the crowds. All this time I still sleeping on he couch. I send Colin to L'Anse Mitan to collect my handbag, some toiletries, my phone. I couldn't face the house. It would be full of memories and smelling like Leo.

When the news hit the papers how Leo from Jam dead, all kind of people crawl out from the woodwork to come on the news and call the radio and say they is Leo family and they shock by the tragedy. Me ent know none of them. Leo was a only child, both he parents dead, and he wasn't close to none of the aunty, uncle, cousin and nennen who show up. Them was only sniffing around for royalties money and the deed to the house in L'Anse Mitan. Eventually, I would have to deal with that, get the deed in my name and thing. Not now, though. First had I to bury the man.

The damn ring still on my finger so nobody couldn't put no question to me. I was Leo common-law wife and he fiancée, so as far as the police concern it was me responsible for Leo and all he business. It was the first funeral I ever see about. I was lucky Colin was there – he help me with everything and was with me right through.

Because it was a police shooting, it get plenty attention in the media. But because it had at least a hundred witnesses to say Leo had a gun in he hand pointing it at me, the investigation was quick. By the Saturday I could bury Leo. We church him by Colin in a private service and cremate him one time by the Cinerary. My next-door neighbours Ty and Natalie and their mother come, and one or two others, plus some of Leo old school friends, and a handful of musicians he used to play with. Jankie and Ricky and Amanda come, and Bobby, Ann and Janelle. Jerry come, too. Tamika didn't come. I ent hear from she since the fete, when she went hospital with Curtis.

Corporal Baker was there too. I see him in the church, but he wait until the casket slide inside the oven before he slide up next to me and say quiet for me alone to hear, 'We had to let Sugars go. Although he was...' he pause, looking at me frank frank '...known to police, we don't have anything to hold him on. He didn't have a weapon on him.' He added, 'Everybody agrees that he was trying to part the fight. Unless you want to say something different?'

I shake my head. He trying to imply I involve in something with Sugars? Or he trying to say is I who call a shot on Leo, my own man? Nah. He not for real. But he stay there watching me in my face until I say, 'No, Carl. I have nothing different to say. I don't know where the gun came from and I don't know Sugars, either.'

Baker nod once and gone, yes. I like him, but I hope to God I never see he again.

And that was the funeral.

It was kind of funny that the dress I wear was the same one I wear to the birthday party.

I staying by Colin, but I know without asking that the parishioners and them had plenty to say about that and so as soon as the cremation done I tell him I had to go home to L'Anse Mitan.

We roll up in the Corolla and I make him promise to wait until I went in first. He try to insist, but I know I had to go inside by myself. Whatever jumbie Leo leave in that house was mines and mines alone to face. I take real long to come out the car. I bite my lip and make myself walk around to the back door. It was my house now. I couldn't fraid it. I open the door and switch on the light. I stand up in the doorway watching the kitchen.

Colin walk up behind me. He see how I feeling dread. 'You want to go somewhere else?'

I step inside. I look around at everything. It look so familiar, but still so strange. On the table I see the envelope from Jankie and I pick it up. I want to go in the bedroom but I just can't force myself to move.

'Maybe just for a day or so.'

'I have an idea.' We went back in the car. He bounce the starter and we drive off.

. . .

231

Colin driving. He see me fidgeting with the ring on my hand. 'What's the matter?'

'I can't get it off,' I say.

'Tried soap?'

'I try soap, I try SqEzy, I try oil, I try butter…nothing. Like Leo will never leave me until this finger get gangrene and fall off.'

He didn't say nothing but he turn in by West Mall and carry me to a jeweller.

'Cut it off,' he tell the man.

It hurt like hell when the man take a small thing like a cross between a pliers and a pizza cutter and slide it under the ring and cut it. As he cut it off I feel the blood flowing in my finger again. Nothing never feel so good.

When I see we driving east I say, 'You not carrying me by that house in Valencia!'

'No, Girlie. Alethea.'

'Well, where then?'

'There's a retreat centre. They have these…camps, I guess you could call them. Counselling camps for trauma survivors, rape victims, domestic abuse…that kind of thing.'

'Oh,' I say. It sort of shut me up. Me ent know if I want to go in a counselling retreat. 'It expensive?'

Colin say, 'No, you could pay whatever. It runs on donations, not fees. Plus, I know the woman who runs it.'

As we driving, my cell phone ring.

It was Tamika.

'Miss Allie,' she say. 'I sorry I miss the funeral.' Then she laugh, short and hard like a dog coughing. 'I not sorry the bitch dead. But I sorry it had to happen so. And I sorry if it look like I desert you.'

'Girl, I say you throw me in the bamboo,' I tell she, smiling and feeling so happy I could burst.

'Never.' She sound like she was smiling too. It sound busy where she was. I hear people talking and music; a car horn beep far off. Maybe she was in town.

'How Curtis? He getting better?'

'He there. When you come back to work we go talk, girl.'

'I not sure about coming back to work, nah.' I look down and spot the card from Jankie sticking out of my handbag. It remind me of what Jankie offer to do. 'Hear nah, I have a opportunity to open a shop. Let we talk about that instead.'

'Way, sah!' she say. She sound even happier than me. 'That is not a phone conversation. We go talk when we see each other. I hope that is just now.' Then she say with mischief in she voice, 'Oh, by the way, somebody want to tell you hello.'

'Family,' Sugars say. In he mouth the word had all kind of lovely, familiar, intimate notes.

'Luke,' I say. 'We don't have nothing to talk about.'

'But—'

'But what.' It had ice in my voice.

He pause a little bit, then like he change he mind and steups and say, 'Okay, family. Whatever you say.'

'Okay.'

Tamika take back the phone, telling me, 'What is this… you now bury your man and he feel you up for a next one already?' She move the phone away from she mouth and tell he, 'You too damn disrespectful!' But I could hear she was still smiling. In she mind me and Sugars was done together already, so what is the harm?

I hush my mouth.

'So when I seeing you?'

'I coming in town soon,' I say. 'I have plenty thing to do.'

'I could imagine,' she say.

We finish the conversation after I promise she I go call she when I ready to meet up. Putting the phone back in my bag, I see Jankie card again. I take it out and open it. I start to laugh.

'What?' Colin ask.

I hold up the papers in the envelope. I was wrong, it wasn't a fancy birthday card. It was a lease to a house near Maraval Road. The card say: *Surprise! Can't wait to start our new business!*

I fumble for a cigarette in the bag, but when I put it in my mouth Colin watch me cut eye so I put it back. I sit there thinking about what I would do with the rest of my life. In one month I went from having nothing to owning two house and twenty acre of land, plus holding a lease to a building with a partner ready to start a new business with me. From a punching bag to a free woman. From a woman alone to one with friends, with a brother. Something inside of me start to grow again.

The retreat centre was past Valencia, past Grande, almost to Toco. It was a plain-looking building, a big flat thing like a school and two buildings to the side just like it but smaller. All around had grass and trees. It look peaceful, and empty.

It had one or two cars park up. We leave the Corolla and went inside one of the small buildings. A pretty woman in a plain black polyester cotton blouse and TetRex skirt was in a office there, typing something on a computer. She look kind of familiar. Is then I recognise she from the other day by the Normandie, the same woman he went to lunch with the day I was there with Jankie.

'Michael?' Colin say.

'One second...' She finish typing she thing. When she turn I see she had a big silver cross, about two-three inches long, on a chain around she neck. 'Father Colin, how nice to see you!'

She hug him up tight tight, rocking from side to side. Whoever she was, they really like one another, boy.

'What brings you here?'

'Sister Michael, I brought someone very special to meet you—'

Before he could even finish, Sister hugging me up too. 'Girlie!'

I didn't know what to say.

'Alethea, Sister. Remember she doesn't like to be called Girlie any more, she said.' Colin look bashful.

'Um. Hi,' I say.

She finally stop hugging me up.

The nun wasn't wearing no habit. She had a short afro, round like she face. Brown skin with deep dimples and a broad smile, salt and pepper hair, and wrinkles around she eyes. She teeth was a little crooked but white white white. If I had to guess I would say she was my age, or a little older. She was wearing tiny silver studs in she ears, but other than that and the cross no other jewellery.

'Alethea, I want you to meet my very, very good friend, Sister Michael Pierre. She was at Convent when I was at Saints,' he say. 'We studied languages and literature together.'

Sister Michael grab my hand and hold it in she two hand. 'Colin has told me so much about you, my dear. I was so glad that he found you, finally.'

It make me good uncomfortable to hear this total stranger say Colin tell she about me, but I ent say nothing. I give she a smile, and give Colin a look from the corner of my eye.

He hold my next hand and say in my ears for me alone to hear, 'I didn't tell her everything about you. Just that you're my sister and that we were out of touch.' Louder, he say, 'Sister Michael works with this group. As I told you, they do counselling and retreats.'

'We have nothing on this weekend,' Sister say. 'What were you thinking of, Colin?'

He watch me, probably wondering how to explain. Finally, he say, 'Better let Alethea tell you herself.'

Both of them looking at me, waiting for me to say something. I spread my hand wide, feeling at sea. 'I don't know what to say. Colin, is you bring me here.'

'Yes...' It had a *but* he wasn't saying.

'Okay,' I say. 'My boyfriend. My fiancé. My husband. I don't know what to call him, nah. He was shot. We buried him today.'

Unless she was living underneath a rock or something, Sister Michael had was to know that already – it make front page in all in the papers, complete with Marie bacchanalist story about how Curtis say Leo used to beat me, and that is what trigger the fight. Add that to the remnants of fame Leo had as a musician, and you had a readymade sensational headline.

But Sister didn't flinch. 'I'm so sorry, my dear,' she say. She still holding one hand and Colin still holding the next one. I was feeling damn awkward between the two of them. It had some hard dining table chairs by the door. I pull away and sit down on one.

Sister Michael follow and sit in a chair next to me. She look from me to Colin and back, talking to both of we. 'What would you like to do?'

'I was hoping she could spend a few days here. Just a few days of quiet. And if she wants to talk...'

Sister was watching me now. 'Is that what you want?'

'I don't know,' I say. 'I just didn't want to go home yet. The house too empty.'

When Colin gone, Sister carry me in a room like a dormitory, a line of ten single beds stretch out on one side and a cheap wardrobe opposite the foot of every bed. It didn't have no mirrors on the wardrobes.

Resting down my bag by the foot of the bed, she give me a little smile and start to talk like a tour guide. 'We generally

236

have residential workshops twice a month, and our guests stay here. This is the women's space,' she say. 'The men have their own space on the other side. But as I said there's nothing on now. You'll have the place all to yourself tonight and tomorrow. On Monday,' she continue, 'we have some guests coming for a corporate retreat. But they will be using the conference rooms, not the dorms. You won't be disturbed.' She finish talk and sit on the bed next to mine and gesture with she hand that I should sit down opposite she. 'Father Colin is an extraordinary man,' she say. 'You must be a really special person.'

'Why you say that?' The bed look hard but it wasn't so bad when I sit down. I watch the nun. This is Colin friend? I feel a little shame that I thought they was together. I could tell she love him from the way she talk about him, but I could see it wasn't nothing sexual. They was really just friends.

'He says you were like his mother until he was thirteen.' She look curious but she wasn't pushy. 'He has a lot of regard for you.'

'Me?' I say. I couldn't believe it. Too, besides, I leave him. I leave him with that monster Mammie and she nasty brother. God know what the two of them could have do him. My imagination stab me with brutal visions of them holding down little Colin, beating him, hurting him.

Grief hit me like one of them wave in Maracas, knocking me down flat without any warning. I start to cry and cry and cry. Sister Michael come by me on the bed and hold me. The longer she hold me, the more I cry, until I didn't have no more tears in me and I fall asleep just so, in my shoes and all.

I was sleeping sound when Sister Michael wake me with a big smile the next morning. The dorm dark, and she look like some kind of dream bending down over me – except she smell like toothpaste. From the dim light coming through the window I see it was just before dayclean.

'I'm going out to the beach to swim and watch the sunrise. Do you want to come?'

I was barefoot. I kick off the shoes in the night. Stretching and yawning, I sit up in the bed. I reach for my cigarettes and the lighter I put under the pillow, and I go to light one, but I see she face and I ent bother. I put the pack and the lighter back. 'I don't bring a bathsuit, nah.'

'That's okay. You want to borrow one of mine?'

I would have feel funny borrowing a complete stranger bathsuit, so I say no thanks. 'Wait,' I say. In the bag it had Colin short pants and he jersey. I jump out the bed and scoop them out. Sister leave me alone to change, turning on the dorm light as she leave. I find the bathroom and strip down naked. I pelt the dress in the dustbin by the sink. I never want to wear that again. I wash my face and brush my mouth, put on Colin clothes and went to look for Sister Michael.

We went behind the compound. The sky was just getting bright, coral and violet streaks lighting up the darkness over we head as the sun get higher. Sister walk in front of me. The back there was open to the sea, and though I couldn't see it I could hear the waves kissing the sand like a sigh. The little breeze was making cold, and the grass between my toes was wet with dew. After we pass the grass it had a steep, rocky track down to the beach. The black, sharp stone jook up my foot until we reach a small bay at the bottom. Even in the dim early morning, the firm sand white white, and the water turquoise blue and crystal clear between two sheer walls of black rock. I walk in the rolling waves a little bit. It was cold. I sit down on the sand while she went swimming, making a good few laps from one side of the bay to the next. She could well swim: fast fast and barely making a splash. I admire how she wasn't frighten at all, she just jump in the water and start to go, like a machine.

'You swim so beautifully,' I tell she, when she come out with water streaming from she afro. Sun well up by now. The light make diamonds on the water.

'Used to be a national swimmer,' she say. 'I still like it, but...' She plops sheself down on the sand next to me. 'I had other things I wanted to do.' We sit for a few minutes and feel the sun get hot on we face. 'You sure you don't want a little dip? The water's cold but it's lovely.'

I study how the water cold no ass, but what the hell. I get up and walk in. Water hit my ankle. Cold no ass in truth at first, but warm and silky on my skin when I get accustom to the temperature. I take another step. It reach my knee. Every step forward was harder, my legs pushing against the current. Then Michael shout out, 'Stop fighting! Let the water do the work.' I take a breath and relax. My body sink down in the sea. I bend my knees. My hair float out all around my face. I stretch out my body straight and come up to the surface, face down in the water. I reach my hand and make a stroke. Then I reach with the other. Another stroke. It was my first time swimming by myself, without Leo.

It wasn't pretty like Sister Michael. I know I was splashing too much and I look clumsy and awkward. But I swim.

I come out the water smiling.

We climb back through the sharp rocks.

Michael carry me in the kitchen and put me to sit down. She put four egg to boil and make two cup of tea. When the egg boil, she put them in a bowl and move to the big dining room, carrying some orange and fig too. It was just we sitting down on two long, empty bench stretching out next to the table. We didn't say much. Even though I had questions about Colin and what he do all them long years when I wasn't in he life, I feel I would wait to ask him and not talk about him behind he back.

After breakfast, I bathe and change and come back outside. Sister Michael was in she office, wearing she TetRex skirt again. She tell me I could do whatever I want, so I just walk around for a while and then I find a shady spot under a flamboyant tree and lie down in the grass, listening to the dry shakshak in the tree shaking when the wind blow through the feathery leaves.

I mustbe fall asleep there because the next thing I know is because Sister waking me up to tell me is lunchtime.

She bring a tray with some cheese paste sandwich and juice and cake and we eat right there, under the tree.

'What do you do all day?' I ask she.

'Secretarial stuff. Maintenance. Administrative things. I write a lot of begging letters,' she say, laughing hard. 'We're run on donations.'

'Yes, Colin told me that.'

'The church gives us some money, but we're a non-profit company and we do most of our own fund raising.' She start to glow, like this really interesting to her. I listen to she, but I was more interested in how she so passionate about the work she doing here. She talk for a good while about how they support the place with community involvement, how they does make their bookings, what they does do in the retreats…

'Sounds…'

'Boring!' She laugh again.

'No, not at all,' I say. 'I just never visited a place like this before.' Imagine, it have a place where you could go and just rest. I never went nowhere like that in my life.

We eat we sandwich and drink we juice and when we finish the marble cake Sister say, 'Oh! I have something for you.'

She trot over to the office and come back with a notebook, one of them old fashion composition books with black and white marble cover. She hand me the notebook and a pen.

'I know we didn't really discuss any counselling, but I thought you might like to jot down some thoughts. We encourage our clients to keep a journal. Not that you're a client—'

'Is okay,' I say, because she was starting to look uncomfortable. I take the book and the pen and put them on the ground next to me. Then, playing with the pen and the book with my fingers, I ask she what I suppose to write.

'Anything. Your thoughts, your feelings, your plans. If you want, I could give you a guided journal. It asks specific questions about your past, your habits, your fears, your hopes. It's like mining, you know. Digging under the surface of your memory to find out why you are who you are, why you do what you do. We all have our demons.' A shadow cross she face but then she flash that smile again. It look like a sunbeam coming through clouds. 'I'll leave you to it. I've got some calls to make,' she say, and get up and dust off she ugly black skirt. She pick up the tray and carry it with she. When she reach by the office door, she bawl out, 'If you need anything, just knock.'

I pick up the pen and open the notebook. The first thing I write is my name.

NINETEEN

I write *Alethea Lopez*. But then I cross that off. If Colin was telling the truth, that name was a lie, and my father never name Lopez. I try 'Reece'. That was my mother maiden name, my grandmother name. But it feel wrong, too. That was my nasty uncle name, my real father name. No wonder Colin change he name to Jackson as soon as he reach America. I cross off 'Reece'. I try 'Dupigny.' My grandfather name, as Colin say. But I really wanted to carry that man name? I never know he, never meet he, never had no connection with he family. It would be a lie too.

Leo never call me nothing except 'babes', as though I had no name at all, as though I was a baby with no sense, no will, no power.

My family call me Girlie. I hate that. I's not just some girl, any girl. I's somebody.

But who?

Alethea Lopez? Alethea Reece? Alethea Dupigny? All of them was lies.

Which leave me with just Alethea.

The book of names in Colin office had Alethea in it. Is a Greek name. It mean 'truth'. That is what you call irony, because my whole life was a lie – lie on top of lie. My grandmother lie to the world when she never put we grandfather down on she children birth paper. My grandfather lie when he never claim he only children as he own because he make them with the maid and not he wife. My mother lie when she make up some Venezuelan man and say is she husband, say is my father, when is she own brother who bull she and get she pregnant. She lie to me and to she self when she accuse me of taking man when I get pregnant. I was fifteen years. She know it was she own brother child. She beat me anyway.

Would I want that child? Would that child even survive? That would be more than incest. Double incest. It have a word for that? A word for me?

Alethea.

After all this time.

The truth.

Funny enough, once I start to write all them thing down I find I like it. It was good to finally get all that off my chest.

I write down everything. All the times Mammie beat me, and make me feel like I worth less than one of the fowl she used to mind. All the time I was late for school because I had to make sure Colin was ready for when the bus passing, as if Colin going to school was more important than me. All the homework I never get to do because I had to cook, clean and wash clothes. All the times the nasty man hold me down, from time I had five years and didn't even know what sex was, until I run away when I was seventeen with pus dripping from my privates and I didn't know what that was either. All the children I go never make for myself.

I write down everything about coming up poor and never having enough to eat, never having nothing of my own, never having clothes and shoes and books like the other children in my school. About how the nasty man would send barrel with food in it and how Mammie would sell it in the market to buy Colin books for school.

I write how I love Colin even in spite of that, because is not he fault my mother was a evil bitch.

I write down how people single me out because my skin whitish and my hair long and straight, and how they would ignore Colin because he skin dark and he hair picky. How they used to do that with Leo, and all, until they realise who he was.

I write down the names of all the man I take, and all the thing I do with them, and whether I want to do it or not. I write down who beat me and who treat me good. Most of them beat me. Leo put me in house and put that damn ring on my finger. But eventually he beat me too, until I was sure he would have kill me if I stay with him. I used to tell myself it would done, that one day he wouldn't beat me no more. But I know that was just another lie, and this book was not the place to write down lies.

I write down everything that make me shame and everything I was glad for. The first list was longer than the second one. But I still write it down. Even through all the licks and the pain I work hard and mind myself my whole life. Colin come out so strong and so smart and so kind. And I not dead. I still here. And people love me.

I write down all the places I live in my life, all the places I work. All the friends I ever had. I write down Liloutee, Jankie, Jerry and Tamika, and Colin. He's my brother but he is my friend too, now.

I write all that down until my hand cramping. The ink in the pen nearly finish.

When I done write so, it was evening. I pick up the book and carry it in the back by the rocks and pelt it hard in the sea.

ACKNOWLEDGEMENTS

This book is the child the village raised. My thanks are many and sincere.

The Bread the Devil Knead began as a manuscript called *January*, which I started in a workshop with the late Caribbean poet, critic and man of letters Wayne Brown. Without that workshop there would be no book.

I later took the manuscript to Monique Roffey's writing group in Port of Spain. Among the writers, Sharon Millar was a rock to me during this period. Over lunch at Living Water, she helped me understand the character of Alethea and her voice – and influenced my writing style, too. Barbara Jenkins was also very supportive. My thanks to all of them.

After that draft was rejected by a couple of publishers, I took it with me to the CaribLit / St George's University Dame Hilda Bynoe Writing Residency in Grenada. There, I scrapped it down for parts and came back with this version, in which Alethea narrates the story in her native tongue, Trinidadian Creole. It too was rejected by a couple of publishers. However, my readers, the people with whom I share my work before it's published, loved it. I put it away, hoping that one day the right publisher would get it, and get it. Thanks to my readers for their feedback.

In the intervening five years, editor Margaret Busby, doyenne of Black British publishing, invited me to submit a piece to *New Daughters of Africa*, her sequel to her seminal anthology *Daughters of Africa*. *New Daughters of Africa* was published in 2019 by Myriad Editions. I stayed on the Myriad mailing list and spotted their call for submissions in the early days of the COVID-19 lockdown. Thanks to Margaret for her encouragement at all times.

Thanks to my thoughtful and thorough editor Vicki Heath Silk, Publisher Candida Lacey, and all at Myriad for believing in Miss Allie and creating such a beautiful book for her. Thanks to Trinidad and Tobago artist Brianna McCarthy, whose painting of a goddess of a woman graces the cover. Thanks to proofreader elisha efua bartels for not letting me make myself shame with bad Creole, and for always being relentlessly positive about the book.

Thanks to the Bocas Lit Fest, without which my writing would have been far worse and my career far less interesting. Through its prizes, seminars, readings, book launches and other support of writers and their work, the festival has given the Caribbean access to the global publishing world like never before. They have become the Swanzy of our generation.

In particular, Bocas Lit Fest Founder and Festival Director Marina Salandy-Brown has been extraordinarily kind to me and generous with her time, resources and networks. I thank her especially.

Picasso wrote, 'We all know that Art is not truth. Art is a lie that makes us realise truth, at least the truth that is given us to understand.' This book is entirely fiction. I don't know Alethea, Leo, Colin, Jankie, or Bobby, and none of this is based on a real story I have ever been told. But this lie shows some truths I was given to understand: brutality is an inescapable inheritance of humanity, but so is love. As terribly as we can be hurt, so deeply can we be healed. And we cannot stand alone.

Finally, thanks to God for all of it.

Petit Valley, Trinidad and Tobago
January 18, 2021

Sign up to our mailing list at

www.myriadeditions.com

Follow us on Facebook, Twitter and Instagram

ABOUT THE AUTHOR

Lisa Allen-Agostini is a writer, editor and stand-up comedian from Trinidad and Tobago. *The Bread the Devil Knead* is her first adult novel. She has written two Young Adult novels, including *Home Home*, winner of a CODE Burt Award for Caribbean Young Adult Literature. She writes and performs stand-up comedy as 'Just Lisa' with her company FemCom TT.